A PARCEL OF ROGUES

Susanna M Newstead

SUSANNA M. NEWSTEAD

PASTMASTERY PRESS

Cover art and design Charlie Farrow

Editing by Gill Whatmough

Published by PastMastery Press
Medlar House
Hanover Drive
Brackley Northants. NN13 6JS UK
sue@pastmastery.com

ISBN 978-1-916244412

A PARCEL OF ROGUES

Farewell to all our Scottish fame,
Farewell our ancient glory,
Farewell even to our Scottish name,
So famed in martial glory.
Now Sark runs to the Solway sands,
And Tweed runs to the ocean,
To mark where England's province stands -
Such a parcel of rogues in a nation.

What force or guile could not subdue,
Through many warlike ages,
Is wrought now by a coward few,
For hireling traitor's wages.
The English steel we could disdain,
Secure in valour's station;
But English gold has been our bane-
Such a parcel of rogues in a nation.

O would, that I had seen the day
That Treason thus could sell us
My old grey head had lain in clay,
With Bruce and loyal Wallace.
But pith and power, till my last hour,
I'll make this declaration;
We were bought and sold for English gold-
Such a parcel of rogues in a nation!

Poem by Robert Burns 1759 – 1796, National Poet of Scotland 1791
This song would, perhaps, have been as applicable in the early 13th century as it was in the 18th.

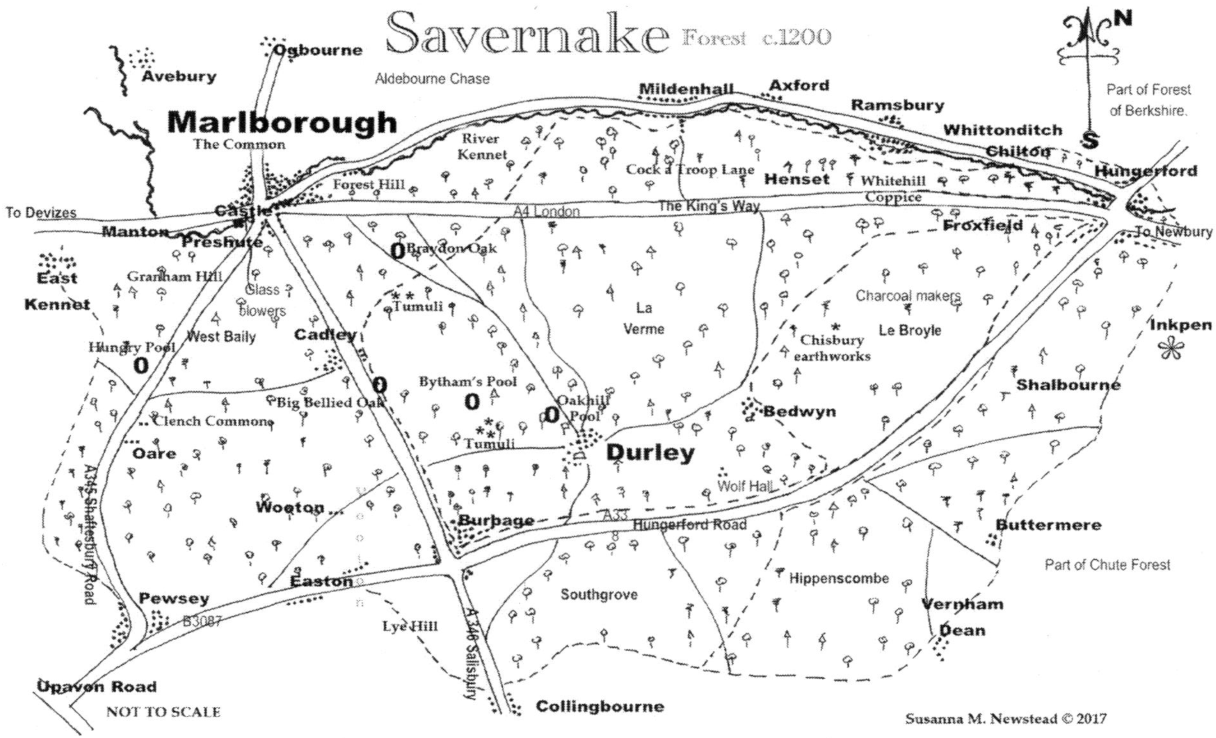
Savernake Forest c.1200
N
S
Avebury
Ogbourne
Aldebourne Chase
Marlborough
The Common
To Devizes
Manton
Castle
Preshute
East
Kennet
Granham Hill
Glass
blowers
West Baily
Hungry Pool
Cadley
Forest Hill
River
Kennet
Mildenhall
Axford
Ramsbury
Whittonditch
Chilton
Hungerford
Part of Forest
of Berkshire.
Cock a Troop Lane
Henset
Whitehill
Coppice
A4 London
The King's Way
Froxfield
To Newbury
Braydon Oak
Tumuli
La
Verme
Charcoal makers
Le Broyle
Chisbury
earthworks
Inkpen
Bytham's Pool
Big Bellied Oak
Clench Common
Oakhill
Pool
Tumuli
Durley
Bedwyn
Shalbourne
Oare
Wootton
Wolf Hall
Burbage
A33
Hungerford Road
Buttermere
Part of Chute Forest
A345 Shaftesbury Road
Easton
Pewsey
B3087
Lye Hill
A 346 Salisbury
Southgrove
Hippenscombe
Vernham
Dean
Upavon Road
NOT TO SCALE
Collingbourne
Susanna M. Newstead © 2017

Durley Village c. 1200

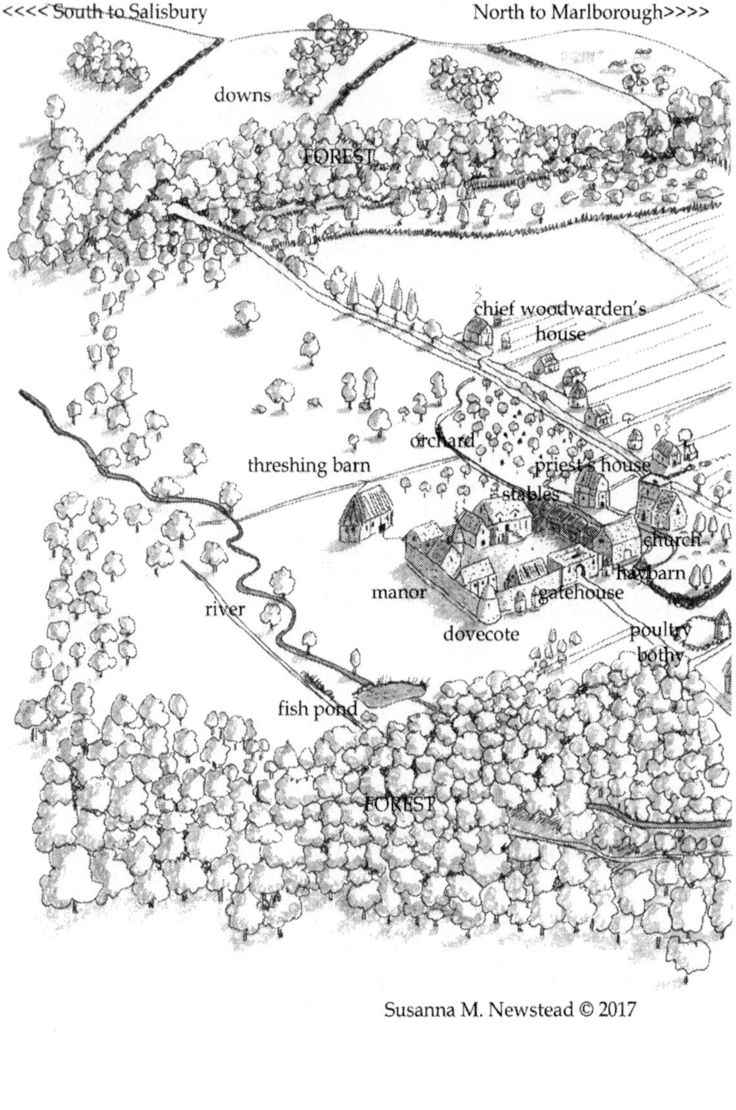

Susanna M. Newstead © 2017

Durley Village c. 1200

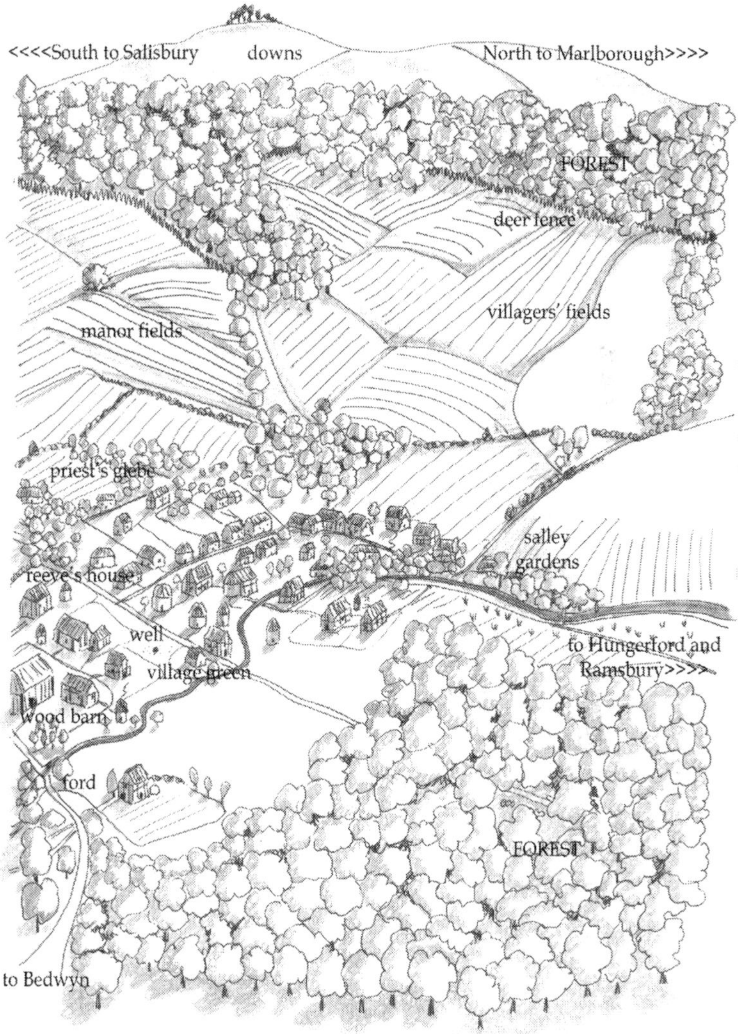

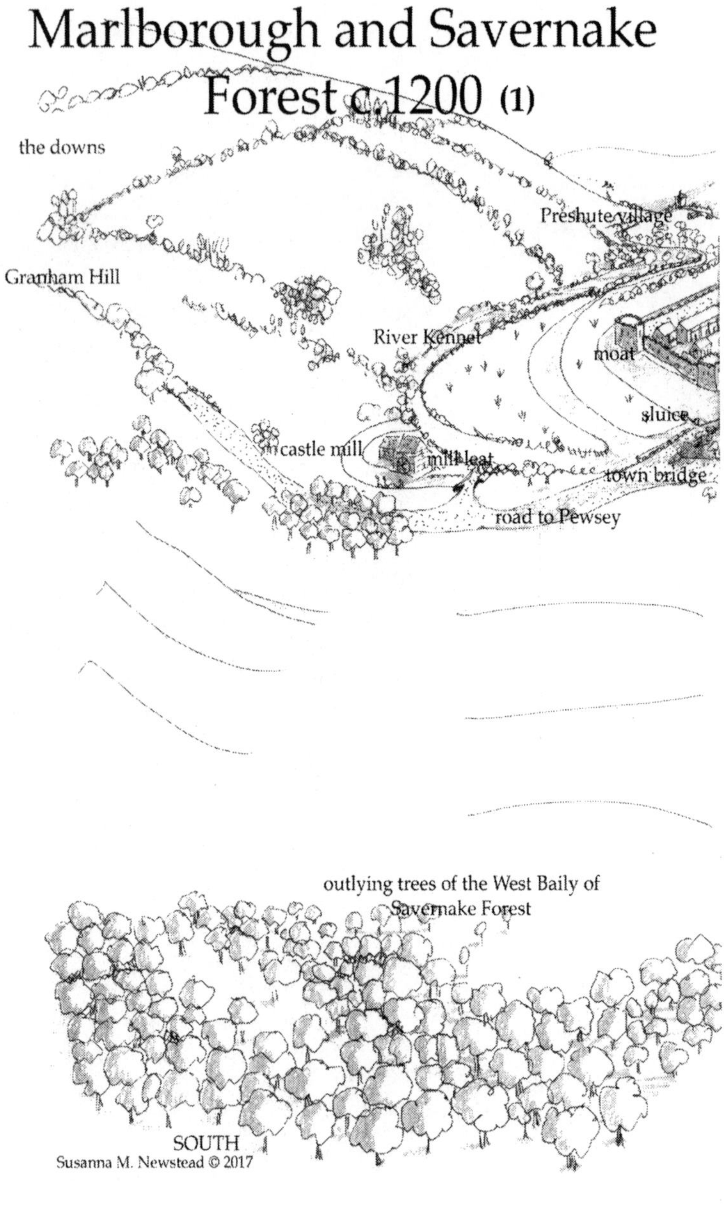
Marlborough and Savernake
Forest c.1200 (1)
the downs
Preshute village
Granham Hill
River Kennet
moat
sluice
castle mill
mill leat
town bridge
road to Pewsey
outlying trees of the West Baily of
Savernake Forest
SOUTH
Susanna M. Newstead © 2017

Marlborough Town and the forest c.1200 (2)

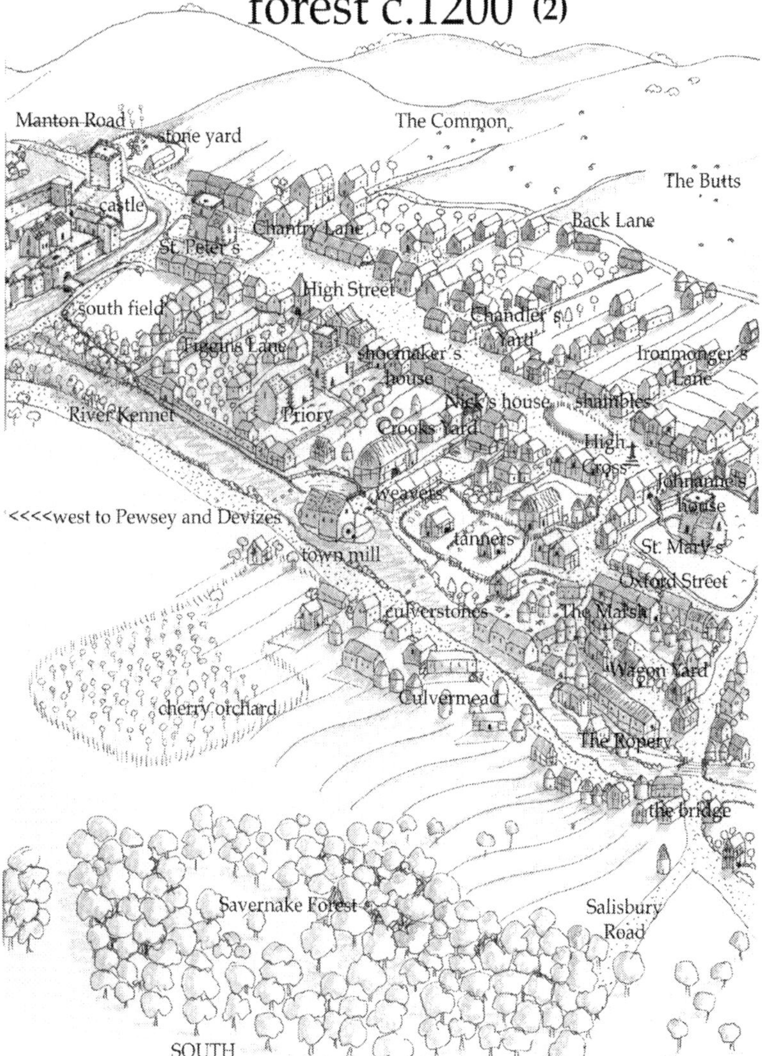

not to scale

Susanna M. Newstead © 2017

Marlborough and the forest c. 1200 (3)

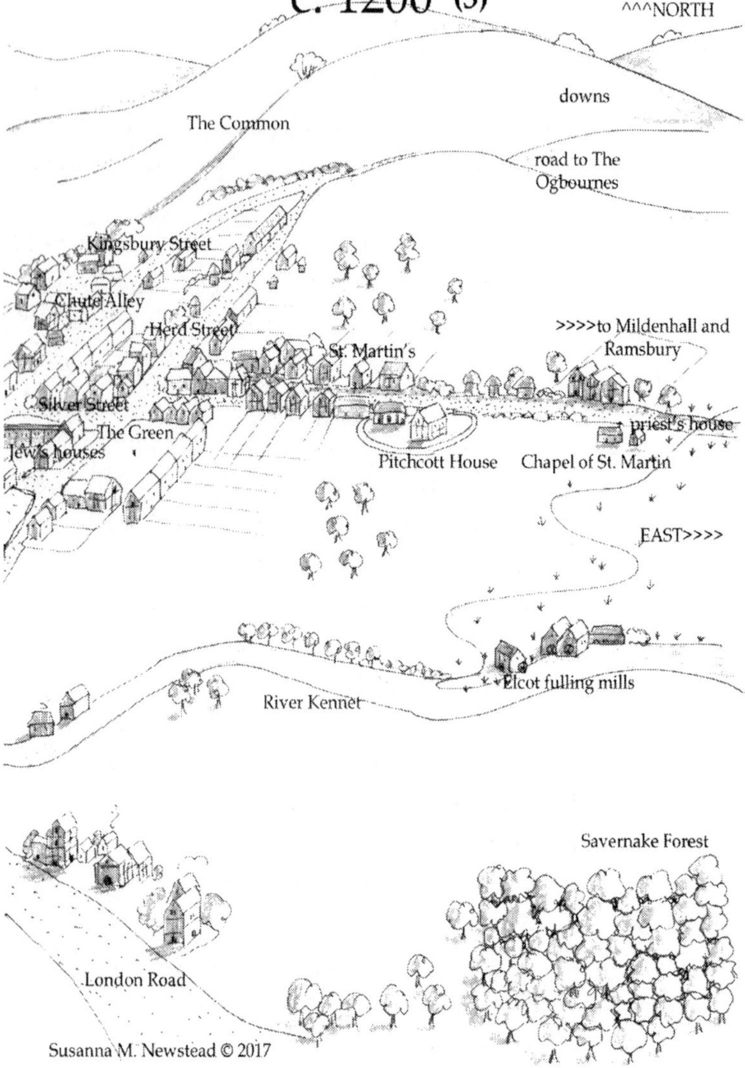

Chapter One

"Everyone is going about with such long faces!" I said, as I sat on my dais in the early spring of 1207.

"Aye, well, we are all soaked and none of us can get dry and warm, even if we bake ourselves in front of the fire each evening." said Hal of Potterne, my man at arms.

"The cold and wet has delayed the manor planting by almost a month," chimed in Henry Pierson, my steward gloomily.

Savernake, the forest of which I was warden, close by the town of Marlborough, in the county of Wiltshire, dripped from above and ran below with little rivulets where none had run before. The bogs expanded; the muddy places multiplied and some areas became cut off. Rushing streams abounded where tiny brooks had once trickled. Dry valleys on the downs to the west of the forest once more ran with water as the spring levels rose, flooding those valleys and emptying into the rivers, whose banks were not able to take it.

"There's widespread flooding in Marlborough town. Nick told John that Newbury road is under water."

"The wooden bridge at London Road 'as near been washed away as were some of the smaller 'ouses along the banks of the River Kennet," said Hal.

"The two churches are opened to take those made homeless. The priory of St. Margaret of Antioch on the High Street has freely opened its guest house to those unfortunate enough to be caught out travelling in such weather," said Crispin Darrell our priest, hugging his robe to him and looking up at the hall roof as the rain drummed above our heads...

We knew some had not made the safety of the town and three bodies of unfortunate villeins were pulled from the swollen river at the Preshute side of Town Bridge. Numerous sheep, their fleeces sodden and heavy, were also washed up.

Debris hurtled down from further upstream, collected at this bridge and had to be quickly removed or the castle grounds would be awash and the corn mill destroyed. As it was, the town mill was flooded on the river side and a new channel started to dig itself into the river bed. Several ground floor rooms were unusable but the grinding room and the store rooms were safe from danger for the moment.

Then as soon as it had come, the rain ceased. On the 25th of March 1207, my natal day, the sun came out and we all gave thanks for the warmth and for the receding of the waters.

I thought I knew how Noah had felt on the day the dove brought back the olive branch.

I walked out onto the meadow at the back of Durley manor, the little place of which I was lord, and scanned our own little stream which wended its way through the forest to join the River Og and thence the Kennet.

Our stream, usually no wider than twenty feet, had burst its banks and had been creeping closer and closer to the walls of the manor. Two houses further in the village had been under water; including the new house of poor Richard Marshall, my head groom, which lay close by the river bank. As the water rose we had managed to lay hands to his and his wife Marjorie's possessions and had evacuated them to a part of the priest's house, a large dwelling by the church up a slight rise and safe from flooding. The priest, Father Crispin, used not a half of his outsized home and so the Marshalls and Geoffrey their young son of almost a year, were accommodated there in comfort.

The other house was that of one of my foresters Robin Woodman and his wife Joan the laundress and they went to relatives further towards the village centre, hanging their possessions from pegs driven into the beams and leaving what they didn't need out of harm's way.

The beginning of April proved to be as warm as March had been chilly and gradually we all managed to dry out a little. However it remained showery.

I bent my brain into thinking how I might prevent this kind of thing happening again in Durley.

I was in my office scribbling and drawing on some parchment with a piece of charcoal late one afternoon when a visitor was announced by my young steward Henry Pierson.

I looked up.

"Show them in Henry." Then I mouthed quietly, "Who is it?"

"The Lord de Neville, sir."

I sat up sharply. Hugh de Neville was the chief forester of all the lands in England, custodian of the castle at Marlborough, a justice and a boon companion of John our King. Of late he had been accompanying the King on many of his journeys to the continent and to the Angevin homelands there, in an effort to regain those lands, threatened or stolen by the French king, Philip. When he disappeared, he left me in charge of the castle. It was true I had many able people to help me and the castle more or less ran itself. Nevertheless, this man was my superior and I had to be on my mettle.

I jumped up. "Where have you put him?"

"In the hall m'lord."

I quickly shrugged on my cotte. I noticed my hands were dirty with charcoal so I searched around for something with which to wipe them. Henry produced a damp cloth. I smiled at him. He knew me well.

"And his men?"

"He has none, sir."

I blinked. Hugh de Neville was an important man. Why would he travel alone?

I gritted my teeth and opened the office door.

*****

"I'll be brief Belvoir," de Neville said without preamble, "and frank."

"I am listening, sir," I said as we sat by the fire and gazed into our wine cups.

"The King has charged me with the job of coming home before him to ask you to make ready the castle to receive an important guest."

"I know the King is at present in Cranborne, Dorset. That is not too far from here…"

"He'll be at Clarendon for a few days, he tells me."

"Near Salisbury?"

"At the palace. He is on his way to Windsor."

"Will he stop here?"

De Neville sipped his drink.

"Unless you know otherwise... no." He looked up at me with hard eyes, "I know you are as thick as pea soup with him."

"In his last letter he said nothing," I admitted. "Nor did he say anything when he was here in December last year. He spent Christmas at Winchester I believe."

De Neville grunted.

King John and I were childhood companions. He was eight years my senior but I liked to think he counted me as a friend and not just one of his royal officers. We wrote to each other often about forest business but John also returned letters to me as a friend; personal greetings attached.

De Neville harrumphed. "The King is expecting a guest."

"To be accommodated at the castle?"

"Quietly."

"As in secretly?" I ventured.

De Neville wrinkled his nose. I formed the opinion that he was not best pleased with this arrangement.

"I will move on with the King. You will take care of the man."

"May I ask who this person is?"

"You may....all in good time."

I winced. "Am I not to be trusted, sir?"

De Neville tossed back his drink. "The King no doubt trusts you. He has asked for you especially as being someone who is…." he made a moue, "intelligent, tactful and discreet."

"But you m'lord?"

Hugh de Neville rose and put on his gloves. "I trust no one. Oh I'm sure you are personally trustworthy enough, Belvoir, but it's best that no one knows anything just yet. Just in case."

"In case of...what, sir?" I asked, cocking my head.

"Much hangs on this, Belvoir. I've managed to get the man safely all the way from the frozen bloody north, by sea round the coast so that his movements were not easily tracked. I'll not have a wagging jaw putting the King's plans in jeopardy."

"Why is he here then m'lord? Can you tell me that at least?"

"Negotiations. Deals. Treaties."

I stored that away for later.

"It's your job to keep him safe. Maybe until the King returns and...."

"Is his life in danger then, sir?"

Hugh de Neville shrugged. "The King thinks it might be so. There has been much opposition..."

"Then I will do my best to...."

"I'll send a runner before, to let you know when he will arrive."

The castellan took up his cloak.

"Sir, what kind of accommodation will the man need? Numbers of retainers? I need to know for security and..."

"The King's House at the castle should suffice."

This was the most prestigious accommodation in the whole castle. It was called the King's House because it housed our King, John, when he came to Marlborough.

"With him only six major men. Six knights. They'll stay with him at all times."

"Only six men?"

"That is correct."

I sighed. "Very well, sir."

De Neville strode for the doorway.

"Sir, why do you not take charge of this task yourself?" I asked. "See to his settling in and..."

De Neville did not turn around. "It seems…," he said through clenched teeth "the King does not trust me...completely. He wants me with him."

"No sir...that cannot be..." I began to say, when he opened the door and bellowed out to the cold air, "This will be the making or breaking of you, Belvoir. Don't fail me." And he was gone.

*****

I sat for a while in the hall before the fire, thinking and turning round my wine cup.

Hal of Potterne, my senior man at arms, came in through the kitchen door.

"Ho, ho, the big man 'imself," he chuckled. Hal had very little time for de Neville. " 'E's back on English soil then? What's 'e want?"

"Do you know Hal, even I, who have been delegated this task, cannot know the whole of it."

"That's daft...plain daft."

"We'll know soon enough."

Hal watched me stare into the flames for a while. "What's your thought on it then, sir?"

I smiled. "The man has been ferried round the coast from the north. He's in danger...possibly....it's all secret. It's all about treaties and negotiations. He's an important man...important enough to be accommodated in the King's House."

"A king himself?"

"Hmmm. No, I don't think so..."

"William the Lion?" said Hal.

I looked up. "Hmm, he's been here before. In the reign of John's father, Henry, I think."

" 'E's an old man, though," said Hal.

"Aye he is...and not in the best of health I hear. John is irked by his constant griping up there on the Scottish border though."

"What would he be doin' 'ere?"

I pursed my lips. "I don't know. They usually meet at York… or somewhere up there in the north."

William the Lion was the King of Scotland. He had been on the throne for forty two years and for much of that time had been trying to annex the strip of land of Westmorland, Cumberland and Northumbria, claiming it for Scotland. The border had been backwards and forwards for years. King Richard and then John had eventually secured it for England some time ago, but William was constantly sniping.

"No, I don't think it's him."

"Someone *for* 'im then?" said Hal, sitting down in front of the fire.

"Someone who warrants royal treatment."

Hal guffawed. "Oh di'n't you just love it when old de Devil," (this was Hal's especial name for de Neville), "said he wasn't trusted. He was spittin' nails 'e was!"

A while ago John the King had warned me against de Neville, telling me that he had become untrustworthy. But then, John rarely trusted anyone these days.

"Well!" I slapped my knees and rose. "There's no point in speculating. Whoever it is, will be here soon enough and we must be on our toes."

*****

Now, Paul, my scribe, my amanuensis. That's the first piece of our tale. We'll have to be very clever how we write this account for it's a convoluted story of the grand political lives of the great and the small mortals caught up in it all.

Thank you for coming from the priory today through the awful rain. It's just like that terrible year. I didn't think you'd come. It's a horrible wet day and so gloomy. Shall we have more candles whilst you write? There; there's the candle box, take out a couple more and place them by your writing desk.

That's better. It's amazing isn't it how much heat a candle puts out. If your hands get cramped with writing then you must tell me. I'm an old man now and although I feel the cold…what's that?

Yes, that's right, seventy three just yesterday. All my children and grandchildren came to see me...oh, it was a grand party. It tired me out of course but I enjoyed it. The children all wanted me to tell them stories....it seems they think I'm good at it.

Ho, no, Paul, I didn't tell them the sort of stories I dictate and you write down. Stories of death and murder. True stories. Those crimes I investigated as King John's constable of the county of Wiltshire, forty years ago with powers to search out and confine felons. Oh no. Those I will not let be made public until after I'm gone. Only you and I know about those.

Now, this story involves treason and murder, cruelty, arrogance, greed and lust and is such a sad tale we shall both have a hard time not weeping at the injustice of it.

So prime your pen Paul. Spring 1207, April the first to be precise, the tale continues.

That day was a blustery, showery but warmish day and Lydia my wife, and I had gone to Marlborough for dinner at the invitation of our good friends Nicholas Barbflet and his wife Felicity. Nicholas was the town miller and the town reeve and a sounder man never lived.

He was wealthy in his own right, quite apart from the mill and he owned several buildings in the town. He'd recently acquired another and had bought up the old Chandler's house on Chantry Lane which he would rent out.

It was his birthday and he was the same age as I was myself. Thirty three. My birthday had been a few days before and so we were to have a joint party to celebrate.

Hawise, my eight year old daughter was friends with their girl Aedelina; it seemed a good idea to have a get together that day.

The children were giggling up in the attic somewhere; we could hear them running about on the wooden floor. We had left Simon, my young son of almost a year, with his nurse at Durley Manor. Lydia was having an afternoon off from him.

We sat at the table which was groaning with food and drink. Myself and Lydia, our host and his wife and one other man and his wife. The servants bustled to and fro.

This was another of the merchants in the town; his name was a byword in Marlborough for wealth and extravagance. I was surprised to see him for I had a feeling that Nicholas and he did not really see eye to eye.

Master Baldwin Caspar was a man of middle age, small with a round middle as befitted a man of such status and wealth. His little eyes were sunk into his waxy face and he bore a small moustache above full red lips. His greying hair was swept over and parted low at the side and his nose was (as Hawise had so aptly noted) as wrinkled as a pickled walnut.

That afternoon, he wore a floor length cherry red gown with simple white embroidery at the neck. He'd taken off his matching round hat and it lay on a side table in the hall cum parlour where we dined. His wife, Isabel, sitting with her chin up and her head forward as if she would miss nothing of the conversation, had said little so far. She too was dressed to perfection in a bliaut of grey-blue with a silken woven belt tied around her waist. Her barbette was pure white linen, topped with a crown shaped ring, also of stiffened white linen.

Lydia wore green, emerald green, and she outshone the other two women there, tenfold.

I sat back and refusing more wine said, "Oh Nick… I can't eat another morsel."

Nicholas laughed. "None will go to waste I promise. What we don't eat will go to the priory to feed the poor of the town, Aumary."

Master Caspar shifted his ample backside. "I'm sure I could do justice to a little more beef, Master Barbflet. None shall go to waste."

His wife Isabel tutted. "Aw, Baldwin!" she admonished, "think of your stomach."

The man laughed. "Aye, I am a martyr to my stomach, it's true. The pain of it some days is almost too much to bear."

"Do you go to Doctor Johannes when it gets too much, Caspar?" I asked.

"Aye I do, m'lord and he sends me up to Apothecary Gallipot for some terrible chalky stuff which tastes like road dust."

We all laughed.

"But does it work?" asked Nick.

"Aye," said the merchant grudgingly, "It does and so it should. It costs me a deal of money." He downed his wine noisily.

"Johannes will only charge those he feels can afford it, Baldwin," I said. "He is a fair man."

"Aye I've no doubt," he replied, though the tone said, he still felt it cost him too much.

Dr. Johannes of Salerno was my good friend and the town doctor. He was a big man, tall, over six foot, near to forty five years of age. He had shoulder length brown hair, scrupulously clean and shining, with just a hint of grey at the temples, which was tied back in a queue and he was clean shaven, contrary to current fashion, which dictated that men wore beards, as I did myself. His eyes were an amber brown, clear and direct of gaze.

He had learned his doctoring in Salerno in Sicily, (where he was en route from the Crusade with King Richard,) the best school of learning in the world for doctoring, he assured me, and though he had some odd ideas as far as the rest of the profession believed, he lost fewer patients and cured more people than others could ever hope to. Cleanliness and orderliness were paramount to Johannes. He had been born in Oxford of a parchment maker and a seamstress but upon his return from Italy, finding it hard to pursue doctoring in his home town, had packed his bags and fetched up here in Marlborough. We were all glad he had. He had been a great help to me in my role as constable, responsible for investigating all odd deaths in the locality. This role had been bestowed upon me by the King a while ago and I have to say I could not have done the job half as well without Johannes' help.

"If you did not eat and drink so well, Baldwin," said his wife, "the doctor says you would not have such a stomach. Then there would be no need for remedies and you could save your money."

So the woman did have a voice and an opinion, after all.

Baldwin grunted. "Hush wife. That's a woman's logic and as such has no place here at this table where we are all enjoying the generous hospitality of our good neighbour."

Ah yes. I remembered now, the merchant Caspar had moved to a larger house on the High Street, almost next door to Nick. Now they were close neighbours.

"How are you settled, Master Caspar?" I asked. "You have been in your new house a scant two months, I think."

"Very well, very well, my Lord Belvoir. There is much more room there. A good hall such as this one. I now have an office at home. We have four separate rooms, one each apiece and a place in the roof for the servants. Now they can live in. They could not do so before, when we lived on St. Martins."

"Most had to come in every day, sir, from about the town," said Mistress Caspar, "and we found that irksome for we had to do so much for ourselves."

Nicholas coughed. "More wine, Mistress?"

Isabel simpered.

"Thank you Master Barbflet, but I do not hold with ladies drinking too much wine. I think I have had enough."

I saw Lydia look at her sidelong through long black lashes and a small smile escaped her lips.

"I hear that you are to marry your daughter soon, madam?" I said.

"Yes," said Caspar "We are most fortunate. I could not have planned it better myself."

"How so?" asked Lydia, her violet blue eyes dancing with amusement.

"My lass has taken a fancy to Anthony Chapman."

"Ah, she's about to get into bed with your competitor then, Baldwin?" said Nick.

"Aye, I'll not deny it, the Chapmans have been rubbing me up wild these many years. But with the two houses joined, no one in the area will touch us."

"Old man Chapman is willing then?" said Nick.

"We have yet to thrash out the details, but aye, he's willing. He sees the sense in it. The two young'uns have set their hearts on each other and who are we to gainsay them?"

"Fortunate indeed," I said looking at my wife over the rim of my cup.

"We shall have a grand wedding at St. Mary's then, sir," said Felicity, Nick's wife. "I do so love a wedding."

"A chance to wear your finery and rings, my love," said Nick, smiling.

Baldwin took another swig of wine. "I'm happy to say that with Anthony as my son-in-law, I look forward to a time of increased prosperity. I don't mind saying though, that I have a feeling that Mistress Chapman is not as set for the marriage as is her husband. I think she feels that her boy could do better for himself but it's not up to the women, is it? It's up to us men of business."

"I'm sure she's thrilled, Baldwin," said his wife. "Really."

"She's nobility, like you, if you don't mind me saying, my Lord Belvoir, and I think she feels that her boy is stepping down a rung."

"Not at all, Caspar. I may have a title but really I am an employee of the King and a businessman too."

Caspar grunted again into his wine cup.

"Well, if we work hard and keep on the right side of the monarch, who is to know what we might be in a few years' time."

The servant brought in some dessert and removed the empty dishes.

"You have a son don't you, Caspar?"

"Aye I do. Cecil."

"That's an unusual name, sir. One I haven't heard before," said Felicity.

"Aye it's from the Latin, you know. From Caecilius which means..." he chuckled, "blind."

Nick frowned. "But your son isn't blind, is he?"

"No, just blind to discipline and hard work."

"Now, now, Baldwin. You know that wasn't why we chose the name," said his wife, smiling.

"Grown into his name though hasn't he?" said the merchant slurring his words a little.

"How does he feel about the merging of the two businesses? No doubt he has some say in the future of the Caspar fortune," I asked.

"Doesn't give a damn... forgive me ladies. Wants to be a soldier. Pah! As long as there's money to spend and time to spend it, he's happy."

"Baldwin!"

"No, it's true my love. He takes no interest in the business whatsoever. My future son-in-law will do me proud I'm sure. Can't rely on my son."

"Oh Baldwin. He'll come round. He's only seventeen!" said his wife.

"And his mother's baby." He chuckled into his wine.

Isabel tutted. "What were you like at his age, eh?"

"Working hard for my father. Ruled with a rod of iron. No nonsense. Minding my own business and looking after his own."

His wife shook her head. "That's not the Baldwin I remember. At seventeen."

We all chuckled at that then.

Baldwin continued "All this nonsense about looking to others… my father — God rest him — would not have stood for all this silly alms giving and setting some aside for the poor of the town. They have to work hard just as the rest of us do. Work hard and keep it in the family."

I saw Lydia look down and take a breath to speak. She would not stand for such meanness.

"Baldwin, you surely can't be saying that you don't believe that for the good of your soul you cannot help your fellow man along a little?"

"Where there is great need or hardship, surely we must all pull together?" I said, catching Lydia's amused eye at last.

"Aye, like we did that winter Aumary, three years ago when Durley village was under feet of snow and starving. The town helped the village then."

"Aye, and we were very grateful."

"Well, I'm sure there's some benefit in *that sort of thing*," said Caspar. "But I'll have none of this looking to those beneath us. The way some folk talk, you'd think we were all equal and had to look to each other like ants do in an ant hill."

"Are we so different then?" asked Nick, sitting back on his chair.

"Aye we are… you know the parable of the talents, Master Barbflet. Some took that money and made something of themselves, others frittered it away. God has ordered us where he wants us. I'll not help a man that treats money lightly."

"Surely Master Caspar, we must all take to heart the words of Our Lord when he exhorts us to 'love our neighbour as we love ourselves?'"

"I only give to those who are deserving."

There was an uncomfortable silence.

Felicity cleared her throat. "Shall we serve the next remove?"

*****

The afternoon went on in much the same vein. Caspar holding forth and the rest of us listening with mounting annoyance. At last we all parted and Lydia and I collected our horses from the back of Nick's house. Nick came round with us.

"I'm sorry about Caspar, Aumary. He almost invited himself. I had no idea the man was such a..."

"Vulgarian? No neither did I."

"I had wondered if he might be town council material but God forbid."

I laughed. "No, no need to apologise."

"Nasty little man," said Lydia. "I hope we *aren't* invited to the wedding."

"The marriage is yet to come to fruition, my love," I said. "We'll see."

"Then if we are, I shall be ill that day. I know I shall."

She kissed Felicity Barbflet on the cheek. "And you shall too Fliss, I forsee it."

Mistress Barbflet giggled. "And miss the chance to wear as my husband said, my finery? Oh no! I shall go and report to you every word that was said and every deed done. Every dress and every jewel."

I clasped Nick's shoulder saying, "Thank you and God keep you," and rode away laughing with my wife and daughter.

*****

The rain continued for the rest of the week. Four days later in the late afternoon, our secret guest came clattering under the gate house and into the castle bailey, with his six men and escort. Five of the King's Flemings accompanied them; so much for secrecy. They disappeared into the garrison lodgings and were gone the next day.

A message upon the previous day had told me they were expected though I still did not know whom I was to house.

I came down the steps of the keep and presented myself as they dismounted and their horses were taken away.

A tall grey headed man with large shoulders, no longer young but still powerful, nodded to me. His hair, it seemed, had once been red for his beard still retained much of the colour. Three men grouped to each side of him. One grizzled old soldier stepped forward.

"M'lord Aumary Belvoir?"

I bowed.

"John of Doune, sir. May I present David Earl of Huntingdon." They spoke in French.

I bowed lower. This was the younger brother to the King of the Scots.

"You are welcome to the county of Wiltshire and to our castle of Marlborough, my lord." I answered in English.

The man nodded and moved away. He spoke no word.

"Please follow me my lord, we hope you will be comfortable in the King's House. There is room for all your men to stay by you."

I turned towards the building which lay close by the chapel.

A voice behind me asked in French where they were to be lodged and another answered.

I opened the door and in French asked for the men to follow me.

A large grin spread over the face of The Earl of Huntingdon, Prince of Scotland.

"Ah you speak French. Good. We shall get along well."

"You have no English, sir?" I asked. I did not believe him. He was a Prince of Scotland, Lord of Garioch but had been born in England.

"Why ever should I speak such a barbaric tongue?"

"Your wife I believe is a Beaumont and you hold the title of an English county, sir," I said. "You have a castle, that of Fotheringay in the English county of Northampton, I believe."

"Pah! My brother gave it to me. It's a God forsaken place. Flat. Full of bogs and water."

I thought to myself, is that not what Scotland is like too, with the addition of mountains, or so I'd heard. I had never been so far north but I didn't voice the thought.

"Well, we hope you'll be snugly housed here." I opened the door to the main room.

The man took in the place. The rush matting, the painted cloths on the walls, the fine painted furniture, the curtained bed, the coloured glass in the windows. His face creased into a beaming smile.

"It will do well, Belvoir."

The men behind him came in and brought in packs and boxes.

"Do you know how long you will stay with us, sir?" I asked.

Prince David scowled. "As long as your King wills it."

I nodded. He did not seem pleased to be here.

"And your King too, sir?"

The man narrowed one eye and stared at me but made no answer.

"Please let me know if there is anything else you require." I bowed and left them to their unpacking.

*****

Andrew Merriman, one of the captains of the castle guard and my good friend, met me at the gatehouse.

"Jesu, Aumary, that was a well kept secret. The King of Scotland's brother!"

"It was one of my guesses when I was told we were to have a visitor from the north."

"Why here? I thought they usually met, John and the Scots, up in the middle somewhere."

"York you mean? Lincoln? Perhaps it's quieter here?"

"By quiet you mean safer?"

"Less, shall we say, local opposition."

"You mean not so near to the disputed lands," Andrew chuckled. "So John and he will thrash out a deal for the border here in Marlborough?"

I shrugged. "That is the only reason I can think of for him being here."

"Why not take him to Windsor, or London?"

"For the same reason...it's not so public here."

"I suppose not. Will you take him out hunting in Savernake?"

"I suppose I shall have to. I have little with which to amuse the man here in the castle. I just wish I knew how long he was to be here."

"You won't know until they've concluded their business, whatever that is."

"What I don't understand is why John isn't here too."

"He will send someone to negotiate for him is my guess," said Andrew.

I stared up at the grey sky. "I wonder who that will be?"

"So no feast for our honoured guests tonight then, Aumary?"

"I have been told this must all stay quiet and undisclosed. Our guests, until I am told otherwise, or instructed by the Scots themselves, will remain discreetly closeted."

*****

All was quiet that night. The next day dawned rainy again and the Scots, as far as I knew, were closeted in their rooms recovering from their journey. I didn't see them all day.

In fact I did not really see them all week until the Friday evening. I'd wandered out of the guard room where Andrew and his watch were settling for the night. The sky had lifted and the rain had ceased and I looked up at the pale silver semi circle of the moon, like a nail paring, though night had not quite yet descended.

If I did not make for home, at night I would stay in the guest house where I had a room set aside for me. I yawned. Davie the kitchen boy was splashing across the courtyard and I hailed him and asked if he might get me some food and bring it to me. I chatted to him for a short while.

Davie had no chance to serve it to me, for as I turned the corner of the chapel a terrible scream rang out.

I was disorientated. The noise was not from the castle grounds, neither the bailey nor the buildings. I turned around and around again.

Andrew ran out from his guardroom. Peterkin Gayle, the man in charge of the gaol and treasury, who also lived in the castle, opened the door of his small room by the gate and popped his head out. A gurgling scream sounded again and the noise bounced across the bailey from the hard surfaces of the walls.

"Outside the gate!" shouted Andrew.

More people were exiting the castle buildings now looking for the source of the disturbance, including the man John of Doune. He stood on the steps before the door of the King's House, sword drawn.

" 'Tis a town matter, sir," I shouted. "Outside the castle. Please do not distress yourself nor disturb your master."

The man nodded and backed into the building.

Andrew, Gayle, one of the gate guards called Castleman and I squeezed through the wicket gate.

Our footsteps rang on the boards of the bridge as we ran under the half lowered portcullis.

Andrew and Castleman drew their swords.

The light was fading but we could just see a small knot of people gathered where the High Street met the Pewsey Road. The bulk of the church tower of St. Peter reared up above them, casting them in almost complete darkness. The open field known as South Field where we held the annual fair lay to the south, a dark, blank shape.

"Constable, Lord Belvoir," I shouted and people fell back. Two or three backed off, turned tail and began a quick walk back down the High Street, looking back once.

One woman on her knees was tending another who was writhing and gurgling on the ground.

Gayle had wisely thought to grab a flare from the gate guard and lifted it above his head.

"God's teeth!" he exclaimed.

Andrew knelt down. "Is her throat cut?"

The woman who was holding her shook her head.

"Run for the doctor quickly," I said to one of the men who had drawn back from the people on the ground. I saw the townsman Wat Fisher turn and run back down the High.

"There will be no fee," I shouted after him to make him aware he would not need to pay anything to get the doctor to stir himself.

Father Columba, the garrison priest of St. Peter, now appeared and knelt beside the stricken woman who continued to gasp for breath and whimper, retch and cough.

"There's much blood, Aumary," said Gayle. "But if her throat is not cut, what…?"

The woman who had been helping now raised her head. I saw it was Grace Cordwainer, wife of my friend the shoe maker. Her wimple was splattered with spots of bright red blood.

"Sir Aumary… the blood comes from within, she is coughing and retching up blood."

"Can we carry her to the castle, to your room Pete; you have a bed close by?"

"Aye," said Andrew, lifting the woman. "She's naught but skin and bone. She's as light as a feather."

"Grace, will you come too?" I asked.

My friend the cordwainer's wife stumbled to rise, catching her shoe in the hem of her dress and Gayle put out his hand to help her up.

Andrew lifted the girl and ran for the wicket, the priest following. We pushed through the throng of castle folk now craning their necks to see what was afoot.

"Out of the way!" I yelled angrily and the three gate guards got everyone back so that we could pass through and turn into Gayle's room.

At the door I turned and yelled at them all, "Go back to your places, now!"

The affected woman was now convulsing, drawing up her knees and retching in a terrible manner. Andrew laid her gently on the bed in the corner and pushed back her long free chestnut hair. She screamed incessantly and quietly with a rasping sound.

I saw Hardcastle shut the door behind us and I knew he would stand guard until the doctor arrived.

Grace loosened the woman's belt and dress and pulled it down at the neck. The front was a mass of blood and vomit, froth and something I did not like to think of.

"Do we know her?" I asked.

"I've seen her about, but don't know her," said Grace Cordwainer, tears in her eyes. "Oh, what can be the matter with her?"

Gayle was lighting more candles. The woman came into view with more clarity.

I say woman for really she looked little more than a girl, not more than perhaps eighteen, nineteen at most. A young woman.

Andrew had found some water and tried to get the girl to drink but she was too far gone to understand.

In a few more heartbeats, we had made her as comfortable as we could though she still continued to retch and draw up her knees moaning and gasping for breath.

Andrew began to try and clear the front of her dress and her chin of blood. She thrashed about.

"Leave her, Andrew," I said, "it just serves to distress her further."

The door opened and Johannes of Salerno ducked under the lintel.

We all backed away though Grace continued to hold the girl's hand and try to steady her in her writhing.

I turned away.

"Nothing to be done now. Go back to your duty Andrew, Castleman. I'll let you know what happens."

The door closed behind them.

Father Columba was muttering his Latin prayers quietly at the head of the bed. His unruly red hair caught the candlelight and turned it to a vivid bloody halo.

I saw Johannes frown and roll up his sleeves. I left them then and went to stand in the cool of the evening and the fading light of the gateway, out of the terrible smell of blood and vomit.

A long while after, Johannes came out and gently shut the door. As the door opened I heard the priest praying ardently and the sound of weeping from inside. Grace Cordwainer.

"I'm sorry Aumary," said the doctor. "I could not save her."

Chapter Two

A short while after, we all sat in the guard room and shocked, pondered on the strange death of the young woman.

Wat Fisher had gone to fetch Gilbert Cordwainer and his distraught wife had been taken home. I told him I would call tomorrow and talk with Grace.

Andrew wiped the gore from his gambeson and pulled his soiled cotte over his head.

Gayle too had been splattered with bright red drops and he had gone back into his room to change and returned wiping his hands on a cloth.

Only I for some reason had managed to miss being splattered.

I had asked that the body be taken to the church of St. Peter until the morning when we would decide what to do.

Now I turned to my friend the doctor and asked "How did she die?"

Johannes shook his head. "I am as perplexed as you, Aumary."

"But surely..."

"All I can say is that, something had been swallowed or introduced into her body and that as soon as it was in the stomach it began to eat away that organ and burn its way through the poor girl's insides."

Andrew looked green and swallowed. "So she was vomiting her own stomach?"

"And coughing up her insides."

"Jesu take her to his bosom," said Gayle, crossing himself.

"Oh the poor girl," said Andrew following suit. "How, Johannes?"

"Like I say, I don't know. I know of no substance which would do that."

"No poison, Johannes?"

"No poison I know works like that. They all, as you know Aumary, work on the body in a slow and insidious way or stop the heart or slow it… or some such thing. They make you vomit but not like that. Many of them are much quicker and…."

"And none of us know her?" I asked again.

Everyone shook their heads.

"Tomorrow we must ask Gabriel if he knows of anything which might do such a thing." Gabriel Gallipot was the town apothecary and a man learned in many arcane matters.

"And, if he knows of anything, where such a substance might be obtained," added Johannes.

"Did anyone hear the girl speak?"

"We came later to the scene, Aumary. I think she was past speaking then," said Andrew.

"Grace may have heard something," offered the doctor. "She was, it seems, quickly at her side after the girl began to scream."

I stood up and stretched. "So we do not know the girl. We do not know what killed her and we do not know why she might have swallowed or been forced to take the stuff."

Everyone shook their heads again.

"Is this murder, accidental death or self murder?"

Andrew shook his head vehemently. "Jesus, Aumary, there must be better ways to take one's life."

"A swift knife in the ribs. Throw oneself in the river. Take a poison which sends one to sleep, you mean, Sir Andrew?" said Gayle.

"Yes. Not that! That… horrible painful coughing and retching one's heart up. It took the time it takes to do a full tour of the castle, for her to die!"

"If it was self murder, perhaps the girl didn't know what the stuff would do to her," I said.

"And if it was murder….?" said Johannes. "Then we have a particularly nasty killer abroad."

We all looked at each other and shivered.

*****

Next morning, after calling the coroner to do his duty and gather together his jury of twelve men over fourteen years of age, I walked down to the cordwainer's house and scratched at the door.

Gilbert let me in.

"Ah m'lord, we thought you'd be along. Go on up. Grace is there. I'll take the girls with me for a walk to the river. Out the back for a while."

I stepped up the shoemaker's steep wooden stairs and came out in the parlour above the shop.

Grace curtsied as did the eldest girl, Gytha. The younger one, Cassandra, was playing on the floor with a small cloth doll.

The two apprentices were already hard at work in the room below, for I could hear Felix whistling and Harry tapping at his shoe making.

Gilbert chivvied his girls down the stairs and then all was quiet.

"I have racked my brains, sir," said Grace without asking. "I cannot work out who the girl is."

"You have seen her about Marlborough?"

"Hmm, I have, but for the life of me..."

"Grace, was she able to say anything to you as she lay dying?"

Grace shook her head. There were tears in her eyes.

"Tell me what happened from the very beginning." I gestured for her to sit.

Grace tucked her hair back into her head cloth and slid sideways onto a bench at the table.

"I had just come out of the church. It was my duty that day — yesterday evening — to sweep and polish. Two of us were on the church duty yesterday."

"Who is the other woman?"

"Mistress Chapman, the merchant's wife. Lady Marjorie."

"Yes, I know her."

"Though she does very little actual work just looks down her nose and.... anyway we were just coming out of the south door when we heard the woman retching and coughing."

"Where was she?"

"At the end of the church path, sir."

"So you think perhaps she was coming *into* the church?"

"Perhaps, m'lord. When we found her, she was outside the wall hanging onto it."

"What then?"

"Marjorie tutted and said that she thought the woman was..."

I waited for Grace to wipe a tear from her eye. "Oh God forgive her, sir. She thought...."

"She believed the girl to be intoxicated?"

"Yes, sir, and she sniffed and went on her way home. I wasn't so sure. I approached the girl and that was when she screamed and all this blood came streaming out of her."

"Then she staggered to where we found her and screamed again?" I asked.

"Yes."

"Did she say anything?"

"Not anything I could understand sir," said Grace, her face crumpling.

"You did all you could, Grace. The girl knew you were there and was comforted by it, I'm sure."

Grace nodded and wiped her eyes on her sleeve.

"Could you tell where she had come from, Grace?"

"I thought she came from South Field or maybe Figgins Lane, sir."

"I shall ask Wat Fisher, he was soon on the scene I think."

"Yes, he was. I saw him. He ran for the doctor."

I smiled "Wat is fleet of foot. Dr. Johannes came back quickly."

"Not quick enough for the poor chit though was it, sir?" and she dissolved fully into a waterfall of tears.

"Come, let's walk down to the river and find Gilbert and the girls. And thank you for your help, Grace."

"I haven't been any help at all. And I was no help to that poor girl."

She dried her eyes and suddenly resolutely lifted her chin. "I shall pray for her. Yes. She may not yet have a name but I shall pray for her. God knows who she is. I'll go to the church now."

"I think she's still there before the altar, Grace. Are you sure you...?"

"Then I must get some of my women friends to help clean her and make her right for burial."

"Can you wait please, Grace? I want Gabriel to have a look first. I need the coroner to see her and then I must make some inquiries into who she might be. She may of course have family. Then you and the priest and her family may do as you wish."

Grace nodded. "Thank you sir. You are so kind."

"Who else was by you, before we came up?"

"Wat of course and Mistress Fleschier and I think it was the girl from the Reeve's house, sir. One of the servants. She had been praying in the church and came out after us."

"Alyson?"

"Yes"

"I suppose they thought that they could do nothing helpful and went on their way."

"When they saw you sir."

"Aye, when they saw us."

*****

I trotted up to Johannes' house and waited for him to finish with a patient who had burned her forearm severely with some boiling water. I knew that she would fare well under his care for one of the guards at the castle, now a member of the priory of St Margaret, had been badly burned in the winter and his injuries had healed well.

"I saw the coroner this morning, Aumary, and told him what I thought about that young woman's injuries. He seemed content that it was an accident for no one, he says, would swallow anything on purpose which would do such terrible things to one."

"Let's hope his jury think the same. I have no wish to see her consigned to a lonely grave in the forest, as a suicide."

"I'll let him know what Gabriel has to say about the matter, if anything and he can make his pronouncement accordingly."

Gabriel did indeed have something to say.

We walked up together, the doctor and I, to Gallipot's little apothecary at Chute Alley half way up Kingsbury Hill. He was serving one of the matrons of the town, smiling and flirting.

I caught Johannes' eye and we both smiled inwardly. This was a very different Gabriel Gallipot from old. He had once been such a taciturn, brusque man who would barely give you the time of day. Since his wife's death, he had positively blossomed.

Gallipot was a small man with a shock of white hair on what looked like a half tonsured head. His face was lined and creased and nowadays he smiled readily. He was smiling now at the Widow Partridge. She paid him some money and exited chuckling like an old hen.

"So Gabriel," said Johannes, "how are you today?" He had been ill at the end of the last year and we had despaired of his life.

"Oh Doctor," said Gallipot coming round to the front of his counter. "As perky as a pig in a pile." He took the doctor's arm and jiggled it up and down.

"My Lord Aumary. Good day to you sir." He bowed.

"I hope I can help you gentlemen? Ah yes indeed...I heard about the disturbance last night. Little Agnes came and let me know." Little Agnes was Johannes' mute, dwarf housekeeper.

"Poor girl... poor chit. Such a terrible, terrible thing."

"We have come to you to see if you might help us identify what the poor girl poured..."

"Or had poured," I added.

"Down her throat," finished Johannes.

"Ah yes. I went to St. Peter's earlier this morning to look at the corpus. What a terrible mess."

"We didn't want to clean her up in case we destroyed anything which might help you," said Johannes.

"You have no idea doctor, what killed her?" asked Gabriel.

"She's otherwise a young, healthy woman, if a little thin. I can't see any injury or evidence of illness on her."

"Not crabs then?"

"If it were crabs of the throat or lungs, I surely would see some evidence besides the loss of blood and coughing."

"Hmm. True." Gallipot fingered his clean shaven chin. "Not an illness which we cannot see then."

"Well, of course it might be. It could be something inside which has burst or which has invaded the lungs or stomach but without dissec….."

"Quite, quite" said Gabriel, glossing over the fact that both of them would dearly have loved to perform an autopsy on the girl to discover what lay inside but the church forbade it.

"Come into the back and I'll show you what I have."

We looked at each other Johannes and I. We had never before been invited into the inner sanctum of Gallipot's apothecary.

The room at the back was twice the size of the shop and lined with small shelves from floor to ceiling. Two apprentices laboured over their work at a small table; one rolling pills, the other pouring a powder carefully into a pot.

"Roger, James," I nodded.

They both bowed low.

"Here I have a small alembic into which I put a little of the, excuse me sirs, blood and gore and liquid the poor girl coughed up. Scraped up from her clothes."

"With a view to?" asked Johannes.

"Distilling it into its major parts."

"And…?"

"I have yet to see the results."

Gallipot searched around for a cloth and took hold of the hot piece of pottery which had been simmering over a small brazier. I'd never seen such a small brazier.

Gently he poured the liquid through a spout into a little dish.

He sniffed. He poured it into another dish, this time metal, and added some white powder to it. The powder sizzled. Gallipot's brow creased. "Hmmm."

He turned to another door at the back of the work room. "Just a moment messires."

We looked at each other and I shrugged. Johannes lifted the small metal dish and sniffed, as Gallipot had done. His sniff was obviously a greater one for he coughed.

"Jesu...that's horrible."

Gallipot returned just at that moment. "Now you will see just how horrible," he said.

On a dish he had a small amount of meat.

"Gone off now. Can't even give it to the dog."

"You have a dog, Gabriel? I didn't know," I smiled.

Gabriel squirmed in embarrassment. "Aye, I do…and Caesar is good company, isn't he lads?"

Both Roger and James grinned.

"And a good guard dog too. I got him from the castle. One of those beasts you rescued a year or so ago, Sir Aumary."

"Well, well," I said. "A happy ending for one of them at least."

As we were talking, Gabriel had been preparing to pour the foul smelling liquid onto the rancid meat.

He retied his apron, donned his working gloves, took hold of the dish and poured very carefully.

The meat sizzled and began to froth. The liquid began to eat away at the flesh. Then it turned black and shrank away.

"Holy Ghost!" said one of the apprentices looking over our shoulders.

"Aye...Holy Ghost indeed, James," said Gabriel, taking off his gloves, "though devil's work more like, I think."

A horrible smell began to waft up from the meat.

"James, open the shutter, there's a good lad," said Gabriel.

A cold breeze blew through the window and the air returned to its musty, herby normality.

"What in the name of Hades is that?" I asked.

Gallipot turned to me and crossed himself. "Something called vitriol, Sir Aumary."

Johannes looked up quickly. "No, Gabriel...it can't be..."

The little apothecary nodded emphatically. "No doubt, Johannes. It's vitriol."

"Holy Ghost," said Johannes, going pale.

*****

We walked the short distance back down to Johannes' house in silence and traversed the alley way to the side.

We came in through the back door into the kitchen and Johannes sat down with a bump onto a bench.

Little Agnes turned from her task of sweeping the floor and laid aside her broom. She looked at Johannes and frowned, her quizzing gaze raking my face. She made her sign for, 'what's the matter?'

"We have just learned what killed the poor girl at the church last evening, Agnes."

Johannes looked up and smiled sweetly at his housekeeper. "Ale I think might help us Agnes," he said, "Though I won't forget…." He caught his lip with his teeth.

"This vitriol. It's the sort of stuff, rather like that substance we saw used earlier last year, I gather, Johannes. Like quicklime?"

"Aye, it is."

"And Gallipot keeps a little of the stuff for...."

"The men at the mint, the moneyers. They use it to clean the coins, I hear."

"They what?"

"Something to do with the cleansing of the coins. Makes it more shiny and takes out the impurities. It's also used by the dyers of the town."

"How, if it destroys so efficiently?"

"Only a moneyer or a dyer can answer that, Aumary."

I nodded. "So our girl could get hold of such stuff."

"Or whoever killed her could."

I rubbed my face with both hands.

"Oh I do so wish I knew who she was."

*****

I asked about the town. I asked Nick Barbflet. He did not know who she might be and resolved to ask his womenfolk. Once again they said they'd seen her but they did not know who she was.

Perhaps, I thought she was a woman just passing through the town. Maybe she was a resident at the guest house of the priory and not a Marlburian at all. Inquiries at St. Margaret's revealed nothing. They had no one staying with them answering her description.

I had to let Father Columba bury the poor girl in a corner of the churchyard.

The incessant heavy rain returned later that day and once again the rivers began to flood the roads and houses were under water. There had been little time for the water to drain away.

I had come back from Durley the morning that it began to pour in earnest. I dashed for cover of the gatehouse roof and gave my horse to an ostler.

Standing there for a while, I began to think that we should start to build an ark, so heavy was the downpour, so prolonged. The courtyard ran with water and the gullies in the walls couldn't cope with the volume. Everyone who was going anywhere in the castle splashed through deep muddy puddles.

Later that day, men came from the town to tell me that it seemed that the town bridge was about to disintegrate.

I donned my most waterproof cloak and dashed out of the main gate and down the Pewsey Road. One of the resident masons followed me out. It would be good to have his opinion. The castle was being rebuilt and strengthened and this man was one of the senior men charged with its works.

Master Lapiss shrugged deeper into his cloak and yelled over the hissing of the rain.

"Debris, my Lord Belvoir..." he pointed, "building up. We must get it cleared."

"Is the stone work sound?" I yelled back over the noise of the rushing of the water.

He dashed to the parapet of the bridge and looked down.

"A crack is appearing just here."

I leaned out where he pointed.

Nicholas Barbflet came running up. "Aumary, they tell me the bridge is going to go."

"Aye. We've come to look."

I turned to the mason again.

"Can we tip some rubble there and divert the water?"

"If we do that we shall just create stress elsewhere. We must get rid of the rubbish and hope that the damaging water will go to the middle where the channel is deeper. Or spread out sideways to the meadows."

"Will that not just put pressure on the...?"

"It's better than nothing sir. It *might* spread out over the meadow."

"Can we shore it up?" asked Nick

"Not in this torrent, sir."

I waved to Andrew who was standing on the drawbridge, and shouted, "Men, Andrew, with pitchforks and poles."

Andrew nodded, waved his arm and a little while later seven men came streaming from the gate.

They ranged out along the overflowing river bank and approached the side of the bridge on the castle side, where lay twigs and logs and flotsam; boxes and bits of furniture and the dross of decaying plants piled up one on another, washed down from upstream. They began to prod and poke. One man lost his footing but his friend was close by and grabbed him before he could fall into the raging torrent. The yeasty water boiled and bubbled.

One of the workers, an ostler I recognised, grabbed a handful of dirty brown muck from the end of his muckfork and threw it over his head onto the ground by the road. Others followed suit. Nick supervised the spreading of the rubbish.

I started to become worried for the men and asked Andrew to run back and fetch a rope in case we might need to throw a lifeline to someone who might be swept away on the current.

Slowly the debris was cleared. Now Master Lapiss could better see the damage to the bridge wall. Hanging onto the stonework, he inched down the steep bank and waded into the water to his knees.

I heard his voice float up to me over the parapet where I stood watching him, much of the sound masked by the rushing of the waters.

"Stones.....dislodged....crumbling mortar...a crack..."

"Will it hold?"

He came struggling up the bank, missed his footing and slid on the mud and slimy plants straight into the rushing water. He came up quickly, his coif missing, his capuchon billowing around him like wings. Luckily the air had been trapped and he floated on the current. Just at that moment Andrew appeared at my side with a thick rope. I threw it to Lapiss who grabbed for it and missed. He tried again and again. The current turned him a circle. At last he managed to grab it and he began to pull himself closer, spluttering and coughing.

Andrew and I manned the rope and we pulled on our end. Suddenly Lapiss let out a cry and dropped one hand from the rope.

"Nigel… grab the rope again!" I cried. "Here… here, hang on and we'll pull you in."

He flailed his free hand trying to find the rope and eventually his grasp caught it and hung on.

Andrew and I pulled and got him to the safety of the roadway by the beginning of the bridge.

"No... one... no one to go on… the bridge. It will go… I think." Nigel Lapiss struggled to say.

I yelled as loud as I could, "Everyone off the bridge… off the bridge!" Nick chivvied everyone along.

Men used to obeying orders began to run onto the road and back onto the clear section where there was less water.

Master Lapiss stood, dripping, breathing hard and started to wring out his clothes.

"Go back to the castle, Nigel and get changed… you..."

"Sir..." he swallowed. "Under the furthest arch...."

"More debris?"

He shook his head like a dog shakes its coat and large water droplets flew out from his hair amongst the driving rain.

"No sir."

"More damage to the bridge… how long do you think we have?"

"A body sir. A man… trapped at the other side in amongst the rubbish."

I blinked the rain from my eyes. "A body? Dead?"

"Yes, sir… I saw him as you pulled me up."

I narrowed my eyes and looked out over towards the furthest arch.

I turned to Andrew. He was holding the rope and I took it from him.

"I shall tie this around my middle Andrew, you stay this side and I'll see if I can drag the man free. If the bridge goes I shall be stranded. If that happens when I yell — pull. Pull us across the water."

"Aumary, you can't…!"

But I had already thrown away my cloak, taken the rope, and was tying it around my waist.

I heard Andrew yell for help to hold me steady against the power of the water.

I ran across the bridge. There was an ominous groaning as I dived into the debris at the furthest side and waded into the cold water, to my waist.

Sure enough there was a man in what had been a good dark green cloak. He was slapping against the stonework of the furthest pier of the bridge with each wave of water coming downstream.

At a struggling swim, I grabbed for him and took hold of the cloak bunching it in my fist.

The bridge gave a lurch.

I hugged the man to me and waded further into the water, then got my arms around him and pulled him backwards.

The stones of the bridge parapet fell above me with a great splash.

One of them glanced my elbow and I groaned. That would be a good bruise tomorrow.

I readjusted my hold on the man and pulled. His cloak was fast on a branch. I tore it and pulled again.

The man's head flopped back.

I took hold of him once more and this time managed to get him onto the lower bank.

Gasping for breath now, I flung the man over my shoulder and struggled up the further bank, slipping and sliding in the mud. Master Lapiss appeared at my side and helped me to pull. We both grappled with the body and at last got it free and onto the roadside.

Once again I flung the man across my shoulder and made for the roadway of the bridge.

The southern side was disintegrating before my eyes. Lapiss had run before me, holding the rope and leaping the holes becoming visible in the roadway.

I ran on, keeping my eye on the ground for holes appearing which would send me straight back into the water.

The rest of the southern parapet fell with a tumbling crash. I leapt for the middle. Hands stretched out to take my burden. I let go.

Suddenly the whole surface of the road had gone. I tossed out a hand and found stone. I grasped it. It fell. I felt the rope around my middle tighten quickly and the breath left me as it jerked me upright.

My legs flailed in nothing. Water bubbled up around me. I felt myself pulled up again.

I threw out my arms and once more found stone. I grabbed it tightly. My arm was almost torn out of its socket as the whole edifice crumbled and I was pulled free of it.

Hands grabbed my clothing as I rose to my knees and crawled.

A voice said, "Aw, Aumary...I thought I'd managed to get rid of you then!"

I chuckled with the breath left in me...

Andrew's face loomed up at me. "Nope...you ain't dead yet. Damn it!" He slapped me affectionately on the shoulder.

Divested of my clothes, wrapped in a spare cloak belonging to Andrew, and drying my hair on a towel, I thanked Master Lapiss and Andrew Merriman for their help.

The body had been brought to the castle, in a cart covered with an oiled cloth; I asked that the finding of it be kept as quiet as possible. Why did I do this? Something in me said that this man was not like the other bodies we had found. This man's clothing spoke of wealth and with the guests we had in the castle, I felt it best to keep his finding to ourselves for a time. The body had been taken to the castle mortuary. I would go to see it later. Nicholas had gone to convene the town council and tell them the bridge was gone.

Andrew told me that it had totally washed away and that Lapiss and I were the last folk to cross it. Marlborough was now cut off from the south. It was likely we should have to ride all the way to West Overton should we wish to move in that direction. Even then we might not be able to cross the sodden meadows.

"There's a deal of rebuilding to do in the town, as a result of all this flooding," I said to Andrew. "Is it still raining?"

"Aye it is. And the river still rising."

He sorted me a shirt, braies, a tunic and some patched chausses. "Try this for size, Aumary. It belongs to Hardcastle." He was the only man of anywhere near my size. My boots were sodden so I borrowed a pair of Andrew's.

I towelled my curly black hair, clothed myself warmly and then Andrew and I sloshed through the watery bailey to the mortuary.

As we opened the door, Gayle came splashing up behind us. "Mind if I join you, sirs?" he asked. "I have some light for us. It's dark in there."

He produced a strike-a-light and two candles.

The candles flickered into life and Gayle set them up, one on a small table and another at the end of the bier where the body of our drowned man lay.

I peeled back the cloth covering him.

His green cloak had been bundled up and stuffed under his head as a pillow. I teased it out gently.

It was napped green wool of the highest quality and lined with red silk. I had torn it as I'd extricated the man from his pinioning branch. The cloak had been held with both strings and brooch, though the brooch, I thought, had been torn off in the water. The cloak showed a hole where this had happened. The silken strings were tied so tightly that the knot was fast. Someone had cut the string to get the cloak off. The man's chausses were dark green wool, his cotte pale rust red wool with a coloured embroidery band at the shoulders, coming down in two panels - two interlacing branches of red and green with small red flowers. The neck had been secured by a small brooch — the hole was there for the pin but, like his cloak pin, the jewel itself was missing.

The man's shirt was fine white linen, rather muddied now and there was some expert white-on-white embroidery at the neck and across the breast where the seams were sewn with it.

The belt was rust red leather. The buckle was oval and bore a buckle plate with fine decoration in red and green enamel; a four petalled flower with leaves. One fine leather glove was stuffed tightly into it. A battered sheath lay at the belt but there was no knife. I noted a strap of fine leather where another had hung, now missing and no doubt ripped off by the man's passage through the torrent.

I turned to his face and took up the candle to gaze at him clearly.

I did not know him.

He was a man of perhaps forty years with light brown wavy hair and no grey at the temples. His face was unlined, though scratched and torn by his watery ordeal; he was clean shaven and he was generally well nourished.

The door opened behind me and I leaned back to see who had entered.

"Ah Johannes, well timed."

"I came as soon as I could."

"We have a very wealthy man here. I think none of us know him...?"

Everyone shook their heads.

Johannes rolled up his sleeves and began to examine the man.

"Many abrasions to the head...concomitant with a water borne body hitting the debris and rocks amongst which he travelled." He peeled off the tunic and shirt with my help.

"Hmmm. More bruising here."

Johannes lifted the body to peer at the back. "Ahhh," he said.

"What doctor?" asked Gayle.

Johannes dropped the body back down and rolled it to the side.

Andrew took in a hissed breath.

"That is a sword cut or I am a Saracen," he said.

"Aye it is. Washed clean by the water."

He took up the white shirt and turned it to the back. There was a slash and brown blood marks faded by immersion in the cold water.

"Help here, Aumary?" asked Johannes.

Soon the man lay naked before us.

"A well made man of forty or so years. A soft life. His hands are clean and the nails pared and manicured. There are no marks to his hands to indicate his role in life. No scars to denote a fighting man. His clothes speak of wealth. Here see, a gash to the lower back as well as the sword slash. The man I think, was first struck with a sword and then finished in the kidneys with a knife."

"Such a man would not walk anywhere. There must be a horse loose somewhere out in the rain and it will be a fine one," I said.

"And men such as he do not travel alone," said Gayle "there will be servants, baggage, armed protection perhaps."

"If there was, they did him no good."

"He was not robbed. His finery was still with him when he went into the water, I think," I said.

"In the river washed down to the town bridge. Where from?" asked Johannes. "He's been in the water a day, I'd say."

We each looked at the other. "West... obviously?" said Gayle.

"Down the Granham Hill?" said Johannes.

"The Shaftesbury road and then tipped in the river dead....to be washed up a mile or so down stream?" I said.

"Or tipped in closer? said Gayle.

I took up the cloak again.

"A very fine man… travelling alone? Why?"

"He has no scrip, no pouch, no purse," said Johannes.

I folded the cloak once more. There came a wet rustling and crackling.

I shook out the sodden cloak again.

"Turn it inside out, Aumary," said Johannes. He too had heard the noise.

I felt all along the seams at the bottom. I reached the place where I'd torn the lining from the jagged branch.

"Ah." I slid my hand up between the lining and the wool. I felt a small package folded in what seemed to be oiled skin and I gently fished it out.

Leaving the cloak over the man again and folding the rest of his clothes in a pile we left the mortuary and went out into the light. Gayle locked the door.

In my office, I undid the seal, simply a blob of red wax on the small packet and unfolded the vellum.

Out fell a large coin. No, it was no coin, it was a large gilded wax seal. I had seen this type many times before.

John's crowned head and seated sceptred body stared out at me from the seal. In his right hand he held a sword aloft.

I gave it into Gayle's hand. He took it to the light of the closed window and flung back the shutter.

I scanned the small letter.

"The man is Alan of Windsor. A King's man. It seems he was here to meet our esteemed guest the Earl of Huntingdon. This is his safe conduct and patent. His warrant."

"Not so safe eh?" said Andrew.

"So where is the rest of his party?"

"If he had one—party that is…," I said, "they are the other side of the swollen river."

"And those they come to meet, are on this side," Johannes said with wide eyes.

"And until the waters subside....never the twain shall meet," I added.

Chapter Three

I was a prisoner in the town. I could not move south into the forest and head for home, for every road there crossed the river and both local bridges were gone. I couldn't ford the river at other places for it had become too dangerous. No boat could paddle against the swell. I prepared for a lengthy stay at the castle.

The following day as I stood looking at the body of the King's man Alan of Windsor, redressed in his cleaned finery and laid out before the altar at St. Peter's church, I felt a presence behind me.

I turned to see the Earl of Huntingdon standing a little way off. He too was staring at the body.

"My Lord," I bowed.

The man of Scotland came forward. We spoke in French.

"I came to see what manner of man was Alan of Windsor. The man who was to try to convince me that my brother's claim to Northumberland was not valid."

"Do you know him, sir?" I asked.

"No. But I was told he's a lawyer. A fine lawyer."

"But not one who is a cleric. He has no tonsure."

The Earl scoffed. "Not all men of the cloth are holy, My Lord Belvoir."

"No indeed. Plenty of them are as secular as you or I, sir."

"He has a fearsome reputation as a negotiator."

"Has he? You know a little about him then?"

"I made it my business to ask about him. It pays to know one's enemy, Belvoir."

"You speak of him as an enemy, yet you'd never met the man."

David folded his arms across his barrel chest. "He was your King's man and as such until we had come to an agreement, my enemy."

"Forgive me my lord, but is that a very fair thought? You come here to dispute a strip of land. Surely the whole point of negotiation is to listen to argument with an open mind and a respect for your opposing counsel's opinions?"

"My brother wants that land. I must get it for him. There will be listening to argument, Belvoir, but in the end one outcome."

I turned to look him in the face. "You are set on this then? Why come all this way if there is to be no accommodation? Why not just fight?"

The Earl tipped back his head and laughed. "Oh yes, there is to be an accommodation, as you put it."

I turned away.

"I will insist. Your King will capitulate. Castles will be handed over. Money will change hands…It's a matter of time."

"Have you met our King, sir?"

"Thrice I think."

"Then I wish you luck." I stepped closer to the bier. "You know that the man was murdered?"

"Aye."

"Then someone did not want him to meet with you, sir. Accommodation or no accommodation."

The Earl shrugged. "They will send another."

"Perhaps one not so skilled in…negotiation," I said carefully. I too wrapped my arms around my chest and faced him again.

"I did not kill him if that is what you are saying," he said.

"You called him the enemy. Sir."

The Earl's eyes narrowed. He looked me up and down. "All Englishmen are enemies. To Scotland."

"Whilst you are here at my castle, my lord, you will be treated as a friend. You were I think, a friend to our present King's brother…"

"Richard? Aye… I was his friend. Once."

"Then you must be treated as a friend."

His lip lifted as if he would smile but then the gesture was gone. "For that I thank you," he said eventually.

I bowed my head.

He turned and stomped off saying, "You Englishmen and your ridiculous sense of honour."

I countered with "Your lady wife is English, sir."

He stopped, and without turning, laughed, then I heard the door bang.

So that was how the land lay. I was very glad it was to be nothing to do with me. This negotiation.

I went off to arrange a lead lined coffin for Alan of Windsor. He would lie in our church until someone was able to come and fetch him home for burial.

*****

I spent some time in my office thinking on the death of the young woman. I couldn't rest until I found out who she was.

I'd nothing pressing to do so I went into the town and ducked into Figgins Lane.

Wat's little bothy was under water and he'd gone, I was told, to the house of his elder brother on Oxford Street.

At last I found the house and scratched at the door.

Wat Fisher came and opened it. His face creased into a smile and he wiped his hands on his jerkin.

"Come in, m'lord. You managed to find me then? You can't mean for me to go out in me little boat, sir, in this weather?"

"Oh no, Wat," I laughed.

Wat and his young son Peterkin Fisher had often helped me when, in the course of my investigations, I had needed someone to dredge the river or watch the banks. He was the town fisherman who fished the river and its pools to supply the fish for Friday's suppers.

"You were at the Pewsey road the other day when the young woman by the church, lay dying. Thank you for running for Dr. Johannes."

" 'Twas nothing sir." Wat shook his head. "Nothing he could do though, was there? Too far gone I hear."

"No," I said sadly. "I'm trying to find out who she was, Wat. Have you any idea?"

Wat gestured for me to sit. "I'd give you some ale, sir, but me brother is out of it...nothing to drink, sir."

"We've plenty of water, Wat," I said.

Wat laughed out loud at my feeble joke. "Aye that we have. Too bloody much - beggin' your pardon, sir."

"I'm sorry about your house."

"Aw… it's nothin' sir. It's not the first time… nor the last. We'll just build it up again."

"Galling though."

"I'll set it a bit higher up next time… though I do need to be near the river, for me boat."

"So, *have* you any idea who she was?"

"I followed her out from Figgins Lane that day, sir. She was moaning and calling out a name."

"A name?"

"When I got level with her, she was leaning on the church wall and Mistress Cordwainer and Mistress Chapman were coming out'a the south porch."

"Yes, I've spoken to Grace. She heard nothing. What was the name Wat?"

"Ah, I heard it the once as she came out of the lane and again just as she reached the wall. It don't make no sense though. To me."

"No, I don't suppose it did," I said, thinking of the nasty damage being done at that precise moment to the poor girl's insides.

"She said what sounded like 'Tracy' sir. Mind you it were mumbled and almost whispered."

"Tracy? The surname Tracy?"

"Well, it can be a man's forename can't it?"

"Yes, it can, Wat, thank you for reminding me."

"I don't know no Tracy sir, in Marlbro. Do you?"

"No."

"But then I don't know everyone. You probably know more folk than I do," said Wat.

I smiled. "There are some folk called de Tracy. They hail from northern Normandy near Bayeux, I believe, but I don't know of any of them around here."

"No sir."

"So she came from Figgins Lane and called out the name Tracy or something like it?"

"Yessir."

"All houses, private houses down Figgins Lane aren't there?"

Wat suddenly looked up at the rafters.

"Yessir... and.." His eyes wandered to and fro.

"And... Wat? What aren't you telling me?"

"Houses, just houses, poorer sort than on the High, sir."

"Yes, Wat, I know. Smaller houses."

"One biggun, sir."

"Is there?"

"You wouldn't know about that seein' as you'm a gentleman sir and a nicely married man."

"Ah yes....Wat. Mistress Ashley's place."

"Aye sir. Known to us all as Madam Meretrix."

I laughed. "I'd forgotten that was there."

This place acted as the town brothel, tucked discreetly down the lane in a court just through an alleyway between two cottages. It backed onto South Field. I knew it for Nick Barbflet had had cause to deal with a dispute between Mistress Ashley and her neighbour and he'd called me in to arbitrate.

What's that Paul? You didn't know there was such a place in Marlborough? Well, of course you didn't lad... you're a monk, aren't you?

"I'll start with the houses nearest and then maybe I'll visit the brothel, Wat,"

I said.

Wat's eyebrows flew into his hair.

"Oh no, sir. I can't be letting an upright man...I mean..." he squirmed. "A man of your good background, sir, go there."

I chuckled. "Don't worry Wat, I won't be tempted by the wares on offer."

"But what will Madam, Lady Belvoir say if she gets to know, sir?"

"Our secret, Wat." I leaned forward and put my finger to my lips.

*****

Some folk were at home along Figgins Lane. Two houses on the South Field side were empty of their occupants. No doubt they had work in the town which could carry on despite the floods. At the last house before the alley to the brothel, a man opened the door scowling.

"Yes."

I told him who I was, what I wanted and I described the girl.

"Aye I seen 'er."

"Do you know her name?"

"Nope."

"When you saw her, where was she?" The water dripped from his eaves and ran down my neck. It had started to rain again.

"Can I come in?"

The man shrugged and moved out of the way. The house was a small, one up, one down affair.

"Your name is...?"

"Warin Deyar, my lord."

"Well Warin Deyar, this is very important. You know that a girl was found dying the other day up the High Street by the church of St. Peter. She has no name. Are you sure it was her you saw?"

The man sniffed. "I dunno. There's many look like her."

"Pretty, eighteen or so, chestnut hair worn free, blue eyes, fair skin, no hat or head cloth, worn brown dress with a black belt. Long blanket cape of fustian in dark blue..." I said again.

"Aye, like I say, I saw her."

"Where, man?"

"Outside 'ere."

"Doing what?"

"She were with a man, sir."

"When did you see her?"

He shrugged.

"Did she come from the house next door down the alley?"

"Madam Meretrix...? Maybe."

"What was she doing with this man? Describe him."

"Talking. He had a cloak dyed with alkanet that I know."

"Colour?"

"Purplish red. And his tunic was a lovely blue. Probably cabbage... I like that soft grey blue."

I looked at the man's hands. They were stained a myriad of colours.

"You're a dyer? Where do you work?"

"At Master Tapiser's. We're flooded. Down by the river. Can't work at the moment."

I nodded. "Besides this man's clothes, did you see his face, his hair?"

"Rich man," said the dyer, "light brown hair. Young. Baby faced. Looked like he was sucking a wasp off a thistle."

I tried not to laugh.

"Have you seen this man about town? Elsewhere?"

He shook his head. "I keeps meself to meself."

"Best way to be, my man," I said as I fished in my scrip for my purse. I handed him a quarter penny.

He touched his forelock then and as I was turning away he said, "Course, there was that older fella came and dragged him off."

"Oh?" I turned back.

"Yeah. Lovely crimson gown. Cost a fortune did that. Madder dyed."

"You saw him clearly too?"

"No, only his gown really. Really good quality it was. Fella was old." The dyer laughed, "Looked so bloody mean and dry, I reckon if he passed wind, he'd fart dust."

This time I did laugh.

"Deyar," I said, call for me at the castle if you see either one of these men here again."

He touched his forelock. "Aye sir. I will."

*****

I turned into the alley where lay the brothel and knocked on the door. All brothels had to be run by a married pair - it was the ruling but somehow, since the death of Master Ashley, the brothel mistress had managed to carry on alone.

It was some time before the door opened. Once again I explained who I was.

A sleepy eyed girl with a robe clutched around her said, "We're closed. Come back later."

I pushed past her.

"No, I'll come in now."

"Here…!" she started.

Then the owner of the house came down the stairs which were open to a large ground floor room. She was a woman of about thirty five with long fair hair and a buxom figure. I knew her from the argument she had fought with her neighbour.

I nodded. "Mistress Ashley."

Her perfectly plucked eyebrows flew up and she stroked the folds of her pale blue gown across her stomach.

"My Lord Belvoir. What brings you to our humble house?"

"The death of a young woman who may have once been resident in your house, madam," I said coldly.

Once again I described the girl.

"And what is your interest in this girl, sir?" asked Ashley.

I explained my role as Constable of the county.

"It is my duty madam, to look into her death and ascertain whether she died by accident or by the hand of another. We do not know if the deceased was a resident of the town, a villein, or a free woman."

Mistress Ashley paled. "Murder, sir?"

I nodded briefly.

She recovered quickly, I'll give her that. "What makes you think she is one of mine?"

"Was she?"

Ashley glided down the stairs and swept into the lower room, dragging the folds of her long gown with her.

"None of my girls are missing, sir."

I looked around. One of them was peering at me from the top of the stairs. The girl who had answered the door stood a little way off smirking. One other spied through the crack in the door at the back of the room. I could see her brown eye.

"Has she ever worked here?"

The mistress sat down.

"No, sir. Never.

I stared at her. Her gaze never wavered.

The girl who had answered the door folded her arms and giggled.

"If I find you have lied madam, the penalties will be severe."

"She was not one of mine."

I turned to leave.

"But...."

"Yes?"

"I caught her outside one evening waylaying my clients as they were coming into the house."

"Oh. Where exactly?"

"At the end of the lane."

"What was she doing?"

"I told you. Trying to steal my clients. I told her to push off. My Lord Belvoir."

"Where did she live?"

"I have no idea." The woman fiddled with her clothing, rearranging folds, tightening pleats, squeezing her breasts into what she considered to be a firmer condition inside her cotte.

"Which clients was she trying to steal?"

The brothel mistress laughed. "Oh my lord. You don't really expect me to answer that do you?"

I thought back to the night I'd met the girl. She really didn't seem like a prostitute to me. But then, what did I know?

I described the man that the dyer had seen with the girl.

"It might have been one of my gentlemen…yes," said Ashley. "But there are so many."

"Who is he?"

"I don't know, sir. He never gives a name."

The doorkeeper giggled again.

"If you remember, madam, I am at the castle. Come there and tell me."

I walked in silence to the outer door, with several pairs of eyes on my back.

The door girl hurried to open it and simpered.

"The mistress don't hold with poaching, sir."

"No. I'm sure she doesn't."

"She told the girl to go and drown herself or if she saw her here again, she'd do it for her." The girl laughed.

I stopped.

"Your mistress threatened her?"

"Aye… like I say…."

"Anice!" shouted Mistress Ashley. The girl tried to close the door on me but I put my boot in the door hole.

"Was this just the once, Anice or were there other times?"

"I only heard her once..."

"Anice! Come here!"

I let her shut the door.

Drown herself.

She had. In a way. She had drowned in her own blood.

*****

I carried on down the lane. The first house I came to was empty; the next, a wizened old crone who came no higher than my breast, answered the door.

Once again I explained who I was and what I wanted. I described the dead girl.

The old woman looked up at me with one milky eye.

"She never came back."

"Oh?"

"She never paid her rent neither."

"Might I see her room, mother?"

"It's right at the bottom. I ain't goin' a get down there. Can't do the steps."

I looked into the dingy house. It was one room deep, three storeys tall with a basement. Tiny windows were set into the wall low down. I'd seen them from outside.

"I'll manage, mother," I said.

She took me to a door at the side of the ground floor room where steps led down into blackness.

"Have you a light, mother?"

She just looked at me as if she hadn't comprehended what I'd said.

I fished in my purse and brought out the candle end I always kept there for emergencies and bending to her meagre hearth, I took flame. Then I turned to the black hole that had been the dead girl's home.

The floor was damp beaten earth. The stone walls too ran with damp. The only time, I thought, this room would be dry was in a very hot summer.

I raked the walls with light and into view came the small windows almost at ground level outside which let in very little light and a lot of the rain.

I saw a rope strung bed and straw mattress, a stool, a chest. Two blankets were folded neatly on the bed.

Some clothes were also folded into the chest. There was a good blue bliaut undarned and whole and a super-tunic of darker blue made from good wool. Here someone had very professionally stitched some small white flowers in wool yarn onto a band around the neck. Under the clothes were some passable leather shoes, now going mouldy and a wooden box. Nothing in it.

I gazed round the place again.

I shouted up the steps. "Mother, what name did the girl give?"

"Eh?"

I bounded up the stairs. "Name… what did she call herself?"

"Oh eh... erm... I think it were the name which sounded like a flower. Royse, yes Royse."

"Did she have another name?"

"Royse, er Royse Fordón… or summat."

I frowned.

"Do I hear you right? Fordón?"

"Aye I'm sure of it."

"Thank you."

I made to leave the house. "I'll send a person for her belongings as soon as I can then you may let your room again."

"That's kind...and the rent, sir?"

"The woman is dead, good mother, you'll not get your rent."

"Then I'll have to sell some of her stuff, won't I?"

I sighed and fished in my purse.

I put the money in her black palm and folded her filthy fingers over it. "The goods better be there mother, when my man comes to fetch them. I've noted them all."

She grinned. "Thank you, sir."

"Where did she come from?"

"I dunno."

I moved to the door. "She were a nice girl," said the old woman. "Quiet and... sorta fine. Like you, sir."

"Was she indeed?"

"Aye… and she could read and write."

I stared at her.

"Aye she could. She showed me how."

"Well, well," I said. "Thank you, mother," and I closed the door.

*****

As I wandered back to the castle, I saw that the men of the town council were exiting St. Peter's where they often had their meetings. Nicholas Barbflet, the town reeve, hailed me.

"Sir Aumary. Are you recovered from your dip in the Kennet now?"

"Yes, thank you Nick," I chuckled.

"Your man. I hear you have identified him."

"Aye, we have. We are however at a loss to know where his party is. Surely he cannot have been alone."

Nick shrugged. "Perhaps he felt confident enough to ride on ahead. The places around about Marlborough have no reputation for trouble. Not at the moment."

"No, but the forest might have."

"You think he came that way?"

"The King was at Cranborne and then Clarendon. If he sent him from there....?"

"He would come through the forest - yes. But I hear he's a man of Windsor?"

"Then why would he be crossing the bridge or even be on the other side of it? His most direct way is the Newbury Road. He could have come, perhaps, from Ramsbury and not touched our bridge at all. Everyone knows what the weather has been like. Word will get round that we have floods and the roads are difficult."

"Hmmm."

"I have today identified our young woman too," I said.

Nicholas stood up straighter.

"Ah."

"Her name is Royse Fordón."

Nicholas' brow furrowed. "I've heard of no Fordón family in the town."

"No, and I do not know of one in the forest."

"Passing through then, Aumary?"

"No. She had a home on Figgins Lane, if you can call it such."

Nick turned back to me. "Then who is she?"

I shrugged. "I am sending for her things. Perhaps in them we shall find something which will tell us."

I began to walk back to the castle and Nick fell in beside me.

"We have had a meeting about the bridges. There is nothing we can do, it seems until the waters recede. However, Tim Roper thinks that we might be able to create a ferry at the back of his yard. Shoot a rope across and secure it at the other side...should we need to."

I slapped Nick on the back. "Good luck with that, then."

"Aye. And good luck with *your* quest."

*****

All that afternoon I sat in my office and thought about the girl.

A little while before supper, Hardcastle brought her possessions to me.

I laid them out on my table. The clothes were of fairly good quality, or had been once. It was as if the girl had at one time a position which allowed her to spend money on fairly superior quality clothes and good things. The brown dress in which she had been found, was not such good quality, as if she was saving this one before me, for better times.

I picked up the shoes. It was the same with these. The upper was worn away in places and the lacings had gone. She was keeping them, I supposed, for a time when she would be able to afford to mend them. They were good shoes. No money had been found on her body, nor at her home. The old crone had perhaps raided her savings. Perhaps the box had contained cash. I looked at the small wooden box; it was empty. I picked it up. It was heavy for its size. I examined the base.

There in a corner was a tiny glimmer of something. Something I'd missed when I had glanced into it in that dark cellar in which the poor girl had lived out the last days of her life.

I fiddled with my nail.

Out came a tiny cross, partly caught in the bottom panel. A beaten silver cross with a raised pattern of dots along the middle and ends which were slightly flared. The thing sat on my palm and measured no longer than the length of my little finger tip. I picked it up and took it to the candle light, staring at it on my palm. It was very thin as if it was well worn and a loop had been fixed to the top for the thinnest of chains. I found no chain in the box. I turned it over. On the reverse was scratched the letter M.

The girl's name was Royse. Why did she possess such a personal thing as a cross with the letter M upon it?

I laid it carefully down on the table.

She had not been wearing it when she died but she had kept it safe. Perhaps it was a relative's; her mother's for example. There was no other jewellery, no rings or pins, no brooches. Nothing of value at all. Perhaps she had sold it to keep her in food?

But this she could not sell. This was a keepsake she could not part with?

I put the cross back into the small box and put it aside and set myself to examining the clothes. A faint smell of roses came up from the wool of the dark blue supertunic.

I brought it up to my nose. There was definitely a smell of roses. Lydia used lavender and rue to line our clothes chests, swearing in their efficacy against moth and beetle. My clothes always smelled of rosemary. Lydia said it was a more masculine scent.

Perfume was entirely another matter. It was very expensive and not readily available.

Where had the girl been able to buy perfume and with what?

I ambled out of my office, locking the door behind me as I always did and made for the chapel at the top of the bailey. I wanted to catch Father Columba, who was priest here and at St. Peter's, before he began vespers.

He was busy supervising the lighting of the altar candles and turned at my step.

"Sir Aumary. You are first for worship. I have yet to ring the bell."

"Good father," I smiled. "The clothes in which the girl in the road died. What did you do with them?"

"I have them still. They will go to the priory for the poor."

"Have you washed them?"

"No, not yet. I haven't had the time and it will be a job to get the gore out."

"Can I see them?"

The priest gave the candle lighter to his young acolyte and took me into the small robing room.

"Here we are. They are good enough clothes but I'm not sure we'll get them clean enough. No one wants another's blood on their clothes, even a beggar. And the front is somewhat burned away."

I turned over the clothes now stiff with blood and gore.

I took hold of the bodice of the dress and found a small part not fouled and put it to my nose. No smell of roses. Were the other clothes those which she wore to see her lovers and this brown dress her everyday wear? I searched through everything the girl had worn. There was nothing to tell me anything about her.

"Thank you, Father Columba."

"I must go and ring the bell now, sir."

"Aye you do that. I'll be along presently."

I examined the clothes again, turning them inside out and inspecting seams and looking for secret hiding places. Nothing. At last I folded them and left joining the garrison filing into the church for vespers.

My mind would not stay on the service. Throughout I fancied I smelled the scent of roses in the air of the church.

Chapter Four

That evening for the first time, the men of the Scottish delegation came into the hall for their supper. They had until now been closeted away in the King's house. They sat, a close knot of men at the far end of the room, away from the press of Marlborough soldiers and workers at the castle.

I watched carefully from the top table. The Earl of Huntingdon did not seem to wish to be accommodated at the high table as was his right. He sat hunched, with his men around him and ate quietly what was put in front of him. I saw the servitors glancing uneasily at me.

I stepped off the dais and approached.

The man John of Doune stood as I reached them. He nodded. "Lord Belvoir."

"Please sirs, come up to the high table and feed on better fare. It's not right that you sit here below the salt and eat that which is reserved for our lesser folk."

David looked up, part of a ham bone in his fingers.

"This fare suits me well and this place, sir."

I nodded. "As you wish but manners dictate that I should ask."

The man snorted with amusement.

"May I then join you?"

John of Doune gave up his place by the royal brother, smiling. I signalled to the servitors to bring some of the food from the high table, down to the place where we sat.

"I have yet to be introduced to all your men, my lord," I said, taking some black bread and breaking it.

Doune had squeezed in at the other side of his compatriots and waved his knife in the direction of the end of the table.

"He with the long grey beard is Sir Donald Baird." The man grunted into his food by way of a greeting.

"This is Tam o' the Dale. He is our lawyer, sir." The man stood and bowed.

"Good evening my Lord Belvoir," he said in perfect English. "Though I have a good French name too Thomas de la Vallée."

He too was bearded but his was red and not as long as Donald's.

"Sitting the other side of you, sir, is Sir Nathaniel MacAlpine. Nattie." This man too was bearded, black this time. "Their name comes from the Dalriadan word for son of the blond one, son of Alpin. Ha, though you wouldn't know it now."

I smiled, "You all sport the most magnificent beards, sirs."

There was a slight rearrangement of buttocks on benches. "Aye. A man who owns a beard, *is* a man," said David.

"It is dishonourable, my lord, for a man to have no facial hair," said Doune, sternly.

I smiled. Inwardly I thought, such beards must make it difficult to tell one man from another.

"He is John of Dunfermline," said Doune, pointing again. "That is Alexander MacFirmin, known to us as Coagie Firmin, sir."

This man sported hair cut perfectly around his round head and above his ears and wore a black beard. His ekename meant basin, apparently.

The two men inclined their heads and went immediately back to their food.

"How are you finding your accommodation, sirs?"

"We are happy there. Aye, we are," said Doune.

"I am only sorry that the weather prevents us from amusing you with some sport in the forest, sir, as the King has instructed me. I am, as you probably know, warden of the forest of Savernake and we have some fine game there. I had hoped to take you hunting but… the fall of our bridges has cut us off."

"Aye, we know it."

"Might you like to go up to the common, sir, and hunt the rabbit from the warrens there or perhaps a deer or two if we can flush some out? When the weather permits?"

"Aye that would be woundily guid," said Tam o' the Dale. "I'm partial to the bawtie," I noticed he spoke a form of English.

"Then we shall organise a foray out as soon as it stops raining."

"We're not women Belvoir that we can't go out in the rain," said David in French.

"Aye, we don't shrink," said Coagie Firmin chuckling, in French again.

"It rains well in Scotland," said David.

There was more of the same but I could not understand it for it was partly in Scots.

"Tomorrow then, sirs." I attacked my meat with gusto.

*****

The rain did indeed stop and next morning the sun came out and favoured us with some warmth.

I collected together a party of six men, including FitzAlan our newest recruit to the castle staff and his man Bunce. I knew he was good with a bow. We should not outnumber the Scottish men but neither would we be outnumbered. I matched them man for man. The Scots fetched their own bows.

Some of the King's hunting dogs, which were kept at the castle, came with us. We clattered down the High Street and turned up Kingsbury Hill. No one really bothered to look at us. This was a common sight here in the town. If they stared, it was at the profusion of long beards.

Once on the common, the large tract of coarse downland above the town, we spread out and allowed the dogs and their handlers to fan out and we made for the warrens up on the hills.

Rabbits were soon sighted and the dogs sent down the holes or set to dig.

We chased along beside the handlers watching the skill of the dogs as they cornered the beasts and took them down one by one.

The skill lay in calling the dogs off at the right moment for they would tear the rabbit limb from limb and we should have little for the pot should they be so mauled.

"Do you not hunt the hare, my lord?" asked the Lord of Doune, as he sidled up to me on a bay horse.

"Yes sir, we do, but at the moment the hare is in defence. That means we let them be, so that they can breed in peace. They have a remarkably long breeding period and we don't begin to hunt them till September. It's mostly an autumn, winter pastime for us."

"Och, you're too finicky with them, Belvoir."

"We shall no doubt turn up some hare here, sir, they abound on the downs. If we take them today it will not be such a travesty but we don't set out to hunt them now. Rabbits escaped from the warrens around here are vermin to us and we have no season in which we can't hunt them."

"I see."

"Now and again we turn out a deer up here. They sometimes escape from the forest and there are a few breeding out here on the downs. It's not their favourite kind of landscape but we hunt them occasionally when we find them."

At that moment a cry went up. A hare had been sighted by the dogs. Off they went at full holler. We followed.

Try as we might we could not catch the beast but we had good sport riding up and down the coombes and valleys, trying.

Suddenly one of the huntsmen hallooed. A deer had been sighted.

Those on foot ran up the hill to see if they could see him.

We lurched, leaning in our saddles, up the steep bank.

"See him?" asked Doune, who had matched me up the slope.

"Yes… a small red dot," I laughed, "up by that copse. Parker, let the dogs go!"

The tracking hounds were let loose and we all cantered after.

The deer turned his noble head and dashed into the woodland.

We crashed in after him.

There was much yelling and barking. I stood down and waited, holding my horse's head until I could see the main huntsmen. I looked around. Two men only were with me; Alexander Firmin and the taciturn Donald Baird. I could see FitzAlan up ahead still mounted. It was hard going on a horse just here in the trees.

A cry went up and we moved towards the sound.

"We've lost him, I think."

"Nay lad." Doune appeared from behind me. "He's gone across that hill to the next copse."

Again we mounted and raced across the open down. I could see only four of us now. The Earl David was already disappearing into the trees whooping with excitement.

The dogs began to snarl and bark up ahead.

My horse shied as the hare we had chased earlier, or his cousin, started from under his hooves and sped off down the hill.

I struggled to control the beast. Bayard would never have been so distracted, I thought. I should have ridden him this day. I noticed that I was behind them all now.

Once more we dismounted and I left my horse and bending under the branches of the copse, made my way into the trees.

Three men came with me. The two Scots, Baird, John of Dunfermline and Bunce, FitzAlan's man.

Suddenly there was a sharp cry, a man's cry.

I leapt forward and tried to locate the direction but failed because there were so many echoes and so much noise.

Then a voice rang out clear and strong. "I'm all right man, will you let me be."

I pounded across the new growth at the base of the trees, jumping across bracken and briars.

Earl David sat with his back to a tree. His hand was clamped on his arm and blood flowed, though not too freely, from a wound to his limb. Tam stood close by him.

I came up slowly.

FitzAlan was standing by, his hand on his sword pommel.

"A stray arrow, Sir Aumary" His eyes scanned the trees.

I looked around the clearing. The deer had been brought down and the huntsmen were waiting for the signal to paunch it.

I leaned over the Earl David. "What happened, my lord?"

"Davie here was going in for the kill" said Doune, "when an arrow came out of nowhere and grazed him on the arm."

I mentally placed all the men I could see at the moment I'd heard the cry.

I signalled to the huntsmen to begin preparing the animal for transport back to the castle.

"Are you sore hurt, my lord?"

"Ach no…'tis but a scratch!"

"It was the unexpectedness," said FitzAlan. "One moment we were all focussed on the deer at bay, the next...."

"Did I get him?" asked the Lord David, gritting his teeth.

"Aye you did, Davie," said Doune.

The Earl of Huntingdon leaned his head back on the trunk of the tree and closed his eyes.

I looked around all those now crowding into the small glade.

"How many were with you in the glade, sir?"

"How the hell do I know," he spat. "I wasn't looking at the damn men. I was killing the blessed buck."

All my men, besides the huntsmen now with the deer, collected together in a party at the centre of the clearing.

They all looked towards me.

"Did anyone see who loosed an arrow?"

They all shook their heads.

"Davie and me… that's all," said Doune.

I looked back. There were two arrows in the beast. One to the throat had killed it.

I stared at John of Doune.

"We shot together," he said smiling. "The Earl's arrow was the killing shot."

I nodded.

"Can you ride my lord, or shall we...?"

"Aye, I can ride."

"Then let's be off for home. We have an excellent doctor in the town who will see to your hurt, sir."

I singled out FitzAlan. "Can you stop off at Dr. Johannes' and ask him to come to the castle, Maurice? Tell him what's happened."

"I can do that, yes," he nodded, his facial expression unreadable.

Doune helped the Earl to his feet.

One of the Scotsmen had torn a strip from his shirt and began to bind the wound on his lord's arm. I noticed it was Tam o' the Dale. The arrow was gone.

"We'll ride slowly back."

Earl David pulled himself up straight. "We'll ride as we always ride. It's a scratch I tell you. Gods, I've had worse."

I smiled.

I took Bunce aside… "Look for any stray arrows will you Bunce. Bring any to me at the castle," I said quietly.

We all trooped back to our horses and retraced our steps across the downs.

*****

When I had settled all my men and asked them individually what they had seen, I looked in at the King's house. Bunce had told me he'd found no arrows.

Johannes was there laughing and joking with the Earl as he bound up his arm.

He looked up as I entered.

"Ah Aumary. It's really nothing. The Earl was correct. Nothing to worry about. It will be as right as the adamant tomorrow."

I smiled. "I'm glad to hear it."

"Just need to keep it covered tonight, then tomorrow, it'll be fine to be out in the open air."

"Thank you doctor," said the Earl.

I looked round the six men. "Can I ask you again? Did anyone see the arrow being loosed?"

Tam looked at his Earl. Doune stared at me with a fixed expression.

Donald and Nattie looked at each other and Coagie and John shook their heads. MacAlpine grinned at me.

" 'Twas an accident, man," said Doune. "Can't you leave it?"

"Accident or no, sir, it's my job to keep you safe. I singularly failed today."

"Ach no. Lord Belvoir," said David with a beaming smile. "It's not your fault."

"These things happen," said Tam.

"No one admits to loosing an arrow, sir," I said. "You don't think that odd?"

"Not at all," said Doune. "The man would be horsewhipped I expect." He looked round his five men, "I know I'd keep quiet about it."

They all laughed including the Earl.

I nodded. "Then I'll see you at dinner, sirs." I turned to go out of the door. Johannes was there before me.

"I'll come back tonight and check, just in case."

"No need, doctor," said Earl David with a sweet smile.

"Oh," I turned back to them. "Please do come up to the top table tonight. The venison will be served there."

Johannes and I left.

I realised that all that day, the Earl had been speaking English.

*****

I walked down to the river later that afternoon just to check the level of the water and found Master Barbflet staring at the remains of the bridge.

"Ho Nick!" I called, "How do you think the levels are?"

Nick looked back over his shoulder at me. "Ah, Aumary. Master Caspar and I were just discussing it. We think that the water has gone down a little."

Baldwin Caspar came into view as I reached the end of the road. He had been on his haunches looking into the flow. Another man, a youngster, now joined him from the wreckage of the bridge masonry.

"My son, Cecil, my Lord Belvoir," said Caspar grimacing and trying to rise.

His son held out a hand and Caspar heaved his round body upright.

"I am pleased to meet you," I said.

Caspar's son smiled fleetingly and it was gone. There was no bow, no word, no deference.

"It will just take another day of rain and we shall be back where we were two days ago, I fear, Nick," I said.

Caspar looked up at the sky. The sun was fleetingly seen in the southwest between grey clouds.

"I have goods coming up from Salisbury, my Lord Belvoir. It will take hours and delay matters greatly if my carts must go up and down the river searching for a fordable place to cross."

I shrugged. "All local fords are impassable, Caspar. My men have been as far as Avebury in the west where the river rises. Your carts would be advised to travel north to Devizes but you will still have to negotiate the swollen River Avon at the bridge."

"Oh this is most tiresome."

"Will it rain again?" asked Cecil Caspar.

We all looked at the sky.

"Aye, I think it will," said Nicholas.

"And greatly," I said pointing to the mounting black clouds behind us.

Cecil shrugged. "Then I'd better get home for my other cloak."

"That is a fine cloak you have there, Cecil," I said. "What's wrong with it? Will it not do?"

The young man took hold of a fold of the red purple stuff, known as murrey.

"It's good enough my lord but it doesn't like the wet. The colour leaches out, I'm sorry to say. Not well dyed."

"Then it's not one of my issue, Cecil," said his father. "I would make sure my dyers had done their work and fixed the colour well."

His son shrugged.

"What are you doing wearing another man's goods anyway, boy?"

The young man bridled. "I buy from whom I wish father. I don't always need to buy what *you* sell. Besides, your stuff is so boringly dull. Brown, grey, dark blue."

"Serviceable lad. All weather materials." Caspar rocked on his heels and stuck his thumbs in his belt.

"A man of fashion, father, has to have colour. You should get your dyers to find some better shades. And anyway you cannot speak to me of serviceable when you too own a scarlet gown in which to be fashionable."

Caspar harrumphed. "I do not wear it to gad about the town in a rainstorm, and it's properly dyed."

Large raindrops were now plopping on the ground around us.

"I think we shall all be drenched and leached of colour if we stay here," I said jokingly.

I turned the young man around by his elbow and began to walk at a pace with him up the Pewsey Road.

We outstripped the older man and the town reeve in a heartbeat or two.

"Talking of a fine red cloak, Cecil. Someone tells me that a man wearing such a cloak was seen in Figgins Lane recently talking to the young woman who died by St. Peter's. Might that have been you?"

Cecil furrowed his brow. "I cannot be the only man in Marlborough with such a cloak, sir."

"Her name was Royse Fordón, I believe."

Cecil pursed his lips. "No, sir. I know of no girl who goes by that name, living on Figgins Lane."

"Did I say she was living there, Cecil?"

Cecil stopped and shook his elbow from my grasp. "No sir."

He looked away. "If you must know, I have frequented Madam Meretrix's girls once or twice on the lane. None of them, I can assure you, are called Royse Fordón."

I nodded. "I suppose your father does not know?"

Cecil looked at me under his eyelids. "You will tell him?"

I waited a heartbeat or two.

"No lad. It's our secret," I smiled.

*****

We were all becoming irritable, penned in at the castle and I was no different. I longed to go home to Durley, see my family, and to travel amongst the trees of my forest but it was not possible. Torrential rain swelled the river once more and it rained all night. The houses along the southern side of the High Street, including my friend Gilbert Cordwainer's shop and the ground floor of Nick's house were temporarily under a sheen of water as it gushed from the higher northern side down the slight incline.

As Gilbert had done before, he took all his precious stuffs up to the first floor, opened the back door and let the water drain down to the priory garden and into the river which lay at the end of the orchard. The priory mopped their floors and prepared to bucket the water out to the back.

One day, later that week, when once again the waters were receding, I sloshed my way to the cordwainer's house and pushed the already opened door.

Everyone was on the ground floor with brushes and buckets.

"Ah," said Gilbert. "Sir Aumary. Come to help us mop the floors have we?"

I laughed. "If you need me to, though you look as if you are doing a very good job without my help."

"I told you years ago that the High needed something to funnel away the water, didn't I?"

"Aye, Gil, you did."

"And still we have nothing. Still the northern side sends its water down to us with ne'er a bye your leave, an excuse me, or a sorry."

"I told you then that you needed to talk to Nick. Besides, I thought that a town councillor, an officer, had been appointed to look into the flooding; Master Glover wasn't it?"

"Aye and he's done nothing."

I looked around. It wasn't just the water. It was the mud too which washed down and into the shop, from the roadway. This was the bulk of the work for today; clearing mud.

Grace was looking fraught as if she might burst into tears at any moment. I cocked my head towards her and caught Gilbert's eye.

"Time for a break, I think?" I said.

"Aye, my love," said Gilbert setting aside his broom and enveloping his wife in a hug. "Shall we take the Lord Belvoir upstairs and have a sip of ale?"

Ensconced in the parlour, now a little crowded with tables, stools and shelves upon which were balanced the tools of the cordwainer's trade, we sat down and I told Gilbert what I had learned in the town about the dead girl.

"Royse Fordón. Hmmm. Royse Fordón, my love. Do we know any one of that name?"

"No, Gilbert… I don't believe we do."

"Is she a Marlbury girl, sir?"

"She had a lodging, in a cellar, just a hole in the ground really, on Figgins Lane half way down, with the old woman who has the tall house."

"Aethel, Aethel Sloghter," said Grace, placing our ale cups on the table. "Her husband was a ditch digger. The house was her father's and his father's. They've come down in the world I'm afraid. Saxon landowners before the days of the first William."

"Could do with her husband here, now," said Gilbert.

The two girls had gone to kneel upon the small shoemaker's trestle pushed up to the wall by the window and gaze out at the High Street. The two apprentices Harry and Felix were sitting on stools close by chatting quietly.

"A young man wearing a murrey cloak was seen talking to her. I've just asked Cecil Caspar if he knew her. He wears such a cloak but he tells me he doesn't know her."

I saw Harry raise his head and listen but he didn't make any comment.

I fished in my purse and brought out the scrap of cloth in which I'd hidden the little silver cross.

"This was in the bottom of a small wooden box that the girl had in a coffer in her room. Do you recognise it?"

Grace took it from me.

"Oh how sweet it is and so dainty."

"She obviously kept it safe for she had nothing else of value amongst her possessions."

"I have never seen it before. I wonder she did not wear it," said Grace.

"There was nothing upon which to set it. No chain or string."

"Perhaps she sold that?"

"That is what I wondered."

"She was a small chit, wasn't she Grace?" observed Gilbert. "Nothing to her, you told me. Thin. As if she'd not had a good meal in a long time."

I shook my head. "She was in a state of desperate distress I think, though things had not always been so bad for her."

"Do you think this is why she took her own life?" asked Grace whispering.

I shrugged. "As far as I am concerned, her death, until I can prove murder..."

"If...," added Gilbert.

"If I can, is an accident and she will not lie in unconsecrated ground."

They both shook their heads.

"I must go up to the silversmiths and see if they have been sold anything lately," I folded the material over the cross.

"So what other news is there in the town?" I asked, putting the little cross away in my purse.

"News...? Weeeell," said Gilbert pursing his lips. "Talking of the Caspars, the girl... what's her name my love?"

"Hilda, Gilbert."

"She's accepted the proposal at last of the Chapman lad and they are to be married. Or rather his father has."

"We are to have a grand wedding," said Grace, her eyes lighting up.

"So old man Chapman and Baldwin Caspar have come to an agreement at last?"

"Taken a while. Chapman, as you know, wouldn't be seen within a mile of

Caspar once upon a time. That man would growl at his own shadow, he would."

"Aye Chapman's said to be a trifle… erm… bad tempered isn't he?" I chuckled.

"As an ant hill poked with a stick."

"The business so formed will be a formidable one."

"Aye it will. They are both rich men."

"Chapman's wife was the daughter of…."

"Youngest daughter of The Lord of Calne; Fulke de Cauntelo's youngest sister. Yes. Bit of a scandal when she married."

"I wonder what *she* thinks of the marriage?"

Grace laughed. "As long as the son is happy she will make no complaint. That child was indulged beyond belief. She's made a spoiled, selfish young man of him."

"I heard from Caspar's own lips that he thought the woman did not approve."

"The lady will approve the satisfactory dowry settlement which her son receives I'm sure." said Grace, topping up our ale cups.

"Substantial eh?"

"Would keep a lesser mortal in fine shoes for the rest of their lives, sir," said Gilbert laughing.

"Hmmm. And what does Cecil, Caspar's son, think about the business being pulled from under him?"

Gilbert shrugged. "Not a word has been said."

"Another spoiled chick that one," said Grace.

"His mother dotes on him. The father ignores him. The lad has an allowance which lets him live like a king but he's still in debt to every tradesman in Marlbury." Gilbert shook his mop of brown curls "I dunno what will become of him."

"Maybe the agreement between the fathers will take into consideration the fact that, as he gets older, he'll need a business of his own. Perhaps they will hive something off for him." I said.

"Cecil…? Work…?" Gilbert chuckled. "That'll be the day."

"What does he do with himself all day?"

"Goes off to London sometimes with his rich friends. Spends time and money there. When he's here he's gambling with the low sort and wenching with girls free with their favours."

"He did admit to me just now that he was a regular at Madame Meretrix's."

Gilbert looked round at the girls but they were pointing out something in the High Street and talking, heads together, oblivious of the adults' conversation.

"Mistress Ashley's, aye... no doubt. He carries on there, he'll be clapped so he will."

I smiled at his candidness.

Some time later I looked out of the window. "Ah, it's stopped raining. I think I'll make my way back to the castle."

"I'll see you out, sir," said Harry jumping up.

We stepped down the stairs and entered the now empty and muddy shop.

I made for the door with a "goodbye then Harry," when the lad took hold of my arm. "Sir, I couldn't help but hear that you were talking about Cecil Caspar."

"Yes, Harry?"

"I must just say sir, that Anthony Chapman has a cloak of that colour too. I asked if it was some kind of kinship, for the two of them shared a fondness for red. I commented on it once, that it was a colour which was unusual and difficult not to be seen in. You cannot blend in, in such a colour."

"Ha!"

"I was told for my pains that, the whole point of fashionable colours, sir, was to *be* seen. The cloak must be laid out behind the rider on his mount for all to see. That was the way of it."

"Hmmm. I'm told that the dye runs...is this true, Harry?"

"Only in the poorly dyed cloths, I believe."

"Why would such a young man, with money growing about his ears, buy such a cheap cloak...even if it is fashionable?"

"I've heard, sir, that Cecil, despite his allowance, is constantly out of money."

"But he still wants the rich life he's been used to?"

"Hmmm. I've also heard but, this is...not to be repeated, sir, or if you must then keep it close to your chest that it came from me....I've heard that now and again, he steals from his father's business. I know one of his young clerks quite well. He told me that one of the funds which he cares for has monies missing and that the only person who can have got at it, is Cecil."

"Ah, now that is useful information Harry…thanks."

*****

I left Harry at the door and turned to walk down the High Street towards the castle.

Two women arm in arm were struggling up the mired road, their hems held up, their dainty shoes held high on wooden pattens. Two bedraggled maids trailed behind.

I nodded, "Mistress Caspar."

The woman peered at me.

"Aumary Belvoir."

"Ah yes. My Lord Belvoir...forgive me, my sight is not what it was. May I present my daughter, Hilda."

"I am pleased to meet you." I nodded slightly. She was a tubby not very pretty girl with a pasty complexion and grey eyes.

"All the Caspar family are out today, for I have met every member upon my travel up and down the High Street," I said.

"Oh?"

"Your husband and son this morning by the river and now yourselves coming up the High."

"We are arranging matters for the forthcoming wedding of my daughter to Anthony Chapman. We have been to St. Mary's. The usual priest is not good enough to perform the wedding, we think. A letter has gone to the cathedral at Salisbury. We shall see if we can procure a better churchman."

I frowned. Poor father Torold. I frowned again; they were travelling the wrong way up the street if they had just been to St. Mary's.

The elder Mistress Caspar saw my perplexity and added. "We have just come from the castle. Letters of course have to be sent out too, to family and friends so that they may attend the wedding."

"I have just heard about the finalising of the wedding from Master Cordwainer. You have my congratulations Mistress Hilda. It's a fine match." The girl simpered.

"We have had our letters written by the castle clerk and left them there."

"Oh of course, you intend to send the letters out by the couriers."

She nodded. "Except a rude gentleman there," said Hilda, with a pouting expression "told us that nothing would go out south until the waters dropped."

"Have you ever heard anything so nonsensical, sir?" asked Isobel Caspar. "The King's post must go hither and thither in all weathers. I cannot think that the King would like it if his letters were to be delayed by such a silly thing as rain, my Lord Belvoir. Hmmm?"

"Letters may go out with the royal couriers if they are going to the west or east of the country, to London say, and even then it is not certain that the men will get through. However they are tenacious men, these couriers. They usually find a way through for they know the country well and can usually find a route but it is by no means guaranteed. Bridges are washed away like our own, and fords are not passable."

"My father is paying for this, sir. They *should* take them," said Hilda. I almost expected her to stamp her foot.

"They will no doubt go out as soon as they think it's safe, yes I'm sure they will."

"It is very irritating, sir."

"We must have the letters get through in good time, my lord, for our guests must have time to organise their journeys. Some are coming from as far away as Winchester, sir," said Isobel firmly.

I bowed my head. "I will see what I can do to expedite matters ladies."

I had no intention of doing anything of the kind and I had a shrewd idea who the rude man was.

"Whilst I have you both, might I ask a question or two?"

The women stood still and stared at me.

"You know that a girl was found dying by the path to St. Peter's not long ago? I wonder if either of you knew of her? Her name was Royse Fordón." Again I described the girl as best I could.

The elder woman shook her head vehemently.

"There are so many young women of her sort, my lord. Stupid young things who come into the town from the country expecting the place to be Heaven on earth for them. They have no skills, no character... my husband turns them away daily when they apply to him for work. They don't spin, they can't weave, they don't sew. They are not fit to train as ladies' maids. What use are they in a town such as this? No sir. I do not know a woman called Royse Fordón."

I saw Hilda catch her lip with her teeth. "You mistress?"

"No. I know no one of that name."

"Ah well...thank you."

They curtsied, picked up their hems again and were off, haughtily, noses in the air, up the High.

I shook my head.

I was about to turn back to the west when I heard a splashing run. Harry was coming at me quickly in order to catch me before I rounded the corner and disappeared into the castle.

"Sir, Sir Aumary."

"Yes, Harry?"

He skidded to a watery halt.

"I forgot. Something I meant to tell you. It's about your girl."

"The dead one?"

"Yes. It's her name."

"Oh?"

"Well, sir. It's not a Marlborough name."

"No, so I've been told."

"Of course, she might have come in from the country around."

I thought about the little lecture I'd just had from Mistress Caspar about girls coming to the town to seek their fortunes.

"It's just that, if it's not a real name, sir, then it might be a kind of ekename."

"Royse Fordón sounds like no ekename I know, Harry."

"It's what it means, sir."

"Means, Harry?"

Harry licked his lips.

"You know, sir, that we are an old Saxon family?"

"Aye, I do."

"My father's family came from the Weald of Kent and years ago we held much land there.

"Your peddler Martyn will tell you sir, I'm sure; he will bear me out. I don't speak the language properly but I do know some words."

"Like Martyn does, yes." Martyn of Summersete was a peddler who had settled and married into a family at my village of Durley. His knowledge of old songs was prodigious and some of them were in languages none of us could understand, including Old Saxon English, the language spoken by our forefathers over three centuries ago.

"So you are telling me this is Old Saxon, Harry?"

"Yessir."

"And it means?"

"An abandoned one sir, a rose forgotten and betrayed, a rose seduced and corrupted."

"So, not a real name at all."

"No, sir. I think your girl had given herself that name. She was giving us a clue. A ruined rose. An ekename."

"Harry, you are a marvel. Thank you."

However, I was now set back several paces for I still did not know the real name of the girl.

Chapter Five

After dinner I walked up to the Jewish houses on Silver Street off the Kingsbury Hill and scratched on the door of Elias, the silversmith.

He was indeed a worker in silver but primarily the Jews were money lenders. The law dictated that all Jews were restricted to the one profession only; that of usurers. In our little town we turned a blind eye to the fact that they also purchased precious metals from us and mended our bronze and silver items.

Elias looked up from his work.

"My Lord Belvoir!" His face lit up. "What brings you to my humble home?" He bowed.

"I am inquiring into the death of a young woman who accidentally took poison, or was fed poison... She died at the castle."

"This is in your role as Constable then? Murder?"

"It might be murder, yes."

"Yes, I heard about the poor girl. News travels, even to us. How can I help?"

"The girl had few possessions but this was one of them."

I unwrapped the tiny cross. "I wondered if you might have seen it before? Or maybe the silver chain upon which it was carried?"

"You ask me if I maybe have the chain held here for the girl to come and redeem?"

I smiled. "Just so Elias."

He shook his head. "No sir. I'm sorry, I've taken no silver chains this past few weeks."

I described the girl again. The man's eyes narrowed.

"If she had come to me, I would have given her a fair price. As it was..."

He looked at me sadly under his eyebrows. "She went to another I think."

"Why not you?"

He shrugged. "I saw the man waylay her as she was coming into the street. I did go to the door but, by the time I got down the stairs, they had gone."

"You know this man?"

Elias momentarily shut his eyes. "Sadly sir. I do."

"What's his name?"

"Gowler, sir. If I'd known she had something to sell, I'd have been out of that door like a squirrel down a tree but I was too slow and..."

"Harald Gowler?" I sighed.

"Yes, sir. Unfortunately."

*****

This man was a villain known to me. He came to and left Marlborough as was his wont, usually to let the furore from his last crime die down. His ears had been clipped so many times, he had little left. He wore his hair long to hide the result. He had also had his nose sliced once for some crime or other and somehow had managed to get a surgeon to put it back together again. I knew it hadn't been Johannes.

The man was into deception, fraud, theft and now it seemed he had gone into buying up marginally precious items, probably as Elias had said, for a fraction of the true value, cajoling and coercing, bullying the owners into selling. Most people were wary of him but folk passing through the town, visitors at the priory or those who were unaware of his history, naive young women like our girl perhaps, might allow themselves to be 'helped' by him.

He came to Marlborough, I'll admit it, fewer and fewer times now, for if any of the watch or the officers of the town and castle saw him, we tended to drive him out, kicking him up the backside for good measure.

I knew where to find him.

When in the town he lodged with his brother on the Marsh, a poorer area of Marlborough down by the river, which of course was quite flooded now. The top houses by the High were still habitable, however and it was there I found the man.

I barged him through the door as he opened it and backed him up against the flimsy wall of the one roomed cottage.

"'Ere..whadaya think yer doin'?" he yelled, as the pot of ale he'd been holding went flying.

"I warned you when you were last here if I ever saw you again, I'd beat you black and blue, Gowler!" I took a handful of his dirty tunic and twisted it up to his grubby little neck.

"I ain't done nothin'." His arms flailed.

"Turn out your purse." I let him go.

He pulled his tunic straight and jutted his chin. I planted my feet wide, my hands on my hips and watched him carefully. He looked affronted but did as I asked.

There were some coins and a few items which he might have either stolen or bought from unsuspecting Marlburians.

"How much did you pay for this?" I lifted a bronze net caul such as ladies wear into which they would catch up their hair. There were real bronze threads in amongst the plaited silk ones.

"You 'ad a complaint about me?" asked the man Gowler.

"Not yet. Give it time."

"The woman what sold me that was proper desperate and I give her a good price. Mind you, a man 'as to live. I'll sell it on fer a small profit, so I will."

"I didn't think your hair was long enough that you would be able to wear it, Gowler. But then it would show up your lack of ears wouldn't it?"

"Ha, ha, m'lord Belvoir," answered the man. "You will 'ave yer little joke."

"What's this?"

"Bone of St. Anthony's finger, so I'm told."

"Pah!" I laughed and threw the thing on the table. "Looks like a mutton bone to me, been coloured with some gold paint."

"Nah...really? Well...and it cost me..."

"I'm looking for a silver chain."

Gowler sat down slowly at the trestle.

"Well, you 'ave come to the right man. I can probably get you a silver chain... for a price."

"I have no doubt you can. This one belonged to a young woman. Pretty, eighteen or so, chestnut hair worn free, no head cloth, blue eyes, fair skin, worn brown dress with a black belt. Cape of fustian in dark blue..."

"Now what makes you think I know such a woman?"

"You were seen talking to her at the junction of Silver Street and Kingsbury Hill."

"Was I now? 'Oo by?"

I made no answer but folded my arms and leaned against the door.

"Ah, a Jew was it? Well, ain't that a sorry thing. They ain't allowed to tell no one what they know are they, under oath? And maybe they ain't allowed to admit they was buying up…."

"Who was she, Gowler?"

"I haven't the faintest idea."

"Where's the silver chain you stole from her?"

" 'Ow d'you know I stole it?"

"Aw c'mon Gowler," I said grinning, "We all know you haven't got the kind of money that girl will have known it was worth. I expect she wouldn't sell and you took it from her by force. That's a crime."

"I di'n't."

"You know the girl is dead don't you? I could have you taken up for her murder."

"You can't do that!" screeched the man, jumping up.

I too jumped. I grabbed him once more by the throat. "Oh yes I could. Of course I could forget all about it, if you were to tell me where it is."

Gowler struggled. I thumped him in the midriff.

"You are a nasty little man, Gowler, I'd enjoy seeing you dance on air."

"I weren't even 'ere when..." said Gowler, retching.

"When what?"

The man gasped and doubled up again.

"When she was murdered? I said. "Have I told you when that was eh?"

"I might only have 'alf me ears, but I can still 'ear what's being said."

"Aw, you listen to town talk? How nice."

"I was outta town that night and only came back the next day. Ask me brother."

I took a handful of his greasy hair and bent back his head. His eyes were frightened.

"Where is it, Gowler?"

His eyes flickered. "I ain't got it...God's truth. Some fella came up behind me and told me to leave off."

"A man. What did he look like?" I let go of Gowler.

"He were tall but not as lanky as you. Good clothes, red cloak. Fairish hair. Small beard. 'Ow do I know who he was?" Gowler smoothed out his clothes once more.

"What happened?"

He sighed in annoyance. "This girl come up the 'ill. I saw 'er take off the twisted silver wire chain and look at it. I come up to 'er and asked 'er nicely if she was goin' to the Jews. She nodded. I was just tellin' this sweet young lady that to let the Jews 'ave it would be a crime an' I could do 'er a good deal on the chain when this fella came up behind me."

Gowler searched round for his ale pot.

"'What are you doin' tryin'a sell that Berthe,' he said, 'Are you short of money... come... come with me.'"

Gowler picked up the fallen wooden cup and flicked it dry.

"Then the man snatched the chain off me an' before 'e could give it back to 'er, she'd run off down onto The Green."

The man sniffed, "it were a nice piece, I could'a got quite a few..."

"The man kept the chain?"

"Aye, the woman what he called Berthe ran off. She looked pretty upset to me."

"She was afraid of the man that she ran away?"

"Nah. I reckon she jus' di'n't wanna see 'im. She was cryin'. Upset she was."

"If I find this is a lie Gowler..."

"God's truth it is, sir."

"Just to be on the safe side and so I don't change my mind, maybe you had better pack your meagre things and get out of Marlborough," I said, feeling for the door.

"Aw, I can't only go north."

"What's wrong with west or east?"

Gowler fingered his crooked nose. "Well see..." he sniffed, "east an' west ain't so - welcomin'."

"Today."

"Aw my Lord Belvoir, 'ave a 'eart… in this weather?"

"Yes Gowler, in this weather."

"I'll catch me death'a cold."

"Oh dear. That would be terribly sad for you. However, it would be a grand day for us in the town!"

And I smiled and left.

*****

Now I had yet another man associated with our girl. Both in red cloaks and the jewellery upon which the girl wore the cross, was still missing. And I had yet another name for her. Berthe.

I walked slowly back to the castle, looking round here and there at all the men I could see. No one had a purple red cloak. They weren't so common. Perhaps Marlborough wasn't a fashionable place and red was not worn much here except, perhaps, by the young.

Ah, yes. Harry had said that the young man who was to be married to the Caspar girl owned such a cloak.

Perhaps I would call in and see if I could talk to him.

The family of Anthony Chapman lived in a new house at the very end of the High Street, opposite the church of St. Peter, near the castle.

I stood by the front door and looked at the building. There was a bell sticking out from the plasterwork. I rang it and waited.

A servant answered and I was taken into the house and asked to wait.

Master Chapman came from a room close by the front of the building.

The man wore a tunic of cream linen which reached his ankles. Over this he wore a surcote of bright blue wool which had been quilted in a diaper pattern. Bands of pale blue embroidery stood out at the hem, wrist and neck and there was a further band on the upper arms. His head was bare and his grey hair cut short.

"Master Chapman. I am Aumary Belvoir, Constable of the castle and of the county. I am looking into the death of a girl who died, possibly by foul play." I told him a few of the details.

The man did not acknowledge me.

"You'd better come in my lord," he said. "Why do you want to talk to me? My wife was there that evening but she tells me she left before the girl was taken to the castle."

"That's right. It's your son, Chapman, I wish to speak to," I said following him into a room which had been recently limed. I could smell the paint.

"Anthony?"

"Yes. Is he home."

"What has he done?"

"Why should you think he has done anything?"

"All young men are hot-heads, sir," said Chapman. "But I doubt he has anything to do with your dead girl."

"She was a pretty girl of perhaps eighteen or so. Her hair was chestnut and she had blue eyes and fair skin. She wore her hair free and she had a dress of brown wool with a black belt. Over this was a blanket like cape of fustian in dark blue..." I said.

Chapman pursed his lips and shook his head. "I've never seen him abroad with such a girl. But then he only has eyes for the Caspar girl nowadays."

"I hear they are to be married?"

Chapman grunted. "Been going on over half a year. Of course I said no... over my dead body. Caspar's a rogue, sir. I'd not have anything to do with him."

"Oh?"

"Then Anthony comes up with the idea that we could merge and make an even bigger business out of two big ones...well...made sense then for the young'uns to get together."

"I hear they were dead set on the match sir, regardless."

"My son is twenty two, my lord. He can do what the devil he likes. The girl is eighteen....old enough I suppose, to decide for herself. With her father's consent of course."

"Is your son at home, sir?"

Chapman turned away. "No he isn't. He went off south on business a few days before the bridge went. No doubt he's holed up somewhere waiting for the water to go down."

"How long has he been gone?"

"The day your girl died, I think."

"Will you ask him to come and see me please, when he's able to return? Meanwhile might you answer me a question?"

"Hmm."

"Does he wear a purple-red, murrey cloak?"

Chapman looked stern. "That bloody thing!" He coughed. "I tell him that a merchant of quality and esteem can't be seen in such things, sir. Does he take any notice… no he doesn't."

I looked over his own bright garb.

"Like you say sir, he is over twenty one and can do as he pleases. Pah! Vulgar thing."

I saw his eyes search my clothes and take in my dark ankle length woollen cotte and my spilt supertunic of brown wool trimmed with embroidered ribbons of saffron and green. He even scrutinised my black boots and my worn grey cloak.

He seemed satisfied. He was actually better dressed than I was myself.

"Well, when he returns, Master Chapman, please send him to the castle."

"What was the name of this girl m'lord?"

"She was I believe called Berthe but sometimes called herself Royse."

He nodded. "I'll ask him if he knew her. It's not such a big town that the youngsters can't know of each other. Whichever class they be."

*****

I rounded the end of the church building deep in thought. Perhaps I was wrong about the girl and she *was* a woman of easy virtue. Two men knew her and it seems knew her well. She went under two names, one of them describing herself as a woman who had been corrupted.

I told myself that was no reason to abandon the search for her killer, if there was one. I just wanted to know who she had been.

One thing really puzzled me. The girl had a cross which was inscribed with the letter M. Now we learned her name was Berthe. Who was M?

And was Anthony Chapman with the girl when he was, according to his father, away from town upon the day she died?

Life went on, the river water fell and was then replenished by more rain at the end of the week.

It was a further full week before the rain stopped, the land drained and we were able to say that the worst was over.

Another three days went by before the river level returned to the seasonal depth. Then the masons were out and about, checking and rechecking, clearing the debris and working on the town bridge. The men of the town would quickly rebuild the other bridge at the London and Salisbury road end. First it would be replaced in wood and then eventually, after an interval of a few years, rebuilt in stone.

At the end of that week a party of men gathered at the far side of the river and hollered across to have the Constable of the castle bought to them.

I stood on the northern bank and shouted across that if they cared to go down the Newbury road, they might cross the makeshift wooden bridge built there just this week. Leading their horses and pack ponies of course. They should then travel the length of the High Street and come up to the castle, where we would accommodate them.

The four men clattered over the bridge of the castle some while later. They looked travel stained and weary. People came out to look at them for these were the first strangers in the town since the floods had cut us off.

One man shook his long black locks and smote his coif on his thighs. He pulled off gobbets of mud which had stuck to the wool of his robe and stroked the muck from his leggings.

The horses were taken off to be cleansed of dirt and fed in the stables.

I approached the first man and introduced myself.

He bowed. "I am Olivier Manches, my Lord Belvoir. This is Perigord Goosens, that is Henri Maas. Our final man here is Joske Tillens. We are all men riding with Alan of Windsor. We had hoped he would be here before us?"

I invited them into the hall and sat them down.

"The man is indeed here before you, sirs. We fished him from the river about three weeks ago. We have him coffined in lead and awaiting instruction as to his burial."

There was absolute silence.

Manches cleared his throat. "We were detained by the flood, turned back and sought refuge at Blount's Manor with the Stancombs, at Potterne. We have tried several times to get through to you but it has proved impossible and now after all this you tell us that Alan is *dead.*"

"He is and I'm afraid it's my awful duty to tell you that the man was murdered."

Manches' head flew up. "Murdered?"

"At first we thought the man an unfortunate casualty of the floods. We found him caught in the debris at the side of our demolished town bridge. However, when we got him to the castle we found that he had died from a stab wound to the lower back and a sword cut to the shoulders. Our doctor thinks he was barely alive as he was thrown into the raging torrent sirs, but that he died of drowning a little later."

"This is terrible. Who would wish to...?"

"We know of his mission, Sir Olivier. We supposed that someone who does not wish the meeting of our Scottish guests and the King's man to take place, disposed of him before he could get to Marlborough."

The other three men began to talk quietly amongst themselves.

"The body of the King's man is inviolate, m'lord," said Goosens.

"Not to mention the fact that he was a church man," added Maas in a heavy accent. I gathered that Maas, Goosens and Tillens were some of King John's favoured Flemish mercenaries.

"He did not look like a church man and he wore no tonsure," I said. "I doubt a wolfshead would have been responsible for his death for his clothes and valuable items were still with him. All save his knives."

"He was a proud and vain man," said Olivier Manches, "and it was his undoing."

"Traitors do not play by the rules, sir," I said. "It is a grave sin to kill a priest, of course, and doubly so if that priest is an envoy under safe conduct from the King but treacherous and violent men have no regard for the law."

Manches snorted. "We warned him but..."

"I must also tell you that an attempt has been made upon the Lord David's life whilst he has been here at the castle." I told them about the stray arrow in the woods on the downs.

There was more arguing back and forth between the four men, in their own language.

"Manches, may I ask? How did the lawyer Alan of Windsor become separated from your party? It seems strange to me that with such secrecy surrounding this event, both on the King's and the Scots' side, it would be hard to come upon either party and...."

"I know it is not customary or wise to speak ill of the dead but..." Olivier Manches sighed and crossed himself. "The man Windsor, if you will forgive me, was as arrogant a legal man, as ever lived, as I've said, sir. We all begged him to stay with us but no, he would ride off on his own to visit, so he said, kin of his mother's close by to where we camped. He would have no company he said. It was the night the rain started and we thought him staying with his family, until we made inquiries at the house. He had left the family the next morning but never reached us. Then we were cut off by the floods. We naturally thought that he had ridden on the few miles here to the town."

"We have been unable to recover his horse, sir. If we could, then we might have some idea whereabouts the man was waylaid. It's a forlorn hope now. Too much time has passed."

"No, there will be no tracks now."

"Someone might have taken the horse in. We might find it locally if we ask about. I will organise a search now the land is clear," I said.

"Especially if we offer a reward," murmured Tillens.

"As I said, his knives were missing too. I wondered if they had been washed away but now I wonder if they were taken by the killer. We might be lucky, someone might bring them in to us."

"Or try to sell them," said Manches. "The money they would fetch, would keep a churl happy for a long time."

"If you can describe them I'll have the description circulated amongst our townsfolk and in the countryside at large. They may turn up."

*****

Turn up they did a day later.

A carter trundling the road from Lockeridge to Marlborough found them, he said, washed up at the side of the road by the River Kennet. The carter brought them to us at the castle.

The brooch which secured his cloak was not found.

I looked carefully at what was left of the straps which secured the scabbards to the man's belt. They had been cut by a knife. How did I miss this when first I looked at the man's dead body?

The pommel of the larger knife was finished with an enamelled globe of red surrounded by a rope pattern of gold metal. The man had garish taste in accoutrements. The smaller knife, probably an eating knife, had an ivory handle carved into the likeness of an apostle. Well, that at least was in keeping with a man of the cloth.

I left them in the office along with the dead girl's things.

I quizzed Manches about the family of the dead priest. Where did they live? Who were they?

"That same family we stayed with whilst we waited for the floods to abate. The Stancombs of Blount Court."

"Did you glean anything from them?"

"Only that Windsor had left them early the morning the rains began to flood the river, intending to ride for the town. Now we know he didn't reach Marlborough and if his things were found where he entered the river..."

"By no means certain."

"Then he was thrown in at Manton."

"Or somewhere close. Why did the person take the trouble to cut off the man's scabbards and knives, if they were only to be thrown in the river after the man?" I asked.

"Perhaps they were going to keep them and thought better of it. They are rather distinctive. Perhaps the killer thought to separate man and knives, hoping he would not be identified."

"He was only identified because we found his safe conduct from the King. If we hadn't found that, we would have had to wait until your party turned up. The body would not have been in good condition by then. The killer has had almost three weeks grace."

Manches shrugged. "It's of no import, the King will just send another in his place."

"Ah, but this man had a reputation. The Scots knew he was a fearsome negotiator, a noted cleric and a clever lawyer."

"The King has other lawyers."

"I'm sure he does but this man, for some reason, was the one, above all others, he trusted the most to beat the Scots into submission," I said. "And he was feared by the Scots, I think."

"I don't know anything. Politics is not my forte, my lord," smiled Manches, "I'm a soldier. It's a much easier job."

*****

After almost a month incarcerated in the town I was preparing to ride out for home when I met two of the Scots coming under the gate arch from the town.

Coagie Firmin and Nattie MacAlpine were walking over the drawbridge.

"Good morrow, sirs. You have been up and about early in the town."

Coagie chortled. "Out late more like..."

Nattie ruffled his hair, which was already somewhat disordered. "Ah well, m'lord Belvoir. It's a mite deadly being cooped up in the castle all the time. We thought to go out and get ourselves a bit o' occupation last night."

"Yer have some fine lassies here in the town, sir," said Coagie.

"Do we?" I dismounted and held Bayard's head. "This means you have been to Madam Ashely's does it?"

"Aye we have supped of the nectar of that establishment, yes we have."

I laughed. "Is this the first time you have been there?"

Nattie chuckled. "The first for me. Coagie here, Johnnie and Tam have been before. 'Twas they said I should go."

"I'm sorry that it has been so tedious for you all. Now that the weather has improved, I hope we might go up into the forest and hunt. I am about to go home to Durley and check all is well there. I'll return in a few days."

"D'ye no play shinty, m'lord?" asked Coagie. "We could have a fine game here in the bailey."

I then had to have a lecture upon this game beloved of the Scotsmen.

"And balls, sir," said Nattie. Surely you play the balls?"

"Er... balls, Nattie?"

"Aye, rollin' the balls."

"No, Nattie...I don't believe..."

"Nattie, Nattie," said Coagie shaking his curls, "the constable does'na' have the time for such giddiness. He's a busy man."

Nattie shook his head. "Well then, maybe we shall have to introduce the man to a wee bit o' the fun of the balls one day soon."

I dreaded to think what fun I was in for.

*****

It was good to be home. I spent as much time as I could with my wife and the children. As always I shared my problem with Lydia and as usual she was wise and thoughtful.

Lydia lay back on the snowy white linen pillows and stretched like a cat. "Have you found out where the awful stuff which killed the girl came from, Aumary?"

"It was supplied by Gabriel to the mint and to some of the dyers."

"How many of them?"

"Sadly most of them use the stuff and there are more than fifteen dyers in and around the town now."

"This girl didn't work at any of them?"

"No one will own up to knowing her," I said, wriggling my toes under the sheets and sighing at the comfort of it. After a whole month of rough blankets and poor mattresses, this was bliss.

"Did the old woman she lived with not help you further?"

"The only thing she could say was that she didn't know what the girl did for a living and she never brought anyone home to her cellar. Well...she wouldn't would she? It was nothing but a pit in the ground and she didn't want to be seen by all accounts."

"She was a pretty girl you say?"

"Yes. Well, she was a bit too thin, I think. At a time when she was a little more filled out, she would be pretty." The poor girl had not been very pretty at the time I'd last seen her.

"C'mon Aumary," said Lydia rising to her elbow. "A pretty young girl cannot go unnoticed in a town. Someone must know her. The men will know for sure."

"I've asked as many as I can."

"Then someone is lying."

I lifted a wave of Lydia's lovely black hair, worn free in the privacy of our solar, and twirled it around my fingers. "The younger men deny it and the older men tut and say she was a trull... what am I to do?"

"They cannot make such judgements. They don't know what has happened to her in life."

"Ah but they will, all the same."

Lydia harumphed and lay down. "She must have bought food at some time. She must have spent money somewhere. They must have met her. If she was a girl thrown into prostitution, she must have had clients. Where did they go with her? As you say, not into her underground home."

"I must see where there might be an empty place in the town where she could take men."

"No Aumary, it would have cost her money to hire somewhere. She would not have spent money in that way. If she had enough money for this, she would have lived there and not in Figgins Lane."

"You're right my love," I sighed and shifted onto my side.

"Are we looking at a girl who has been the mistress of a wealthy man," said Lydia, "who has been abandoned?"

"The name she chose for herself, Fordón seems to indicate she was seduced and abandoned."

"Then we are right," said my wife. "Someone is lying."

"Or they all are," I said.

*****

I spent four days at home. Promising to come home within a couple of days, I then returned to the castle. A message was waiting for me. Anthony Chapman had returned home.

I called in at the Chapman's house and once again I was taken into that front room with the new limewash.

A young man entered and quietly closed the door but not before making sure that there was no one in the passageway or on the stairs close by. The servant who had shown me in, had melted away.

The young Chapman was almost of my height, with wavy, very light brown hair and dark eyes. He wore a dark green short tunic, embroidered with a pattern of yellow spots, over black chausses and these were pushed into black ankle boots.

He bowed. "My Lord Belvoir. I am sorry that you had to wait for me to return to the town."

"Thank you for seeing me so promptly upon your return, Master Chapman."

The young man laughed. "My father would have it no other way, sir. He is a stickler for propriety. "

"I am glad to hear it."

"I can't see how I can be of any help to you, sir. My father explained what it was you wanted and I cannot..."

"She was a very pretty girl, Anthony. I'm sure you are the sort of man who enjoys looking at a pretty girl. I know I did when I was your age."

Anthony smiled a rather forced smile "You will have heard that I am now engaged to be married to Hilda Caspar. She is the only pretty girl I have eyes for now, sir."

"This girl was much prettier than Hilda, Anthony." I watched his face. It was set like stone.

"She went by the name of Berthe."

"But I thought you said that her name was Royse."

"Yes, I did. Like many girls who experience, shall we say, difficult times, she seems to have taken several names. After a time of being Berthe, she took the name Royse, Royse Fordón, Anthony. Maybe she'd had enough of her old life and changed her name as she changed her place of work and abode."

The man moved to the window and looked out. "I don't know any girls in the town called Berthe, or Royse for that matter."

"Do you have any idea what the surname means, Master Chapman?"

"No, none. None at all."

"It means seduced and abandoned. It's a Saxon word."

The young man swallowed.

"It means forsaken, sullied, deserted. It was a name she took for herself."

"You do not know her real name then?"

"No, not yet. I cannot even, as yet, guess at what happened to her to make her change her name. It must have been something quite...as my wife pointed out - drastic, for a girl's name is important to her."

The young man licked his lips.

"As is a man's honour," I added, watching the young man's back stiffen.

"Anyway, you tell me you do not know her and that is that."

Anthony turned back to me. He had become quite pale.

"I hope you find out what happened to the poor girl, sir."

I put my hand on his shoulder, "I shall."

As I was exiting the house, shown out by Anthony himself, I turned and put up my hood for there was a spot of rain beginning.

"Oh dear...it's going to rain. Again."

"At least now I'm not from home and shivering in a barn," said Anthony, smiling.

"I must remember to bring my waterproof cloak to the castle," I said.

I looked up as I fastened the ties of my old grey cloak. "I hear you own a red cloak, Anthony. Is that one good against the wet weather?"

Anthony Chapman blinked. "I have such a cloak, sir. I wear it rarely now."

"It's just that this girl, Berthe, was seen with a man wearing a red cloak. Several times I think. The last time was on Silver Street when the young man met her and managed to take a piece of silver jewellery from her."

"I did not…No, sir...it wasn't my cloak. There are several men who wear red. Some of my friends have such cloaks."

"Your brother in law to be, Cecil Caspar, has one, I hear."

Chapman blinked again, "And you have asked him if he knows the girl?"

"Aye, I have, and like you, he has never seen her."

I looked down the street towards the castle keep. "I really find it hard to believe that such a pretty girl has not attracted the attention of the young unattached men of the town. Or even some of the attached ones eh?"

Chapman swallowed again.

"Well, good day, Master Chapman and thank you." The door was closed a little too quickly. No footsteps receded briskly down the passageway. The lad was still standing behind the door.

There was no doubt he had been lying.

Chapter Six

The threatened rain did not materialise, thank the heavens. We had had enough to last us a lifetime.

I threw off my cloak and lolled in the chair in the office.

Annoyed with the lies I had been told, I pulled off my wet boot and threw it across the room. It bounced from the door and landed on the side table where I had laid the things belonging to the girl and to the dead lawyer.

The little wooden box fell on the floor with a clatter followed by the knife with the ivory handle. My boot chased them, sliding slowly after them.

I took off my other boot and stood to retrieve my first boot and the box.

Gayle opened the door just at the moment I bent to pick it up and the wooden board knocked me on the head.

"Christ Pete!" I rubbed my sore pate.

"Oh, sorry, Aumary... a message for you."

He looked at the things scattered on the floor. A few pieces of thin vellum had followed them, fluttering down and they blew around as the breeze came in through the open door.

"Shut the door for goodness sake!" I said. "There's enough mess in here."

Peterkin Gayle closed the door and bent to pick up the fallen items. He gathered the vellums together and placed them back on the side table. He picked up the box, a small book and the knife and replaced them, then he handed me my boot.

"Things not going well eh?" he said smiling.

"I am irritable this afternoon Pete!" I said, "I own it. I'm sorry."

"Not like you."

"No, maybe not. I just do not like being lied to."

"Aw no...I can see that would make you angry. It would make me angry."

I sighed. "What have you for me?"

"A note, from the clerk.... the Scots clerk."

"Tam o' the Dale?"

"That his name?"

"He gave it to me as I passed their door a moment ago. He seemed a little agitated."

"Thanks Pete." I broke the seal.

The note said simply, 'Sir Aumary come quickly, our Lord is poisoned.'

*****

I retrieved my boots, jammed them on my feet and ran across the damp bailey and charged through the door of the King's house.

John of Doune let me into the inner chamber.

"I came as soon as I got your note."

Doune nodded to me and I saw the burly John of Dunfermline take his place behind the portal.

"What has happened?"

We walked through to the separate room which was the sleeping place. The figure of Nattie MacAlpine was lying on the main bed, his knees were drawn up and he was moaning.

"Like I say sir, poison," said Tam.

"I thought you said it was the Earl? What has he eaten?"

"Nattie tastes all food before our Lord eats it, Sir Aumary. He's eaten duck in a sauce and bread and drunk ale."

I turned to John of Doune. "Fetch the doctor. The gate guard will tell you where he lives."

John wavered and then nodded to Tam o' the Dale, who sped out of the door.

"When was this?"

"About the time we saw you come back through the gate," said Doune.

"Not long then."

Then David of Scotland came forward.

"Have you eaten any of this, My Lord Huntingdon?"

"Do you think when I saw Nattie going a funny colour, I'd eat any of the shite myself?"

"The food came straight from the kitchen?"

"As it always does."

"Where was it served?"

"Here on the side table."

I marched up to the long, narrow linen covered side trestle table and peered at the dishes there. Nattie MacAlpine gave a lurching moan.

"Who served it?"

"I did," said John of Doune.

I stared at him for a moment or two.

"Please sir, will you empty your purse?"

There was a cry of outrage from the other men in the room, but strangely, not from Doune.

Holding my gaze, he took the purse from his belt and poured the contents onto the side table. My eyes raked the heap of things. No small bottles, powders or anything which might be used to poison.

"Thank you."

I asked every man in turn. They grudgingly threw the contents of their scrips and purses onto the side of the bed, one by one. There was nothing I could find which might have poisoned Nattie.

"He ate the food and how long after did he, as you say sir, change colour?"

"A heartbeat only."

"He was perfectly well before this?"

"Aye, he was and boasting of his prowess at Mistress Ashley's," chuckled Coagie.

I looked up from the stricken man. "You have been there again?"

"Aye, last night."

"Did you eat or drink anything there?"

"Aye, we were well fed and watered."

"What did you eat?"

The man told me. It seems that three of them had been out that night, Tam included and none had felt any ill effects either in the night or this morning. It was only when Nattie ate the food destined eventually for the Earl, today, that he fell ill.

"From now on, there will be a guard at all times in the kitchen," I said, "when your food is prepared. It will be brought to you by a trusted person each day and we shall make sure it cannot be tampered with."

"I'll do it," said Doune.

"No sir, I will appoint someone of the castle, whom I can trust to do it."

Doune's hand went to the hilt of his sword.

"What are you saying, lad?"

"I'm saying that someone is trying to kill the Earl, John. It might be anyone. No one is above suspicion."

"Not even my best friend, my lord?" said the Earl sadly.

"Best we do not inspect our friendships too closely."

"You...!" John of Doune drew his sword and made to swipe. I ducked. I would not, if I didn't have to, draw my sword on an honoured guest.

The sword was parried by that of the Earl David.

"Put up, Johnnie," he said. "You know he's right."

I swallowed and stood upright again.

"Don't be so carnaptious man!" said the Earl to his man.

"I am not particularly implying that any of you are the culprits. You may however be blamed, by having the poison or stuff hidden amongst your belongings by the true killer. This way we avoid any mishaps. If you handle the food, you are suspect."

"Aye, no one can be blamed if we don't," said Coagie.

"The culprit now knows we are aware they have tried. I doubt they'll try again but just in case…."

Doune slammed his sword back in the scabbard.

"Aye...well."

Johannes knocked on the door. The other John opened it.

The next hour was taken up with poor Nattie being induced to vomit what he had swallowed and us retiring to the next room to mull over what had happened.

"No one saw anything out of the ordinary?"

They all shook their heads.

"The same person came from the kitchen to deliver the food?"

"Aye, yon spotty faced lad with glassy, fish eyes," said the Earl.

I smiled. Davie the kitchen boy.

"All food and drink must be taken away. Some will be retained by Dr. Johannes for examination."

"You'll no take me uskebeaghe," said Coagie. "Aw no… you cann'a have that."

"Your what?"

"Nah, Coagie. Dinna be afraid. It's not that which Nattie took, is it? If he had, you'd have his scalp off him wouldn't you?" said Dunfermline.

"Aye, that I would."

I learned this uskebeaghe was a fermented spirit beloved of our northern highland cousins.

A little while later Johannes poked his head out of the sick room.

"All is clear. The man will live. We caught it in time."

"Thank you doctor," said the Earl. "I really thought he was beyond help."

Johannes smiled. "I will let you know later what I think was used to poison him."

I followed the doctor to the door and whispered.

"Let me know first, Johannes."

"Why, Aumary?"

"Because I think the Earl's life is in danger, from one of his own men."

"No! How can...what makes you think that?"

"No one in the castle, as far as I know," I whispered carefully, "has any real interest in what happens on our northern borders. No one here knows our Scotsmen."

"No but..."

"I could be wrong but, I do know that there is some opposition from some Scots to this constant spending of coin and effort on trying to annex the northern counties of England."

"How so?"

"In some quarters, William the Lion's constant draining of the treasury to fight this battle is not well liked. There are other areas of Scotland, some believe, which need subduing..."

"Such as?"

"I don't know. But I'm keeping my eyes and ears open. We may have a Scottish murderer here in the party."

"But that would help John's cause, wouldn't it?"

"Yes it would. It would greatly," I said.

"Then…" Johannes came closer and mouthed, "Why interfere?"

"I do not like murder, Johannes. Neither do you."

The doctor pondered. "Ah… yes… I see." He fingered his smooth chin. "Hmmm. I see indeed."

*****

I returned to my office and shut the door.

Two attempts on the Earl's life and the negotiator for the English, dead. The Scots had been here nigh on a month and no word about the disputed land had been exchanged between John's representative and the party for William the Lion.

The longer they stayed, the more desperate the killer would get. The talks had to be scuppered somehow.

I had no doubt that a new negotiator would come trotting into the castle soon. Then we should see more fun.

I sat in my chair, leaned back and balanced on the two back legs, resting my boots on the table. I stared at the rafters.

My eye strayed to the side table where, before I'd been called out, the things stored there had fallen to the floor.

The wooden box was back on the surface, turned up the right way, its lid closed. The knife had been laid upon the vellum to weigh it down. A small brown book rested on the lid of the box. I stared at it.

Where had this come from?

I searched the table before me. Nothing was missing from here. I tidied it up a little. Again my eye strayed to the small book.

I really didn't remember this being in the room before.

It was about five inches by three and bound in the thinnest calf leather. The skin was sueded, a light brown in colour, and a little discoloured with a thin strap securing it. The pages were tiny and the script thereon, minute. Written in graphite were crowded words, many to a page as if the person who had written it had poured it onto the surface and made sure that every inch was covered, no space wasted.

I put the book down and took up the small wooden box.

There in the bottom, the base had been dislodged. When first I picked it up, I'd thought it heavier than its size really warranted. Now I knew why. The little book had lain under the base. The silver cross had been caught in the crack as the base was refitted.

This book had belonged to the girl Berthe.

Except her name was not Berthe.

According to the little book it was Merewenna.

A very pretty name for a pretty girl.

Now I understood the meaning of the letter M on her silver cross.

It took me till almost supper time to read the whole book.

There were still four pages unwritten, clean; however, the story was finished. Ended, and as I read the girl's last words - yes the old woman had been right, she could read and write and write well - I felt such an anger boiling up inside me, I had to walk out of the confines of the castle, as the light faded in the west, over Avebury, and go down to the river to watch the now harmless and clear trickling waters spill and bubble over the stones of the bottom.

I now knew what had happened to the girl. It was not a happy story and yes, the poor creature had taken her own life. Taken her life in that awful way for she felt defiled and worthless and at that unbalanced moment, this way was her own choice of punishment. She felt she needed to be punished and there was no one else to do it.

I felt she had already been punished and punished for something she did not do.

I would have justice for her. I would.

Chapter Seven

I did not feel like supper.

I watched over and over, in my mind's eye, the girl's suffering as she struggled with what she had done to herself.

I had no doubt she had not truly understood what the vitriol would do to her. She knew that it would be painful but I do not think she knew it would take her so long to die and in such agony.

I needed to have redress for her but I could not tell the world that she had taken her own life for then they would dig her up from her comfortable resting place by the wall of the churchyard at St. Peter's and drag her body to the forest and bury her there in unconsecrated ground with a stake through her heart, so that her spirit could not walk and bother the living.

Whoever had decided this ridiculous thing, I do not know. Some pious long dead churchman I suppose. You will not prevent a person who is dead from rising from the grave by pinning them to the ground with a wooden stake, of that I was sure.

Yes, Paul, I know that is not what most people think. But I do.

What was I to do?

I needed to get together all those responsible for her death and make them see how they had contributed to her terrible end. They had not physically murdered her, but together they had certainly killed her.

I sat alone long into the night planning how I was going to do it.

The next day I peeped in on Nattie MacAlpine. He was looking much better and had regained some colour. He thanked me profusely for sending the doctor to him so promptly.

I told him he was in the wrong job.

He laughed. His lord's life was a greater one and of more value than his own, he said. He was dispensable, his lord was not.

I found that very difficult to answer so I did not try.

I organised the food to come from the kitchen with an armed guard for it was not to be kept hanging about. The Scots would not come into the hall for their meals but would stay in their quarters now, making it easier to contain the food and the people and keep them from harm.

Whilst the Scots were at their devotions, Gayle and I searched the rooms they were using. Stuffed down the back of the serving table, under the table cloth, was a folded piece of parchment. We had found the remnants of the poison used to try to kill Nattie. I kept it in my purse to give to Johannes.

Then I sent a message to the house of those I felt had questions to answer, about the death of the girl Merewenna. There was one other to add to this number and that message was duly delivered and the person asked to attend at a given time the following day. I made it clear that I would not countenance absence.

The next day, I dressed carefully in my best clothes, or at least the best I had with me at the castle. I paid attention to how I looked. My beard I trimmed with a tiny pair of shears, looking at my reflection in a polished piece of steel which always sat on the side table in my room. My teeth I cleaned with salt, sage and birch bark.

I combed my hair till the black curls were completely untangled.

I wore my lovely blue surcoat, the one which my first wife Cecily had made for me with fabric given to me for my birthday in that last year she lived. She had embroidered a band at the neck and at the edge of the short sleeves with small blue forget-me-nots and trailing green leaves in wool. The effect was not unlike the Belvoir seal which I wore on my right hand or that which was embroidered on my gambeson. Three small five petalled flowers surrounded by tiny oak leaves.

At the appointed time I walked down the road to the house on the High Street and scratched at the door.

I had not told the occupants what I wanted. They would hear soon enough and they wouldn't be pleased.

The servant ushered me into the hall. The family were seated around a large linen covered oak table. Before them was the remains of a meal. It seemed as if they had just shared a joke, for they were all smiling and laughing. Master Anthony Chapman was the only one standing, his back to me. It was obviously his joke for he did not turn but carried on speaking.

"My father was livid, I can tell you!"

"And so would I have been, my boy," said Baldwin Caspar. "I'd've put you over my knee and..."

He looked past his soon-to-be-son-in-law, and saw me.

I nodded. They all rose from the table. Caspar's eyes widened. "Ah yes, my Lord Belvoir. Do come in - wine?"

"No thank you, Master Caspar."

Chapman swivelled to face me. His jovial expression fell. He bowed, "My lord, I came as you requested."

I simply nodded. "Perhaps you would all like to be seated."

Caspar signalled to the servant who had let me into the room that the remains of the food should be taken away. There was silence as several other servants trotted into the room and cleared the table. The door closed. I remained standing.

"Why such a dour expression, sir?" asked Master Caspar senior. "You cannot come into this house today with such a long face. We have just been celebrating my daughter Hilda's nineteenth birthday and of course, her forthcoming wedding to Master Chapman here."

"You have already had my congratulations, Mistress Hilda, but you have them again. And you also, Master Chapman."

I moved to the head of the table. Of course Caspar had been seated there and he had had to change the position of his chair in order to still keep me in his sight and not to crick his neck.

"You all know that some time ago, a young woman was taken ill whilst passing the door of the Church of St. Peter."

"Yes" said Caspar, "It was all around the town. Can't keep that sort of news quiet. I'm sure it's very sad but what has it to do..."

"Dr. Johannes of Salerno did everything he could to save her life but sadly a short while later she died."

Cecil Caspar looked across the table at me. "I heard she had been poisoned. Is this right, sir?"

"I suppose it is, in a way."

"What was it that killed her?"

"She had swallowed a good deal of something called vitriol," I said.

"What's that?" said Hilda, smiling up at me. She was nearest to me, at my left elbow.

"It is a liquid which burns. Like quicklime. It corrodes and destroys."

The smile left the girl's face and her hand came up to her mouth. "Oh that's horrible."

"Where had she managed to obtain this ...vitriol?" asked Caspar senior.

"It is freely available at dyers' workshops for they use it in their fixing process," I said. "And a moneyer uses it to clean his coins."

"She took her own life then?" sniffed Mistress Caspar.

"Yes, mistress, she did. In the most horrible way."

"Then she should be excommunicated," said the mistress of the house flatly.

I glared at her. "She died in the most horrible agony and for a year or so before she died, she left a record of her life. It was all written down in a small book."

"Written?" said Caspar. "Surely the girl could not write."

"Oh yes. She could write. She was a clever girl. She could read, write and also do minor household accounts."

"Pah!" said Mistress Caspar. "I don't hold with all this education for the lower classes. Especially girls."

"There I cannot agree with you, madam," I said. "I have the children on my manor educated where I can. And yes, this includes the girls. I have my daughter educated. Educated women make helpful wives. And helpful, educated wives make educated children. There will come a time, one day in the future I think, when all men will be educated. And all women too. All classes, as you put it."

"God Forbid!" said Mistress Caspar, hunching her folded arms below her bosom.

"What was this paragon, this girl's name?" asked Caspar, smiling at his wife, "and what is she to do with any of us that you must get us all together like this, sir?"

"Her name, sir, was Merewenna Broder."

Caspar frowned. "No, no, the name means nothing to me."

"Sir," said Anthony Chapman, "First you tell my father that the name of the girl was Royse. Then it's suddenly changed to Berthe - you told me that. Now it seems it's Merewenna. What is going on, sir?"

"I also told you, Anthony, that the girl changed her name several times. Her given name was Merewenna. When she no longer had a use for that name she changed it to Berthe and latterly to Royse."

"Whatever for?" giggled Hilda. "I'm sure I know I'm called Hilda. Did the silly girl not know what she was called?"

"Her life changed beyond recognition one day last year and that brought about the first change in her name."

"Last year, you say?" asked Anthony.

"Yes. When she was dismissed from one of your workshops, Master Caspar."

The man slid forward on his seat and put his hands flat on the table. "My workshops?"

"One of those which embroiders fine works for the church and for wealthy folk."

"I don't remember....her...her name." But I could see that the man was suddenly coming to understand who the girl might be.

He took a deep breath. "I have dozens of women employed in my workshops and in their own homes. Dyeing, carding, weaving, sewing, embroidering. I cannot keep track of them all, sir. They change like the moon."

"Ah but this was a girl, Master Caspar, in which you took a *great* interest. A great interest. She was a very pretty girl. A little out of the ordinary, you might say. Charming, spirited, educated. Oh yes, sir. You'd remember her."

I saw Mistress Caspar cast a quick look at her husband, under her eyebrows and then down at the clasped hands lying in her lap. She smiled a small, secret smile.

Likewise, Master Caspar favoured his wife with a quick sideways look.

He stood and drained his cup. “There is nothing untoward about this, my Lord Belvoir,” he said. “I remember her now. She lived, I believe, in Mildenhall and walked into the town for work every day. She was trouble.”

“Trouble, of what sort?”

“She would not do as she was asked.”

I laughed out loud then. “No, I don’t expect she would.”

“Look, my Lord Belvoir. Can we not go and discuss this in private? This is not the sort of thing my wife and daughter should hear. It’s too delicate for their ears. I…”

“No. No. Everyone shall hear,” I said.

“M’lord…” Caspar gave a nervous laugh and opened his arms. “You are a man of the world, you….”

“No one will leave the room.”

Caspar sat down with a bump.

“So, Master Caspar. What was it that this girl would not do?”

I saw Cecil pour his father another cup of wine, then one for himself. Baldwin reached for it. He drank.

“I asked her to take on a special project. One which required her to be alone in one of the workrooms. It was a large piece and required space. She refused.”

I took out Merewenna’s small book from the breast of my cotte and turned to the second page.

I read silently. “No, no sir, I must disbelieve you. That is not what it says here.”

“Then what it says there, sir, is a lie!” bellowed Baldwin Caspar.

“Baldwin!” said his wife with a slight smirk. “That is no way to speak to my Lord Belvoir.” She turned to me and smiled sweetly. “I apologise my lord, for my husband’s churlish behaviour. What does your book say?”

“I’ll read it.”

I lowered my eyes and began.

" 'My master asked me to go into one of the smaller rooms with him. He said he had something to discuss, which was to be to my advantage. I naturally thought that it was to be an item of work which he would like me to execute. Previously, he had told me that he would pay me extra, for my work was excellent and I was a fast worker and I was to be lifted above the ordinary working girls of the sewing room. I did not think it shameful to go with my employer into this room alone. I trusted him.

Oh that I did.

Once there and the door closed, he tried to force away my clothes and put his hands upon my body. I managed to tear myself away. He asked me to lie with him. He wanted, he said for me to be his mistress for he was mad with lust for me and I must allow him to...'

"Here the account breaks off," I said.

"See here my Lord Belvoir. You cannot think that..."

"Oh but I can, sir."

"You cannot take the word of a...a strumpet girl against that of a respected townsman..."

"At this point, she was no strumpet. Why would the girl lie, sir? This is her own book. She made it herself with her own hands. No one was meant to see it, I think. She was after all, simply writing for herself."

"Father?" said Hilda, shock in the utterance of the one word.

"It's untrue. Untrue I tell you!" Caspar was perspiring. "Every word."

"Yes, because she would not do what you asked of her and she fled from you, you dismissed her."

"She was trouble I tell you."

"I think perhaps if we ask... ask your other workers, they would tell us differently."

"If anything is said by any of them, I'll...."

"You will dismiss them all?" I chuckled. "Oh Master Caspar. You would, as they say, cut off your own nose to spite your face."

Caspar subsided into mutterings.

I looked at the shocked party of people in front of me again.

"So the girl is thrown out. She has no work. She has nothing with which to get herself another position, for you have sent her off without a 'good conduct.' No one will take her on for they will know that she has come from you and she now has a reputation, which no doubt you with your vindictive nature, will feed."

"No father. You wouldn't?" said Cecil.

"No, of course I wouldn't," spluttered Caspar. "All of this is utter nonsense. It's her word against mine."

"I know who I am inclined to believe," I said quietly to myself.

Caspar shifted his ample rear end. "You have to be strong with this sort of person, my Lord Belvoir. If they refuse your instructions once, there's no telling what they'll do. You'll never get them to work hard again."

"That's true, sir," said Anthony Chapman. "My father is of the same opinion."

Caspar looked up at me with a stern face. "How do you get on with your superior, Sir Aumary?"

"The Lord de Neville? Arguably well, Master Caspar."

"He's a friend of mine you know. Yes, we have known each other for years..."

"As I have John, the King, sir," I said smiling. "We are boyhood friends."

Caspar's head dipped. There was an embarrassed silence.

"My Lord Belvoir...?"

"Yes, Mistress Caspar?"

"This girl did not kill herself because my husband allegedly attacked her?"

"No, madam."

"Though I have to say, it's a scene I can imagine. Oh yes... I think there may be some truth in what the girl says."

"Isobel!" shouted Caspar, rising to his feet.

"Tell me to be quiet, Caspar," she said, smiling. "Go on."

I grinned at her. "Madam. Thank you for your...support."

She inclined her head.

Caspar sat down again. "I don't have to say anything more to you, my Lord Belvoir. I told the girl to leave and never come back and that's the last I saw of her."

"Where did she go, sir?" asked Cecil.

"In good time Master Caspar, I will tell all."

"No more, Belvoir, my wife and daughter need not listen to any more of this rubbish. The girl did not kill herself because I dismissed her and there's an end to it."

"No, she did not kill herself because you took away her livelihood but you began it, Caspar. You began the process which led to her death."

"Then sir, if you will forgive me, this signifies nothing," said Chapman. "Master Caspar cannot be held responsible for what happened to the girl after she left his works."

"Was she a very pretty girl, my lord?" asked Hilda suddenly, twisting a piece of her hair around her finger.

"She was extremely pretty, mistress."

"Oh! Prettier than me?"

I simply bowed and left the question unanswered.

"We cannot help you, m'lord, because we have no idea what happened to her afterwards," continued Chapman.

"Are you sure of that sir...any of you?"

Caspar cleared his throat. "Are you suggesting, my lord, that my daughter or my son, or Master Chapman knows something about this terrible affair?"

"Yes, sir. I am."

There was silence as they all exchanged puzzled glances.

"I did not know anyone called Merewenna Broder..." said Chapman sitting down and filling himself a cup.

"Nor I," said Cecil.

"There you are then, sir," said Master Caspar. "Now, will you have some wine?"

"No thank you." I said plunging on.

"Master Caspar knew the girl as Merewenna Broder." I walked to stand behind the girl Hilda.

"She then became Berthe. The poor girl tried her luck at the other establishments like yours Caspar, in the town. At Master Chapman's for example. There was no work. So the girl walked to Ramsbury and thence to Hungerford and tried to find a job there."

"It says this in her book, does it?" asked Hilda.

"Yes." I opened the little calf skin cover again and read aloud,

" 'I lived with my grandmother in a small cottage in Mildenhall. Now I had to leave the aged woman in the hands of our neighbours. I did not want to do it, but there was no work to be found in Marlborough.'

This is why folk do not remember her well for she did not live in the town to begin with. She walked each day to work and back to Mildenhall again," I said. "Now she was known as Berthe Croft, taking her grandmother's name."

Master Chapman's head cocked at the name but I ignored him. I noticed that Hilda had seen the gesture and was frowning.

I continued to read, " 'It was not long before I had word that my grandmother was gravely ill. She died in August. Now I was totally alone. I sought work in the town of Hungerford. It is not as large a town as Marlborough and has not the industries which we have there.'

"There she was, you understand, a girl alone, in an unknown town, lonely, living in one small room somewhere, her savings dwindling away," I said, "and no prospect of the sort of work she was used to."

"Then she must do something else," said Hilda blithely.

"Yes, she must. And she did."

"She walked from door to door, trying to find something which she might do. Then she had, what she describes in her little book as the 'most wonderful piece of luck.' She was taken on by a family in the town. A good family, who needed a girl to fetch and carry, clean and sew, and we know she could do that, don't we? And they needed someone to look to the younger children."

"Their previous girl had died suddenly and they were at a loss what to do without her. There were several younger children in the house and help was very much needed. Berthe came at just the right time. They liked her. She liked them. She lived with them in the attic of their house and all went well for a while."

"I have a friend in Hungerford," said Hilda suddenly, as if nothing had gone before her outburst.

"I saw her last March. She's the eldest of five girls! Can you imagine five girls, father. And you think yourself chased about by just one daughter! Pah!" and she snorted like a pig.

No one added anything to that, so I carried on.

"All was going so well. She really enjoyed her job and the place. Then suddenly, for no reason, she was asked to leave."

"Got herself disliked there too eh?" said Caspar. "I told you she was trouble."

"Perhaps the girl was not good at what she was, ahem, asked to do by the lord of the house, my lord," said Isobel with a grin.

"No, when asked, they could give no real reason for her expulsion, save that something had been said by a visitor and that if she did not go, the family would see that visitor no longer. The visitor threatened to tell her father that the goods which the family made; the business which supported the family, was not to be indulged by her own father's business."

I saw Caspar look at his daughter.

Hilda looked round at me standing behind her. "When does she say this happened, this girl? Is it written in her book?"

"Oh yes. Every word is there, mistress."

"What does it say?" she asked, clasping her hands in her lap.

I opened the book again,

" 'I was happy with the Gorings...' "

Hilda gave a small cough.

'And then unexpectedly one morning in November, I was asked to collect my things and leave. A complaint had been made about me. A visitor to whom I'd spoken for a very short while, had gone to Master Goring and said that I had been rude and discourteous.'

There was silence again as I closed the book.

"I suppose you are going to say that..." began Hilda, pouting, an expression she was good at.

"I am not going to say anything, young lady," I said.

Everyone looked away.

At last Hilda said hurriedly, "It was me. I complained. It was me."

Everyone else shifted in their seats.

"Well, don't look so surprised. You are all thinking it anyway!"

"Hilda!" exclaimed a shocked Anthony Chapman.

The elder Caspar stood up and walked to the window.

"Hilda told me she'd been insulted by a...servant girl living at the Gorings. The Gorings have a weaving business in Hungerford. I buy from them. They weave the special two tone twill which we....anyway." He rubbed his hands over his face." I give them a very good price but I could go elsewhere, if I wanted. I'll not have my girl discomfited by a servant. I told Edward Goring he'd better get rid of the creature or I'd..."

"Cease to buy his cloth?"

"Aye.That's right. Perfectly good business sense."

"So poor Berthe had to go."

"Ah! She was known as Berthe there was she?" said Caspar. "You see, I told you. Trouble! What had she to hide that she kept changing her name, eh? And of course, I didn't know it was the same girl I'd....."

"For Heaven's sake Hilda, what did the girl do? Asked her brother sharply.

Hilda lifted her chin. "I was in a bad mood that day."

"You're in a bad mood every day," chuckled her brother who'd had just a little bit too much to drink. "You'd better be aware of that Anthony!"

"I went to see Gilda. We had been talking about wedding clothes. Gilda Goring was to be at the wedding of course. We wanted to talk with a seamstress about the fashion at court. There wasn't anyone in Hungerford who could tell us what was being worn."

"And that made you angry?" I asked.

"Yes. I wanted to know."

"Why did that make you cross with Berthe?"

"The girl was there folding up linen. She was listening to us. She had no right to listen in to our conversation, what we were saying. I asked her what she thought she was doing.

She said she had been an embroideress in Marlborough and that she was interested in dresses and such.

"I didn't believe her and called her a liar. 'What are you doing, a servant in this house,' I said, 'if you are an embroideress?' Of course she couldn't answer."

"How did she insult you, as you say she did?"

"I asked her, mistress clever clothes, what was the fashion at court, if she knew so much about dresses and she told me that a wide necked, sleeveless gown, a supertunic lined in silk, which showed an undergown of another colour was becoming the most fashionably worn dress there."

"And that made you cross?'

"No. That would be silly. I said that I would have such a gown for the wedding then."

"Yes?"

"Mistress Goring had such a new gown, she said and that she'd let me try it on. Before I put it on, Gilda was saying spitefully that she didn't think it would be right. I tried it on and..."

"Yes?"

"Even before I saw it myself I knew it was wrong."

"And this made you angry with Berthe? I furrowed my brow.

Hilda answered me quickly. "The girl smirked...she actually smiled nastily over my shoulder and I know she was thinking that I looked fat in the dress.

"I tore it off and Mistress Goring put it up against this servant and...."

"It looked better?"

"How dare she? I know what she'd been thinking. She was so very pretty and slight, but still with a good figure. The dress was a beautiful blue and the thing would have suited her..." At last Hilda looked a little contrite.

"She made me feel fat."

Hilda was, it has to be said, a little too well padded.

"And ugly."

Oh that makes you giggle does it Paul? Well, I must admit, I had to stifle a smile.

Isobel Caspar came up and put her arms around her daughter but Hilda shrugged her off.

"I told father that the girl had been impertinent. That she had laughed at me..."

"Which was not entirely the truth, was it, Hilda?" I said.

Hilda shrugged. "And I said that I would never marry Anthony if father didn't get the Gorings to get rid of her."

"Hilda… you didn't mean that...?" started Anthony, looking a little confused.

Hilda stood up and faced her betrothed across the table. She stamped her foot. "Yes, I did!" she shouted.

"Oh ho!" snorted Cecil, into his wine cup. "I warned you, Anthony."

"So poor Berthe Croft loses yet another job. What is she to do?" I said.

"I'm sure, sir, she can have got another one," said Isobel Caspar.

"Again she has no 'good conduct,' madam. That's two places now. It isn't easy to obtain work without some sort of recommendation."

Caspar senior came away from the window. "You surely can't think that just because she lost a second place we are responsible for her death, sir?"

"Both your daughter and yourself have played a part in her demise, sir."

Hilda turned to scowl at me.

"Once more, according to her little book, she goes off in search of work. Now she is in a much smaller place, Hungerford. It's not so easy. As she said, there are fewer places, fewer industries. She decides to return to Marlborough. It has been weeks now and she can't find work. She is starving and none too strong nevertheless she walks back to the town and seeks alms at the priory for a while."

"She was a beggar?" cried out Hilda.

"For a while, yes. What else was she to do?"

"Ugh!"

Young Master Chapman looked at the floor with a face full of disgust. I wasn't sure then if it was at the girl being a beggar or at his betrothed's reaction to the news.

Suddenly Hilda jumped up.

"Come on Anthony!"

"What?"

Hilda put her hands on her hips and threw her head to the side.

"WHAT?" said Chapman again.

"Oh don't think you can fool me. You betrayed yourself as soon as the Lord Belvoir said the girl called herself Berthe!"

"*I* didn't know the girl."

"Yes, you did...I saw your face."

"I must say mistress, I too think your young man has some explaining to do," I said.

"There, see!"

Anthony looked from one to the other and then threw up his hands. "Oh! All right. I knew her. Are you satisfied?"

"No. I — am — not!" said Hilda nastily. "How did you know her?" There was a further silence.

Anthony had time to calm down and think.

"Look Hilda... there's nothing… I didn't know her well. Honestly sweet one..."

"I don't believe you."

Anthony took in a breath to speak and then sighed. "I met her one day when she was at the door of the priory, seeking alms."

"Aw, how kind of you," said Hilda sarcastically.

"She was obviously uncomfortable being there. There was a lot of shoving and pushing going on, as there always is when the food is handed out."

"She would not push herself forward?" I asked.

Anthony shook his head. "She was frail and tired and oh so beautiful."

The tubby Hilda sat down with a bump and stared open mouthed.

"Some women have that ability, I believe, to become more beautiful and delicate when they are in extreme circumstances," I said.

"I promise you Hilda, that it was all over before we ever met."

"When?"

"Hmm?"

"When was this? When did you meet her?"

"November. At the priory. She was cold and shivering and I lent her my murrey cloak."

"How chivalrous of you!" sneered Hilda. "And anyway we knew each other before then," she murmured, pouting again.

"Well, I was more kind than you!' snapped Anthony.

"Children, please!" said Mistress Caspar.

"What happened after that?" I asked.

"I took her to a place I know where she could be warm and have some food."

"Where?"

"Does it matter?"

"Yes," I said. "It matters."

"If you must know, it was a room at Mistress Ashley's."

Hilda hissed, Caspar groaned. Isobel smirked.

I nodded.

"I didn't want her to stay there. So... I got her a place out at Manton, by the Grange. Two rooms of good quality."

"Anthony… are you telling me that this girl became your mistress?" hissed Isobel Caspar.

Cecil began to giggle.

"You've had too much to drink, Cecil!" said his mother.

"He always drinks too much." This was Hilda.

I walked closer to Master Chapman, "Sir, perhaps you'd like to tell us how the girl Berthe became your mistress."

"She didn't."

"Aw c'mon Anthony," said Cecil, slurring his words. "You don't get a girl lodgings, keep her in food and clothes and not take something in return."

I leaned over and took away the cup Cecil was about to lift to his lips. He shrugged and sat back.

"It was all over by the end of January."

"Oh… it lasted *that* long did it?" said Hilda.

"It's all in the little book. I can read it out if you like," I said. "But I'd like it from your lips, Master Chapman."

Anthony looked down at the table top and drew his finger along some spilt ale dregs.

"Like I say, I took her to Manton and found her two rooms."

"You paid for them?" asked Caspar senior.

"Yes. She stayed there until she felt better and could go about a bit more, though she hated to go into town."

"And you visited her, bringing her food and other things?" I asked.

"She told me that when she'd been begging at the priory, some men had approached her and asked for...favours. She wasn't like those usual beggars you see. She still had dignity and..."

"Looks?" I offered.

"Oh yes. She was very beautiful," Chapman sniffed. "I couldn't bear the thought of her being pawed by the lewd old men of the town. Some of father's lecherous friends, so I offered her my protection. She was all alone, see, sir, no one. No one at all."

"Yes, this is what she writes in her book and if it's any consolation to you, young man, she writes very favourably of you."

Anthony suddenly covered his face with his hands and began to weep silently.

"Oh for Heaven's sake!" said Hilda and sat back on her chair, looking up to the rafters.

"At first I didn't mean to do anything. I did love her. I did," snivelled Chapman.

"Oh no, of course not. No, you didn't *mean* to seduce her," chuckled Cecil.

"Be quiet boy!" shouted his father.

"I had no intention of...keeping her as my mistress but as time went on...I was really sorry for her. She'd told me a little of her history, she gave me no names and so today was the first I knew of the truth of it all. I knew she was desperate and poor and as I say..."

"I think, from what she has written in her book Anthony, you gave her the happiest time of her short life. There's no doubt in my mind that she grew to love you. You say you loved her. But not for long eh?"

"She gave me a warmth I didn't get at home from my parents. I gave her security and companionship when I could. She was very grateful."

"That isn't a good base upon which to build a life together, Anthony though, is it?" I said. "Being grateful."

"No, I know that now."

"Did you love her, really love her, Anthony?" said Hilda suddenly serious.

"Not as much as she did me, I think."

"No naturally. You were the knight who saved her from the wicked monster. Oh how you must have loved it."

"She was young and beautiful and any man with a heart would have wallowed in it," shouted Anthony.

I cleared my throat.

"So this went on until February?"

"And all the time you were courting me and..."

"No, Hilda. I never seriously looked at you until I had finished with Berthe."

"No, I agree with you there. You were decidedly half hearted. What changed your mind?"

Anthony licked his lips.

"The old man. My father. Until then he had been saying, 'over his dead body'. You and I could never be married. Then suddenly, somehow I knew that Berthe and I could never be."

"Berthe knew this, Anthony. In her book she writes that she could not stand in the way of your future happiness. She knew that you would have to make a good marriage eventually. You could never marry her. She knew it wasn't possible. She was all prepared to let you go. That is how much she loved you."

Anthony swallowed and tears appeared in his eyes. "She was a fine girl." He sneered at Hilda.

"I had suggested to my father that if Hilda and I got married we could merge the two businesses. Any sniff of money and my father is there with his tongue hanging out. We approached Master Caspar and eventually it was arranged."

"Berthe moved from Manton?"

"She went away... I don't know where. I'd given her some money so she wouldn't be without but I had no idea what she would do with herself."

"You let her go… just like that, Anthony?" said Mistress Caspar. "You must have guessed how a girl like that would end."

"No madam. I did my best for her. She didn't want me to make a fuss. One day she was at Manton and we discussed the future, the next day she'd gone. I didn't know where."

Hilda flounced up.

"We are finished Anthony Chapman. I will not marry you."

"Now see here girl...," began her father

"No father. You cannot make me."

"When all this is over, we shall sit down and talk sensibly...."

"No. I will not marry him."

"You think I think any better of you, Hilda Caspar, after this afternoon, after I learned what you did? You spoilt little brat. You think I want to be wed to *you*?"

Hilda leaned over and slapped Anthony hard on the face leaving a pink hand print.

She then fell onto her seat and stared at the wall. Chapman simply glowered at her.

"Hilda, you must understand that, even though you might be married, men are... inconstant things," said Isobel Caspar placatingly. "They must have their dalliances." She threw a look at her husband. "Do not think them perfect my dear. They can never be so."

"Mama I..."

"Hush now, child. Anthony has only done what countless men have done in their lives. They have mistresses. They visit brothels. If you believe they will not when you are married, then you are a fool."

"Isobel…!" began Baldwin Caspar.

"Be quiet dear. I know what your father is like. You now know what Anthony is like. It is no reason for me to leave your father nor for you not to marry Anthony."

Hilda sat with her mouth open.

I coughed. "So, you say that was the last time you saw Berthe?"

Anthony sat up. He too cleared his throat. "Yes. Yes it was."

"Not quite true, is it?"

"Hmm, sir?"

"The day on Silver Street?"

Anthony furrowed his brow, then his expression changed. "Oh yes. The last time I saw her was the day I left for business in the south. I'd gone up to the Jews who keep monies for us so that I could go on my journey well provided for in coin. There she was being busied by that creature…"

"Gowler."

"Aye, sir, him. Foul monster. I thought he was trying to steal her chain. I'd given her the chain for Christmas, sir, so she could wear a little cross which had been in her family a while. Gowler had it in his grubby little hand. I was going to give it back to her but she ran away saying she didn't want to see me."

"You also gave her some perfume, didn't you?" I asked.

"Aye, I did."

He fiddled in his purse.

"She was so thin and tired looking. I just wanted to help…"

Into my hand he dropped the fine silver chain and I reunited it with the delicate silver cross.

"By the end of the next day Anthony," I said, "she was dead."

Chapter Eight

I paced around the table.

"So now we have the young woman, abandoned, used and forgive me ladies, no longer a virgin. Now she thinks to herself, 'if I am worth so little, then there is no shame in using my looks and my body to keep me.' It was all she had left."

"When was this?" asked Caspar senior.

"Master Chapman finished with her in February. She was going to sell the chain to Elias the Jew in April. She died in early April. She changed her name for almost the last time to Royse Fordón. It was a name she chose specially. A Saxon name to reflect her Saxon heritage and one which means a rose forsaken, abandoned and sullied."

They all shifted on their seats and Master Chapman held his head in his hands.

"She now took a small room at Mistress Sloghter's house in Figgins Lane for it was all she could afford. You cannot imagine what that place is like. It was a far cry from the comfortable rooms she had known with Master Chapman. It's a dingy damp cellar with an earthen floor, and rough stone walls. She had simply a bed, a chest and a small stool. Nothing more. It was a not a place she wanted to take her clients.

She would spend her days there, for she would not go out into the town in the day, in the light, lest someone see her and recognise her. This is how ashamed she had become. She preferred the hours of the night, of the dark time as the sun was going down and rising."

"Why sir, did she not apply to Mistress Ashley for help? I'm sure the woman would have aided her," said Chapman raising his head.

"She did, Chapman, and was turned away."

"NO!"

"Mistress Ashley had taken against her. She was your lover, Anthony. She had taken you away from the house on Figgins Lane - albeit for a short while. You were previously a good customer, were you not? Mistress Ashley is not a forgiving woman. She threatened Royse."

"Threatened?"

"Royse lived close by. Mistress Ashley had seen her a few times on the lane and thought that she was poaching her custom."

"Which of course she was," said Hilda in disgust.

"I'll read from Royse's little book again. 'I took the lodging because it was the cheapest I could find in the town, close by the brothel. I had not thought Mistress Ashley would be so unkind. When she saw me one evening, she threatened to throw me in the Kennet and drown me if I as much as looked at one of her regulars. I had not taken her custom. I did not approach the men who came to her establishment but rather went to other parts of the town.'

I read, "Mistress Ashley would give her no place at her home and she would not allow Royse to linger anywhere for long, close by, in case her customers thought Royse much prettier than her own girls."

"Then how did she make a living, sir?" asked Chapman. "And where did she take her clients?"

" 'At first I took the poorer sort of men and could do nothing but couple with them in barns and deserted buildings, those further away from the town and up in the forest,' she writes. 'I took what monies they offered me. I was desperate and could not seek more.' "

I put the book down on the table. Hilda looked over at the tiny writing. I knew she could not read it.

"She tells us that she waited on the roads to the outskirts of the town, begging and offering herself to passing men. It was not a lucrative business but then, it kept her in lodging and some food at least. I will read a little more."

I picked up the book once again and flicked over a few pages. " 'One day I was walking quite some way from town, on the riverside road to Manton. The river had risen quite a lot with the rains and I stood and gazed into it for quite some time thinking how easy it would be to wade in and disappear...."

"So the girl was thinking about taking her life even though she was not quite at the end of her resources," said Isobel archly. "I think that tells us what kind of girl she was, don't you?"

I ignored her and carried on reading. 'Something then happened which made my heart leap, for I met a fair young man, a little younger than myself who became really interested in me. Not just as a harlot with which to couple, but as a friend, I thought. The poor young man's family was wealthy but he told me that his father kept him short of money and that he couldn't do as he wished. I felt very sorry for him. Each time we met, I learned more about him; that he would have to go into the family business and that was not what he wanted at all, for he wanted to become a soldier and go and fight for the King.' "

I saw Cecil sit up straighter.

"This affair went on some while. The young man bought her clothes and housed her decently for a duration in an unused room in one of the properties owned by his father, up at the back of a building at the top of town. Here she could entertain a better class of men and did so for the young man understood that he could not keep her as a mistress, he did not have the funds - unlike you, Master Chapman," I said.

"How did she get from there to the desperate plight she found herself in later, sir?" asked Chapman.

"Now that thing happened which all girls in Royse's business dread...."

"Ha! She became with child!" scoffed Isobel Caspar.

"That is so, mistress. The young man who had taken a liking to her, got her with child."

"And could not marry her, naturally," said Hilda smiling.

"Oh God!" said Cecil quietly, pulling his father's cup to him and taking a swig of wine.

"Now she did not know what to do," I said.

I turned over a page. " 'I thought,' she writes, 'about trying to get rid of the child and approached a woman in the town who said that she could help. She wanted a lot of money. It is a grave sin to take a life thus and a further sin to aid a woman in such a thing. I knew that and so I paid her what she asked.' "

There was an uncomfortable silence.

"Wicked girl," said Isobel under her breath.

I looked up from my reading " 'I could not do it,' she says."

Anthony Chapman sighed.

"The girl could not get rid of the child and when she asked this helpful creature who was willing to perform the abortion, to return her money, she would not give it back. Royse was no longer going to avail herself of the woman's services. She needed her money back for now, she would have a child to support. The woman declined."

"The man who got her into this condition must be made to look to her," spat Isobel Caspar.

"This wasn't Anthony's child was it?" asked Hilda... "It was too late for that."

"No, it most certainly wasn't," answered Chapman with great bitterness in his voice... "Not that you should care now."

"And I repeat the man should have been made to marry the girl. It's nonsense that he could not be made to do so," added Isobel.

"Royse had to give up the fine room at the top of town and she disappeared back to the cellar on Figgins Lane. She left her lover, the young man who was the father of her child, and disappeared," I said.

"This book tells you all, my Lord Belvoir, why ask us... we don't know who this filthy beast of a man is," said Isobel, lifting her chin defiantly and straightening the folds of her perfect pink gown.

"Mother!" warned Hilda.

I'd had enough of Mistress Caspar's superiority; I launched myself at her.

"Mistress, you do not remember the name Royse Fordón?"

"I most certainly do not. Why should I?"

"There is, in the town, is there not, a group of charitable people, both men and women, who seek to aid those Marlborough folk who have fallen into difficulties of one sort or another. I remember Nicholas Barbflet telling me that it had been set up at St. Peter's by Master Roper's wife and a few others, including Felicity his own wife. I know that Mistress Fleschier is one such member and Master Baker's wife also belongs. Funds are taken from the town guilds' dues and charitable donations are made."

"Yes, that is so, my Lord Belvoir."

"You are a member aren't you, madam?"

Isobel stayed silent and fiddled with her dress.

"Aw c'mon, mother," said Hilda. "You can't hide it. Remember he has the book."

Isobel looked up at me, her face stony.

"You are quite correct, my Lord Belvoir. There is such an organisation and I have, at the moment, the honour of being the leading lady of the group."

"You do not remember the meeting of about four weeks ago?"

"What of it? We have done some very good works in the town in the past year or so. I cannot remember every meeting we've had."

"You cannot remember then, meeting Royse Fordón?"

"I have never met the girl in my life, I tell you!"

"Mistress Caspar, you have met Royse. Not quite a month ago you met her."

"I have not, I tell you."

"You met her as Mistress Royse Losod."

The woman paled and look up at me, blinking.

"It's another of her little names and means, in the Saxon tongue again - lost, madam."

"Why did she feel it necessary to give a false name yet again, sir?" asked Chapman.

I shrugged. "By this time she had been so disillusioned with her previous lives, she wanted again to be someone else. And asking for help, she wanted to appear...respectable."

Isobel's mouth twitched.

"She told a pack of lies about being a married woman whose husband had died. I saw through her immediately. She was with child, she said, and needed help to look after it."

"Which was not untrue was it?"

"In the end I did get the truth from her."

"Which was?"

"That she has taken a young lover, as you said, who was too young to marry her...Pah...I told her if he was old enough to get between her legs and get her pregnant..."

"Isobel!" shouted Caspar senior, shocked.

"...then he was old enough to marry her. She said it wasn't possible for there was no love in their relationship and she simply did not wish to ruin his life. Besides he was, she said, above her in her own station in life. His family would never sanction it."

"What a lot of nonsense," said Baldwin Caspar, coming round to the side of the table. "I agree with Isobel. A marriage should have been arranged. It was not up to the girl. Her wishes should not be considered. The young man must be seen to do the right thing." He put his hands on his wife's shoulders.

I picked up the book again.

" 'I told the woman at St. Peter's that I could not marry the young man for he was silly and often drunk and I would take no more of his money. He was a sweet boy but I could not marry him.' "

"She had taken his money? For more than just the, ahem, the services she provided?" asked Caspar.

"He had kept her in the house and when he knew that she was with child he had given her money, yes." I said.

"Why did Berthe...Merewenna not want to take his money? He was after all the father of her child?" asked Anthony.

"Because he had admitted to her that he had stolen it."

"Stolen it?" exclaimed Isobel and Baldwin together.

"From his father."

"A girl of her kind, refuse money...never!" exploded Isobel Caspar. "I knew she was a liar the moment I set eyes on her."

"So she came to the fund to ask for help, because she could no longer take stolen money and she did not want the young man to get into trouble for taking it. That, I think madam, is very commendable."

"Nonsense...it was nothing but lies."

"It was the truth, madam," I said forcefully.

"Well, we refused her aid and there's an end to it."

"I think you had a great influence on that decision, madam," I said, "There were few to gainsay you. The meeting was not, I'm told, well attended that day because of the rains."

"Humph."

Isobel Caspar pouted. Like mother, like daughter, I thought.

"Well, then, we must lay the blame on the stupid young thing who was the father. If, as she says, he was above her station in life, then he must be some besotted, drunken, lecherous sluggard and should not escape penalty. If he will not marry her, then he should be set in the stocks...and..."

"Mother!" shouted Hilda who, all the while this speech was being delivered, had been staring at her sibling. Cecil sat rigid and pale faced, his lips clamped together.

"Think what you are saying."

"He ought to be handed over to the authorities and whipped."

"So you think we should try to find this young man, make him confess his wrongdoing and punish him?"

"I do. Severely. Obviously he cannot marry her now but..."

Caspar senior took his hands from her shoulders. He too had seen his son's face.

"Isobel. Shut up."

She turned on him.

"Don't you speak to me like that, Caspar!" she screeched. She turned a pink face to me.

"You should be out there constable, on the street, trying to find this reprobate instead of interrogating an entirely blameless family. That would be doing your duty to us all. My lord Belvoir," she added as an afterthought.

Caspar shook his head and sat down.

"Oh Madam," I chuckled. "I will do my duty, of that there is no doubt."

"Make him confess in public, make an example of him," she added, jutting her chin.

Hilda giggled. "Oh mother, you really are the dimmest..."

Isobel glowered at her only daughter. "You can keep quiet, Hilda Caspar. This is none of your business."

"Oh but mother it is, it's all our businesses...can you not see?"

Isobel looked round the table.

"You are telling us..." said Caspar in a weak voice, "that our son..."

"It was me," said Cecil suddenly. "It was me, mother. I was the father of Royse's child."

There was another moment of complete silence.

"I don't believe it," said his mother, rising from her place slowly, her white knuckles balanced on the table top as she leaned over to confront her son.

"It's true, every word the constable says. It's true."

Baldwin Caspar sat shaking his head... "Never… never..."

"And for your information, mother, I did ask her to marry me. I don't know how I thought we'd be able to manage it. It was a bugger's muddle but I thought..."

He put his hands to his face. "God. I wish I was dead too." He dragged his hands down his face exposing his pink lower eyelids.

Isobel Caspar was just standing staring at her son with an open mouth.

Hilda started to titter and then it became a fully fledged laugh. "Cecil! You took up where Anthony left off! How vile."

"Shut up Hilda!" shouted Chapman, "You're not helping matters."

"You took money. Money from me?" was all his father could think to say.

"Yes, I took money from you, you old skinflint. Royse had no money. She had no job. She was going to have my child. So I gave her money to keep her going until..."

"My money?"

"The business's money."

"For your whore?"

"She wasn't a whore!"

"Well, what else can you call her? She wasn't your mistress...that I might just understand. She went with men of the town, not just you. She was a harlot."

Cecil glowered under lowered brows. "Anyway she wouldn't take any more of the money."

"I fetched you away from Figgins Lane, my lad, that day just as the rains began in earnest and the river flooded the town didn't I? Where had you been then, eh?"

"I had been, if you must know, to Madam Ashley's."

"Cecil," exclaimed his mother, "you didn't go in?"

Hilda guffawed, "Oh Cecil, you lecher!"

"Yes, mother. I went in. It wasn't the first time."

"You saw Merewenna there, didn't you?" I asked. "On the lane."

"She was loitering on the corner. I didn't know that she lived on the lane. Yes, I saw her."

"Did she see you?"

"She saw me coming from Madam Meretrix, sir.'"

"Did you speak?"

Cecil nodded his head. "Aye, we had a few words."

"What did she say?"

"She told me she was all right and that she had enough money. She had taken a rich lover."

"She described him to you?"

"Aye, she did, but I didn't know him."

"He wasn't a Marlborough man," I said.

Cecil licked his lips. "No, I suppose not." He looked down at his hands.

"The money can't have been enough for later that day she was trying to sell her chain, wasn't she? She lied to me."

"No, it wasn't," I said. " She sold everything she owned. The clothes you and

Anthony had given her, the jewelled rings. All except the little cross and one dress. The cross she kept and even then at the last moment, she was going to sell the chain for she had really felt the bite of hunger and it was the last thing she had. And the lover was a figment of her imagination."

No one said anything.

"She lived quietly and frugally for a while in her damp dark cellar. And one day she went out to the river, when it was beginning to be in full flood. I'll read a little more of her book.

'I was sitting at the roadside. I had more or less decided that I would walk into the river and that would make an end of me. God would not, I was sure, censure me but take me to his arms when gently clopping along the road came a man on a fine horse. He stopped. He spoke to me kindly. He said he had an important job to do. I could believe it, for he was very wealthy to look at, with his huge cloak brooch and all his silver horse trappings. He said he had been riding to Marlborough trying to be ahead of the rain which was now coming down in torrents. He suggested that we go into the Grange barn close by to get out of the wet and when we were there—well, one thing led to another. He was gentle and kind and he gave me more money for that one bedding, than I'd earned all week.'

"Still a whore then," said Isobel, straightening her dress.

"What else could she do?" Cecil jumped up screaming, "You have no idea at all about hunger, about desperation, mother, about deep sadness. Nothing! You with your fine clothes and your full belly, with your idiotic friends and their stupid small concerns. You have no idea how the lesser people suffer!" He was breathing hard.

"Don't speak to your mother like that," said Caspar.

"You're not much better, you old lecher. If it hadn't been for you, Royse would not have reached such a state."

"Sit down Cecil," I said "please...and I will finish the tale."

Silence drew down again.

"Merewenna never saw the man again. She did not kill herself that day. The man she lay with in that barn told her things which she did not understand and things which I will not lay before you for, though they are pertinent to her death, they do not concern you.

No, Merewenna Broder did not see the wealthy man again but I think she did see another, another who knew of him. And that was her undoing."

Chapman looked up. "I thought you said that Merewenna had killed herself... if another was involved, then, it's murder and cannot be our fault."

"Yes, I did say that. She did kill herself but it was as a result of something that was said by the second man she saw, after our wealthy traveller. This was piled upon what you had done to her, all of you, and tipped her over the edge."

"Does she say who the man was?" asked Cecil.

"I wish she had, for that would make my job of finding a murderer, much easier."

"She said no word about what the man had told her?" he asked.

"In her book she says it was such a secret that it must not be written down. And so—she did not. It died with her."

"Who was this rich traveller...did she say who *he* was?"

"No, but *I* know who the man was."

"Who?" chimed all of them, their faces lifted to me in curiosity.

"Again I'm not at liberty to reveal anything yet. It will all be town gossip 'ere long."

"Gossip has it that there have been Scots visiting the brothel...is it anything to do with them?" asked Chapman.

I did not answer.

"So now you have destroyed our family, my Lord Belvoir, what do you intend to do next?" asked Isobel.

"Leave you all to sort out your differences and come to understand what you have done—all of you and perhaps make amends."

Isobel Caspar scoffed. "Some of those differences will, I fear, never be resolved."

She looked pointedly at her daughter.

"I'll not marry him. Not for all the money in his father's coffers."

"You know what Hilda..." said Cecil, leaning forward on his bench, "I think you should be cast out without a penny, onto the streets to beg and to whore like poor Royse. That will teach you...."

"How dare you! You thief! I wasn't the one stealing from father's coffer."

"I will pay back every penny."

"How?" said his father. "You have no money of your own. Everything that is yours is mine."

"Well, then. Ha, ha, see you don't know everything. I have some money of my own. Just you wait and see."

"And how did you get that? More stealing?"

Cecil pulled his face into a gargoyle like smile. "Wouldn't you like to know?"

"A sobering thought, Master Caspar," said Chapman. "Since Hilda is set against marrying me now, you have only one son, Cecil, to take into your business. Think on that."

"We shall see about that," said Baldwin through gritted teeth.

Chapman rose. "If you have finished with me, my lord. I shall return home. On the way I will go to St. Peter's and pray for the soul of the poor girl, whatever her name was, who was so ill used by us all. Like she said in her book, I think God will be merciful and take her to his bosom. She may have killed herself but I do not think our God is a vengeful God. He will understand."

I picked up the small book, stowed it away in my cotte and walked around the table in silence, opened the door of the hall and stood in the door hole for a heartbeat.

"There is nothing I can do to any of you, even though I may wish to. You have broken no laws. You have however, all of you, broken the laws of human decency and humanity; you have not an ounce of tolerance or kindness between you. Some of you are worse than others." I glared at the women. "Master Chapman at least had good intentions, to begin with.

"Confess your sins to your priests madam, mistress, sirs. You are in great need of God's forgiveness. If you cannot sympathise with the poor dead girl now, how is God to pity you? I am a mere man. I cannot forgive you."

I saw Isobel Caspar look down at her hands and open her mouth to speak. No, madam, I thought, you will not have the last word.

"We do not live in isolation here on this earth. God has put us here to live side by side with our fellow men: those flawed, weak companions who travel the road beside us. If we do not come to realise that each one of us is bound up in our neighbour, whoever that may be, each one dependent upon his or her fellow for our own well being, then there is no hope for us. And the last of days will be upon us, sooner than we think. God save us all. Good day."

And I left, banging the door for good measure.

*****

I stomped up to Johannes' house. I had to go and explain the story to him. It would make me feel better to share it with him.

I went in through the front door, often left open for clients to come in and out. I rarely entered that door, preferring the back door from the courtyard into the kitchen. He was with a patient in his workroom and the door was open. I poked my head around the door jamb.

"Be with you in a moment," said Johannes, his back to me.

"It's only me" I said.

Johannes turned and looked up from dropping some sort of liquid into a man's eye. He frowned.

"You look like a man who has swallowed a wasp," he said, laughing.

"As well I should," I chuckled. "I've just been in a hornet's nest."

"Ah..."

"Sorry to interrupt John," I said, as I recognised one of the clerks from the castle record office.

"Bathe the eye twice daily." I heard Johannes say as he turned back. "For five days and then we'll see how it is."

I went into the kitchen. Something delicious was bubbling in the pot over the fire.

I took a look and a sniff and replaced the lid of the pot. Sitting down I poured myself ale from the jug on the kitchen table.

Johannes entered a few moments later.

“So, this hornet’s nest...?”

“The Caspars.”

“What have they done to annoy you?” he asked, looking puzzled.

“You too will be annoyed when you hear the tale,” and I started on my story.

The bell for compline was ringing out from the church tower when our conversation ended, Johannes asking questions and looking at the little book which had belonged to Merewenna Broder. We stopped and stared into the fire.

“There is nothing you can do to them.”

“Only make it a public story and shame them...”

“And then you open up Merewenna to censure and a possible digging up.”

“I cannot do it.”

“No.” He chuckled. “Be careful one of them does not come up behind you on a black night in a dark alley.”

“The only one with the guts to do anything would be Isobel and frankly, I can’t see her taking a knife to me.”

Johannes chuckled again, “No.”

He tossed back the rest of his ale.

“Did you know she was with child?” I asked. “Merewenna?”

Johannes grimaced. “Yes. I did. I did not, as you can no doubt imagine, make a thorough examination of the girl when she was still alive, but after she was dead, I did have a good look at her to see if I could find any trace in any other part of her, of what might have killed her.”

“Other things save this retching and coughing.”

“Yes. Other signs. That is when I realised. I didn’t say anything because I thought that there was nothing to be gained and anyway, I wasn’t going to add fuel to the fire. If it was to become known she was an unmarried gravid woman, the fact that she might have taken her own life became more feasible.”

I nodded.

"I still have the mystery of what she was told. I have no idea but that it is connected to this man Alan of Windsor and the visit of the Scots."

"I've been thinking about that, Aumary," said Johannes, getting up and reaching for a small waxed tablet and a stylus, always left somewhere in the kitchen for Agnes to write with.

"You tell me that Wat Fisher heard the girl mumble a name, before her throat became too burned to speak further."

"Yes, he was on her pretty quickly."

"He followed her from Figgins Lane..."

"Where she was living, yes."

Johannes took the small stick and drew the tablet closer to him. He scratched a word.

"This is what he said he heard."

The word he had written was Tracy.

"I have been thinking about that word, Aumary. I know no Tracys here in Marlborough. I know it can be a family name *and* a given name. I've asked about but no one in the immediate area is known as Tracy. However..."

He scribbled another word.

"In the course of my asking, I had cause to mention the name to one of the old'uns of the town. I asked Will Chasier..."

"The cheeseman."

"Yes, the elder. He's a good age and has lived here all his life. I asked him if he'd ever known a Tracy? A man or woman, with the name as a surname. Or a man with the first name Tracy."

"And had he?"

"No. But you know how deaf he is..." he chuckled.

"Ha, yes he is...it's a hard job getting him to hear anything properly nowadays."

"His eyebrows almost flew off his head. He looked shocked and said to me that most certainly if he did, he'd report it to the authorities..." said Johannes.

"Hmmm? What...?" I asked, screwing up my face.

"Exactly. I repeated my question and the man chortled and said that he'd heard me awry. No, he didn't know of any Tracys. He never had."

"What did he *think* you'd said?"

"Traitor, Aumary." He turned the tablet round to face me. There, he'd written the word.

I leaned back and rolled my ale cup in my fingers. "Yes, it makes sense."

"It does, in the light of what is happening at the moment at the castle."

"So the girl, upset with something she's been told ..."

"Or had seen..." added Johannes.

"Feels responsible?"

"It's a possibility."

"And in her desperation mouths the word 'traitor, or traitors', twice."

"Whether she was trying to communicate it to anyone who at that moment could listen or whether it was just in her head, we shall never know. She was not in her right mind, Aumary, in absolute agony and very afraid."

"Yes. I know. God rest her." I made a moue. "Why should it make her kill herself?"

"She was close to it anyway. She had been thinking about it for quite a while, we know this. She says so in her book. This was the thing, the very last thing, which made up her mind."

"Feeling responsible for the death of Alan of Windsor?"

Johannes shrugged, "Maybe."

"Someone she knew, a client perhaps, was a traitor?"

"It's not impossible. But a traitor to whom?"

"And she had, perhaps unwittingly, aided him?"

Chapter Nine

A few days later, as we lost the party who had travelled with Alan of Windsor, a pair came trotting under the gate arch.

Two men, on small palfreys, those even gaited amblers which ladies and priests prefer, brought their pack horse trailing behind them, their crotal bells jingling in the confined space of the tunnel under the gatehouse.

I bowed. "Sirs, you are welcome to Marlborough."

"Sir Aumary Belvoir?"

I bowed again.

"This is Stephen Argentum, my lord. I am Richard Lingan."

"Welcome gentlemen."

"We come from the Justiciar."

"My letter was received then, despite the floods."

"Yes, indeed. It was surprisingly quick in delivery considering the parlous state of the roads. Furthermore it was received with great disquiet. We are all saddened to hear of the death of Alan of Windsor. He was a great man."

I had penned a message to go out to London with one of the couriers who frequented the castle, telling of the murder of the lawyer Alan of Windsor. The Justiciar had sent me another man as requested. Or maybe two men.

I looked them over.

The first man through the gate sported a coif and a small highly decorated hat, the other was bare headed and wore a tonsure.

The taller man was dressed in a gown of watchet with a sleeveless supertunic of tawny gathered at the shoulders; the priest wore a brown split cotte with a black sideless gown over. His legs were bare and he wore pointed shoes.

"Come, you must be tired. We have quarters prepared for you where you can refresh yourselves and rest."

These two men were most unprepossessing. Fellow travellers would have given them not a second glance, unlike the flashily dressed Alan of Windsor.

I checked their credentials and read the letter penned by the Justiciar, Geoffrey FitzPeter, the Earl of Essex. He had asked me to return the body of Alan of Windsor to London.

I learned later, before supper, that Stephen was a royal clerk and Richard a King's lawyer. They were quietly disposed men, self possessed and of few words, unless they were discoursing on the law, naturally.

The tables were laid for supper and I escorted our two newcomers to the top table. The Scots were already ensconced in their usual place at the bottom of the hall. I tutted for I'd asked that they stay in their quarters and eat what was brought to them. As we passed, John of Doune and David of Huntingdon rose and bowed their heads. The other Scots followed in ones and twos.

The two royal clerks bowed deep.

"My Lord David, may I present our King's men, Stephen Argentum and Richard Lingan."

Lord David rose up to his full height. His swept back his cloak to show the large knife at his hip and put his hand on the pommel, as many men who wear swords do, to prevent it swinging. I thought this an unnecessary gesture as neither clerk nor lawyer wore swords. And strictly the Scots should have been unarmed at supper.

"Sirs, the Prince David and his men."

A conversation in French now ensued.

David introduced his right hand man John of Doune and his lawyer Tam o' the Dale but gave him his full name in English, Thomas atte Vale. The others did not warrant individual introduction.

The rest was mere formality. A smile once or twice crossed Stephen's face. Then the conversation broke away from polite talk about the journey and apologies for the wait.

"So sir, you think you can persuade us to return home empty handed?" said David.

Stephen had turned away to walk up to the dais, but turned back.

I watched him consider his reply and there was a small silence.

"I have been charged by my King with the task of listening to argument. Listen I shall. I shall listen and then make a judgement within the law, my lord. If that judgement does not favour your King's claim, then the law must prevail. If, conversely, I find that my own King is in error and the disputed land does indeed belong to the Scottish King, then I shall withdraw to inform him of this fact."

"You're not the first to come here to try. You know that?" answered David.

"We know that, my lord," said Richard Lingan.

"You know what happened to the man?"

I lifted my eyebrow. Was this a veiled threat?

"What happened to Alan of Windsor is...regrettable my Lord David, but the roads are so uncertain and dangerous in this land of ours, the weather pernicious...."

"Have you brought a cart load of gold with which to bribe us then?" grinned the brother of the Scot's King, looking round his men.

"Why should we need to do that, sir?"

"Surely we shall reach agreement without bribery my lord," said Richard.

"Aye, I suppose the money comes later," said Coagie quietly in English.

"There will be, I am sure, many things to speak about, including money, sirs," said Stephen Argentum, his mouth fleetingly smiling. "But for the moment, my belly is telling me, it is supper time."

He bowed and left them.

We sat ourselves at the top table.

"The Scots do not eat with us?" asked Lingon.

"Yes, why do they chose such a lowly place?" added Stephen Argentum.

"There has been an attempt on the life of the Lord David, sirs. I am surprised they are here in the hall at all. I bade them stay and eat in their quarters in an effort to keep them safe from poison."

"Poison? Oh dear me," said Stephen Argentum.

"The Lord David's taster was poisoned but happily recovered."

Lingon grinned at me. "I suppose their curiosity got the better of them.

They must come and see what manner of men are the King's negotiators, eh?"

"I have no doubt," I said smiling. "And to answer your question, sir. If anything... untoward were to happen, here in the hall, sitting where they do, they can be the first from the door can they not, being so close to the outside."

Stephen Argentum turned to me and smiled over his silver goblet.

"Sir Aumary, surely nothing untoward will happen. You are cynical, sir, about your Scottish guests."

I too smiled. "My safety may depend upon theirs, sir," I said.

*****

Two large rooms, known as the Queen's House, in the bailey of the castle were made available to the negotiators and I supplemented the guard of the Scots with men of my own choosing so that we might have an even number on both sides.

Then, next morning I left them to their discussions and retired to my small room by the gatehouse.

I sat turning my pen round and round for a short while, thinking of the death of Alan of Windsor. The arrival of the English negotiators had brought him back to mind.

I went over everything I knew about the meeting of poor Merewenna Broder and the churchman, for there was no doubt it was Alan she had met on the riverside path.

I took out her small book again and read once more the passage she had written about meeting him on the road.

"I was sitting at the roadside, when, gently clopping along the road came a man on a fine horse. He stopped. He spoke to me kindly. He said he had an important job to do. I could believe it, for he was very wealthy to look at with his cloak brooch and all his silver horse trappings. He said he had been riding to Marlborough trying to be ahead of the rain which was now coming down in torrents. He suggested that we go into the Grange barn close by to get out of the wet and when we were there - well one thing led to another. He was gentle and kind and he gave me more money for that one bedding, than I'd earned all week."

She had not said exactly where they had met, but the barn at Manton was known as the Grange for it was the barn belonging to the castle where the fodder for the horses was kept. It was not far from the town on a westerly road which ran alongside the river.

As the rains began, the road had been just about passable and as the river flooded the meadow, road and riverpath were under water. Then the bridge collapsed.

Not far from here the man's knives had been found when the waters receded. I read on.

"I thought to myself, I did not need to lie with anyone for a week for the man's money would keep me and so I paid my overdue rent, until the next quarter day. However, habit made me think about seeking more coin for I knew that it would not last me long."

The old woman on Figgins Lane had lied to me, then. The rent was not overdue. Merewenna had paid it with Alan's money. At that point the girl had not desired death, for no one who contemplates killing themselves in April, pays the rent until June.

The girl had written, "The next day I went back to the riverside. The floods had taken the path and I could not walk where I'd walked the previous day. A man I met there told me that the bridge was unsafe and that I had better go back to town or I would be isolated here on this southern side of the river. He had been to Preshute he said and the banks were unsafe."

So, was this the day before Alan's body was washed up? He had been killed just after he had met with Merewenna, it seems, and tipped into the river as it rose.

I returned to the last page of writing.

"I walked back towards the castle gate with the man. He spoke oddly and I had to listen carefully to him to be able to understand what he said. He said he would like to lie with me and so I took him to the South Field close by, where there was an empty bothy, just above the rising waters. Afterwards, I told him about the man I'd seen on his fine horse, in an effort to make him pay me more, for if that man had paid me so much, surely I was worth more than this man had offered me. He insulted me by offering me a coin I did not recognise. I asked for silver pennies, coin I knew. I said I would find my kind rich man again then I would not have to lie with the likes of him.

He struck me, then laughed and called me names. My fine man was dead he said, and dead men do not pay whores. Did I not know who my fine man was? He was a priest. An ordained man of the cloth. What a wicked girl I was to lie with a priest. What a terrible sin I'd committed. He tossed me the coin and left. I wept then, for my fine and kind priest on the beautiful horse and for myself and for my baby."

After this we do not know exactly what happened.

We did know that later that day Merewenna tried to pawn her chain and then she was not seen again until night was falling and she was dying by the church gate.

I read to the end of the page. She had managed to procure some vitriol by walking past a dyer's yard as they were closing up that night. She pretended to be begging, she said and they chased her out of the yard. However, she managed to get what she had gone in for.

The very last page of writing was simply a denunciation of someone...not I feel the man who had refused to pay her what she thought herself worth but some other man. It was also an onslaught on herself; how stupid she had been, how wicked and how thoughtless. The word traitor did not appear and I was surprised it did not. Then the pages were blank.

I needed to find the man she had coupled with in the bothy on South Field. I wanted to find out how he knew that Alan of Windsor was dead. We ourselves, did not know that until the day after, when we fished him from the river and we found his safe conduct.

If this man knew and had told Merewenna, then it was likely he was Alan's killer or knew who had killed him.

I flung on my cloak, exited my room and threw a glance to the Queen's House. My guards were still standing outside the door. With a yell into the guard room of "Andrew keep an eye on matters. I'm on South Field." I made my way over the drawbridge. I was not going far away.

The bothy was one which Wat Fisher had built to house his equipment and store his boat when not in use. It was rather ramshackle now and had been flooded by the river. I picked my way across the sodden ground.

Much of the daub was gone, washed away by the flood. The house had been flooded to the measure of about two feet. The door had just about remained intact; a wattle panel secured by leather hinges. It scraped on the ground as I pushed it for it was still swollen and damp.

The walls were nothing but mud and wattle, the floor was mud. The whole building was leaning forwards where the river had undermined it as it had gurgled its way over the meadow. It was a few yards from Wat's home, a similar building but a little larger, higher up.

Wat still had a few things stored in that bothy. A net or two, not good ones, hung from the roof beam; a leather bucket; a lethal looking spike, another wooden pail with a hole in and a heap of rags were piled up at the side wall where the water had pushed them. I scuffed up the mud floor. The smell of fish, mud and river came up into my nostrils. I looked around the bare walls. Nothing. I pushed the door further back. It screeched. I looked down. I pushed again. The door stuttered to a halt and wouldn't budge further.

With two hands I lifted and pushed it closed again. Now it was gloomy in the place, for there were no windows and only a little light came in through the ill fitting door and the holes in the walls.

Something glistened in the drying mud.

I fished it from under the door where it had been driven when I'd pushed it back.

Stepping out into the light, I looked at it with a furrowed brow.

It needed cleaning. I took the small piece of rag I kept in my purse for such small tasks and rubbed the thing between my forefinger and thumb.

I looked carefully, tilting it to the light.

It was a coin. Like a silver penny.

Silver pennies had John's father Henry on the heads side. The King had never bothered to alter the pattern and so his father stayed on John's coin. The reverse, the tails side bore a short cross and lettering.

This was not an English penny for Henry's stern face did not stare out at me. This was an equestrian portrait of a man in a conical helmet. The coin was worn but I could just make out the words 'Dei' and 'Scottorum'.

This was a coin of Henry the Lion.

*****

I jogged back to the castle.

As I crossed the drawbridge, Andrew nodded his head in the direction of the Queen's House.

"Long faces, Aumary," he said.

The Scottish delegation were just leaving the building. Tam O' the Dale was grinning from ear to ear but David Lord of Huntingdon was grimacing as if he had been once again pinned by an arrow.

"Oh dear," I said "That didn't last long."

"Four hours."

"No, surely not that long."

Aye, that long," said Andrew Merriman. "If they hadn't stopped now, they would have to break for dinner soon anyway."

Stephen Argentum came out of the Queen's House, stretched like a cat and turned his face up to the watery sun.

He saw me and sauntered across the bailey. "My Lord. I must thank you for providing such a congenial dwelling for us. We are most comfortable in the accommodation and the negotiation rooms are perfect for our needs. Thank you too for the very capable clerks."

I nodded. "Thank our King, messire, for it is he who has built up this castle to the fine place it is today."

"He speaks lovingly of it, as he does highly of you, sir."

I smiled. "The castle was but a poor apology for a fortress only a few years ago. John has lavished effort and money on it."

"He was married here, was he not?"

"Yes he was, to Isabella, his cousin of Gloucester. However, that marriage was dissolved on grounds of consanguinity. He has his second Isabella now. That marriage took place in Angoulême."

"God keep her," said Stephen. "You will have heard of course that the lady is with child?"

"Yes. John wrote a postscript to me, on a scrap of parchment which came with an official one, sealed with the privy seal, boasting that at last he too would have a son."

"Oh?"

"I have a son born last year. It was a source of friendly rivalry between us."

"It's good that at last we shall have an heir."

"In the eighth year of our monarch's reign," I said. "Yes. With an heir comes security."

Stephen smiled and looked down at his feet.

"How goes your work, sir?" I asked.

Stephen Argentum smiled again. "Just because something is repeated over and over my lord, does not make it truth."

"They hope to wear you down?"

"They ask too much."

"Do they have evidence to substantiate their claim?"

"Oh yes....all spurious."

"Did not Richard the King take coin from the Scots for his crusade? Did they not pay for the privilege of owning their own lands?"

"Indeed they did. But these lands about which we speak now were never really Scottish. Richard sold back to the Scots what were the Scots' in the first place."

"The King will not give them what they want, will he? Cumberland,

Northumbria and Westmorland?"

"No, sir. He will not."

"Why do they persist?"

Stephen Argentum wagged his tonsured head. "They have for years disputed this land. The King seeks to prevent an armed incursion into Northumbria..."

"Surely..."

"Which will no doubt happen if we do not parley."

"You play for time, sir?"

"The King seeks to avoid war. The Scots raid, burn, pillage and destroy at the least provocation, those lands they would annex. Men, women and children lose their lives. Ordinary folk. John wants to prevent this. War is a costly business, my lord, in money and lives."

"But he will not give in."

"No. The land is in England, sir, and will stay there. Perhaps next year, the King tells me, he will go up there and sort it out for all time. He's talked about building a castle there."

"He has been distracted by other matters these last years, has he not?"

"Yes, he has. With the treaty between Philip of France and himself and the nonsense over church matters...."

"You will talk until the Scots lose their voices?" I chuckled.

"Talk is all we *shall* do. But of course, I did not say that," said Stephen Argentum, whispering. The King has some plan or other. I am a humble priest and servant, sir, I am not party to John's long term schemes."

"He is a wily old fox."

"Oh I know it. He will have something under his crown I'm sure."

"I do not understand why William the Lion has made such a protracted job of trying to relieve us of these lands, Master Argentum. It has taken him the best part of his forty year reign and much money and endeavour. First he took on John's father and failed, then Richard his son, who let him have them at a ruinous cost. He lost them again and now he's trying John. This pastime of his has beggared his country."

The priest shook his head. "It has become a habit with him. It's almost a compulsion and it's cost him the loyalty of some of his lords and of course, parts of his own country."

"I heard that some lords were in dispute with him."

"That is correct. Ross and Moray were beyond his control, Galloway was rebelling. The islands...well....!"

"John will never forgive him for supporting Arthur of Brittany, will he?"

This was John's sixteen year old nephew who had, at the beginning of John's reign in 1199, set himself up in opposition to John and had himself declared King of England. William the Lion had backed the wrong man.

Stephen smiled. "John never forgets a slight, does he?"

"But he's good to his friends," I said, as I looked up at the sky with its scudding clouds.

"So… have you any idea how long all this will take?"

Stephen Argentum laughed. "William is an old man. Not in the best of health. John is a vigorous young man with much stamina and sticking power. Eventually, the Scots will lose heart. If I must sit and talk till the last trump...I will. But I hope it will not take that long."

"Please no!" I laughed. "I'd like to go home sometime."

"Ah yes. To your lovely forest."

"Savernake...yes. And my lovely wife."

The priest nodded.

"Will you come sir, and sup with us one day, in Savernake?"

"I will indeed, my Lord Belvoir. I would love to. It would be an honour."

"Meanwhile take care please, messire. We have a murderer abroad who is trying, any way he can, to scupper your talks."

Stephen Argentum put his fingers to his cheek. "Can you scupper, my lord, a boat which is already holed and sinking?"

I laughed out loud. "Our murderer does not know that, sir."

"I shall paddle, Sir Aumary, I shall paddle hard for the bank."

*****

I'd reached my room and was unlocking the door before I realised the thing I'd singularly so far failed to see.

Alan of Windsor had been the English delegate. He'd been killed.

There had been an attempt on the King of the Scots' brother's life.

For Heaven's sake! Whose side was this murderer on?

Did I have two murderers?

I sat in my room and stared at the coin. A Scottish coin.

I reread the passage written by the girl Merewenna.

She'd had difficulty understanding the man's speech. He'd given her a coin she did not recognise. Did she leave this disdained coin in the bothy or was this simply money washed up there in the floods?

I had been to one place the girl had visited. I needed to go to the Grange barn at Manton.

*****

A little while later, as dinner was being taken in the main hall and the delegates of both parties were engaged in eating, I left the castle and headed for the road to Manton, a small lane on the southern side of the river. It was but a mile from the town boundary and Bayard made short work of the distance.

Everywhere there was evidence of the flooding.

The road was a mass of puddles. The hedges were littered with streamers of vegetation washed up when the banks of the river had burst.

Here and there were barriers of flood debris left high and dry. More vegetation: logs and twigs, whole trees, water animals drowned by the raging torrent: voles, birds and otters. Land animals too, caught out by the rising waters. The stinking, rotting remains of a fox sat in a dip in the road and further along, closer to the Grange, a cat who had exhausted his nine lives, lay mouldering on the bank. I looked up. A kite was mewing above. No doubt calling to his mate, passing on the fact that that he had found dinner.

I dismounted at the barn door and hollered. No one came. It was sufficiently far from the main farm for them all to be at dinner and not hear me.

The barn lay on a slight rise and the building had escaped the floods. It was a typical double doored building of stone, like the hay barn I possessed at Durley manor.

There was very little hay left now for the castle beasts and their visitors' animals had eaten their way through that laid down last summer.

I pushed open the door and there was a scattering of rats, their little feet scratching on the beams and rafters, the remaining hay rustling with mice no doubt.

Perhaps the cat I'd seen was the barn cat and the mice and rats were happily playing here now, like children in a meadow.

I hollered again just to make sure. I didn't want any surprised and irate peasant to think I was up to no good and swipe me with a billhook. However no one was about.

I began to look around. Mind you, I didn't know what I was looking for.

As I said, there was little hay left. Just one bay had half a filled bank.

I looked along the dusty floor. There were a few sacks of some sort of grain; some had been spoiled by rats, others were whole and untouched. Someone had been at work here, for a pitchfork was stuck into the hay close to the beaten earth ground of the barn.

I heard a buzzing of flies. Strange. It was early in the season for so many flies.

Although we'd had a deal of rain, the weather had remained mild. Today was positively warm.

Flies, could be out and about in the warmth, especially so close to the water.

I searched about. I was methodical. I quartered the floor and picked up the three pronged pitchfork with which to toss about the remaining hay.

I'd made a couple of passes when I realised that the hay was sticking to the tines of the pitchfork. I pulled the business end towards me.

All three tines were deeply covered in blood.

I stepped back and looked carefully at the remaining hay. My eye travelled up to the cloud of flies.

Casting aside the fork, I bounded with difficulty up the face of the hay and stood looking down at last at the top of the pile.

I held onto the rafter with my left hand and balancing with the other out beside me, I scuffed the hay with my feet. I sank a little further into the sweet smelling dried grasses and let go of the rafter. Falling to my knees I pulled apart the stack.

There, staring up at me, was the face of Lord David's food taster, Nattie MacAlpine. A trickle of blood had dried on the side of his lips. His eyes were open and staring glassily.

Now I would never have a demonstration of the game of balls, he'd so kindly offered to show me.

Chapter Ten

I pulled away the remaining hay. Nattie's body came into view. He had been stabbed twice through the middle with the hayfork. The first had pierced his lungs it seemed, the second his lower abdomen.

I dragged him across the hay and laid him on the floor. I searched his body. His purse, with Scottish and English coins inside it, was intact. His dagger lay in its sheath, his sword undrawn in its scabbard. Not robbery then.

He wore the clothes in which I'd seen him the day before at meat in the hall.

The flies followed the body and hovered in a ring above him. I looked around for a cloth with which to cover him and found some sacks which had been piled up at the side of the barn and I used these to wrap him, apologising to his shade that it was all I could find.

Then I walked the short distance to the farm house and yelled through the door.

*****

The body was covered and carted back to the castle and when we arrived and found the Scotsmen, all the demons of Hell broke loose.

Accusations were levelled at the English delegation. The Scots swore in three languages.

"They were both in your sight all day, sir," I said to Prince David. "They are not responsible."

The Scots fell silent.

"Nattie did not go into the talks this morning with you my lord. Did you not think it odd he was missing?"

"Nay. He'd had a skinful the night before. He was sleeping late. I knew he'd surface eventually" said John of Dunfermline.

"What might he be doing out at the Grange barn?"

"Nowt. He'd no reason to go there," said Coagie. So, Coagie knew where the barn was.

"Who else was missing?"

They all looked round like wide eyed children accused of some misdemeanour.

"I will ask the doctor, if he can tell me, when he thinks that Nattie died. Then we shall have to know where everyone was at that time."

"I take exception to that, lad," said Sir John of Doune with barely concealed anger.

"Why would one of us kill our own?"

"Why would any of *us*, kill Nattie MacAlpine? He was a guard...not a negotiator," I said. "The Lord's taster."

"Aye, and a friend," said the usually unforthcoming Donald Baird.

John of Doune glared at me. "You should've kept better watch on us."

"You are grown men, sir. You can come and go as you wish. I cannot, even if I tried and, yes, I have tried...to keep you in, like hens in a coop, safe from the fox. You disregard my suggestions, which I must say are all designed to keep you alive. You are not children."

John of Doune took one step forward.

"Johnnie! He's right. Leave it," said the stern voice of David, Prince of Scotland.

John of Doune subsided but kept his hand on the pommel of his sword.

"The Englishmen were here all night. I know it, for I posted a guard at the door of their room. They did not stir all night. Then as I say, you saw them. They were in full view of you all for the rest of the day."

Aye." David rubbed at his grey hair. "We cannot think...."

"Robbers," said John of Dunfermline.

"Nattie's purse, clothes, sword and dagger were still with him so it was not a chance meeting with a murderous thief. No thief leaves such pickings."

"Then why?" moaned Coagie Firmin.

"I can only think he was silenced for something he knew."

The Scotsmen looked at each other in disbelief.

Johannes came running up the steps of the King's House. I turned.

"The body is in the mortuary, Johannes. I'll accompany you there." He nodded.

I wheeled round and stared at the Scots. "You will all stay here..." I bowed, "my lord, until we return."

*****

"He died about the seventh hour of the night, Aumary, just before or after."

"That means whoever killed him was out of the wicket gate of the castle at the sixth hour or so. It takes no great time to jog to the barn."

"Did they go out together, Nattie and his killer, or separately?" asked Johannes.

"The gate guards must be quizzed," I said.

"By the way it was aconite."

"What was?"

"The poison given to Nattie. Inexpertly done too. Not prepared properly. The leaves dried and ground down."

"Hmmm. Someone not used to poison then," I said.

We found Maurice FitzAlan and asked his guards on duty that night, who had gone from the castle after curfew.

It seems there was a steady trickle of folks out.

First, Master Gayle went to visit his lady friend on the Manton road.

My eyes widened. "I didn't know Peterkin had a lady friend."

"Oh aye...he never stays out all night. He just goes for a while," said the guard

"Then that fella the Scotsman, Coagie. He went out and give me a wink that he'd be returning in the mornin' early. He was off to the Mistress Ashley's. That John of Doune went out too. He was to join that Firmin fella at the ladies."

"Nattie MacAlpine, when did he go out?"

"Ah that were before dark, sir. He went before curfew. I took it he too were going to the broth... ladies. Them girls are goin' a feel the pinch when these fellas go 'ome, sir."

"Anyone else?"

"Castleman went to see 'is lad at the cordwainer's. It was Friday see, sir. He always goes Fridays." The man tugged on his beard. "Two stablemen went to The Green Man. They came back before matins. I saw 'em go into the chapel later."

"How many didn't come back till the morning or came back in very late, in the hours of the morning?"

"The Scotsmen. Master Gayle. That Nattie fella never turned up at all. Castleman was back after a short while or so, as usual. "

"Anyone else?"

The guard scratched his head. "A coupl'a the masons went out but they were back right quick... I reckin as 'ow they'd gone for some food somewhere and brought it back."

I smiled. Generally the food in the castle refectory was abysmal.

"That lad what lives on the High came into the castle...on curfew. Asked for the Scottie man."

"What lad?"

"Aw, I cannot remember his name."

"What was a man from the town doing asking for a Scotsman? They have no contact."

"Only to and from the brothel it seems," said Johannes, smiling.

"Which Scotsman did he want?"

"I dunno, sir. He just asked for the Scotsman. And I played dumb, sir and... like you said... I didn't say nuffin', pretendin' I didn't understand."

"Well done Bradfield," I said. "Think about this lad please and see if you can recall anything about him. Let me have a description of him."

"Aye, sir."

"We shall now return and see our Scotsmen. See what they have to say."

*****

Johannes and I returned to the King's House. On our way there I chanced upon Peterkin Gayle, the man responsible for the treasury, security at the mint and the gaol. Pete had been out on Friday night.

He was a dapper, small man of late middle age with a ring of white hair and a pate like a tonsure. He was quite an attractive man still.

"Pete! I had no idea you had a lady love in the town - you old rake, you."

"A lady love?" Peterkin looked outraged..."Who told you that?"

"I got it from Bradfield. You go out to see her sometimes I hear, in the town. Of an evening."

"Are we to have a wedding soon then, Pete?" asked Johannes folding, his arms across his chest and chuckling.

"Wedding...?" Peterkin looked shocked. "No... no… of course not. I have a cousin in the town... if that is what you mean?" He looked affronted. "If you must know I go to see her since her husband died to... make..."

"Ah!" said Johannes

"Well, it is allowed with cousins...," I added, nodding. "Under certain circumstances…"

"Sometimes," said Johannes, laughing. "With a dispensation from the Pope."

"Make music with her…" finished Pete.

"Ah, is that what they call it nowadays?" guffawed Johannes.

"She plays the harp you see....and I...well...I sing."

"Sing?" said Johannes and I together.

"I'll have you know that it has been said that I have a very fine bass," answered Pete, puffing up his chest. "And Alice is an extremely good cook. I go twice a week or so, for food and music."

"Well, well," I said, wiping my eyes of humorous tears. "And here were we thinking..."

Pete harrumphed. "Her food is a darn sight better than the slop they serve here of an evening, I can tell you."

I clapped my old friend on the shoulder. “We’re sorry for ribbing you up, Pete,” I said. “When you were out last Friday, you didn’t happen to see anyone you knew out and about around the castle, did you? Before curfew perhaps.”

“Castleman went out of the gate with me. He is often there waiting as I go out.”

“Yes. We know about him.”

“The usual crowd...”

“Masons and stable lads and the like?”

“Aye, them. As I was going up to Alice’s on Church Street, I saw that lad of Caspar’s.”

“Where was he going?”

“He crossed the road before he met me and went towards Figgins Lane.”

“Hmmm. Still visiting Madam Meretrix, I suppose. You’d’ve thought he’d learned his lesson,” I said.

“No one else, Aumary. Why?”

“And coming back?”

“It was later than I usually return. I saw no one at all. Alice’s is only a few steps from the west door of St. Peter’s and I had my head down and my hood up. I was hurrying as it was well beyond curfew.”

“Thank you, Pete.”

“Again, why, Aumary?”

“Someone has killed one of the Scotsmen, Pete. Shhh, no news abroad yet. MacAlpine was killed in the night and found at Grange barn. I wanted to find out who was out last night.”

Peterkin looked aghast. “The taster? You cannot think...?”

“No, no we don’t suspect you...how could we? No. We just wondered if you had seen anything.”

“And I have not been much help. Sorry.”

*****

Most of the Scots were sitting sullenly around the table in their room. The Lord David and John of Doune were playing chess. Coagie was sharpening his knife with a stone. Donald was asleep on his pallet on the floor. Tam o' the Dale was staring at some parchments.

As we entered, no one stirred.

"Nattie was killed, the good doctor tells me, about the sixth or seventh hour of the night. I will need to know where you all were then."

David turned from his game. Putting the flat of his hands on his knees he looked up at me. "I was here in my bed as all good Christians should be at that time of night," he scowled. "Donald was here with me."

I looked at John of Doune. He cleared his throat. "I too was abed. But the bed was not my own. I lay in the arms of a buxom young wench by the name of Clarice."

"And I was in the next room, a snorin' me head off," said Coagie. "Or at least that's what the girl complained."

"Madam Meretrix'?"

"Aye… mind you she never complained before that when I..."

"Tam; where were you?"

Tam rolled his parchments before he answered.

"I was here with my lord David. Unlike the rest of them I was looking to the welfare of my soul, not my body. Ask your priest. I was in the chapel for every service through the night."

"Where is John of Dunfermline?"

The man came in from the next room. "Here, sir."

"Where were you?"

"Dicing till late in the stables then abed here. I didn't go out at all."

"He came in on midnight," said David. "I heard him. He sleeps closest to my bed."

I scrubbed my face with my hands.

"I shall ask around and make sure you are telling the truth."

Sir John of Doune stood upright and scowled at me. "You'll not take our word?"

"No, sir, I cannot do that."

"You best not be callin' us liars, my lad," he said.

"Wheesht Johnnie," said the Lord David, "Don't be so quick to catch offence. The man is only doing his job."

I bowed and left.

Before supper, Johannes and I walked down to the large house on Figgins Lane. The doctor would later walk up to his own house at the top of the High Street.

The same small young woman let us in, grinning this time. The mistress of the house had to be fetched from elsewhere. Today her face was painted and her hair decently done up beneath a white veil.

She curtsied. "Lord Belvoir. Another visit. My, you are getting quite the regular."

She leaned and looked past me "And Doctor Johannes. Well!"

"Mistress Ashley," I said, "We have been told that on Friday, two of the Scottish men who are residing at the castle visited your establishment."

"Indeed; the Scots have become good customers, sir."

"Can I ask you if they were here all night with your girls? I believe one of them was called Clarice?"

Mistress Ashley then nodded to the grinning girl who went to the back door and bellowed.

A woman, she looked more of a girl really, of about fourteen, came from the back room, smoothing down her skirts. She had raven black hair and her face was oval and dainty. I pictured the large coarse John of Doune with his long grey beard in my mind's eye and shuddered.

"The man you entertained on Friday, was he with you the whole night?"

The girl gave a quick bob. "Yessir. We had something to eat and then..."

"The man in the next door room?"

"Oh I didn't do him, sir..."

"Who was with him?"

"I think it was Sela, sir."

"Fetch her please."

The girl looked at her mistress and was given the nod. Off she went into the back room.

"Why are you asking such questions, sir?" asked Mistress Ashley as she flounced in front of me.

"I need to find out where they all were on Friday night."

"Why, sir?"

"I will tell you mistress and you will keep this to yourself. If I find it has gone around the town I will ask the town reeve to find something with which to charge and fine you. Your establishment will be no more. Is that quite clear?"

The woman blinked slowly. "Perfectly."

"A man is dead. Murdered. I am trying to find his murderer. So I want to know where everyone was on Friday."

"One of the Scots, sir?"

"One of the Scots."

"He did not die here; that I can tell you."

"No, I know he did not," I said.

The girl called Sela arrived. She was a little older, perhaps nineteen or twenty with copper hair and a freckled face.

"Sela, the man you entertained on Friday night. Was he with you all night?"

She curtsied beautifully and then asked, "Why do you want to know, sir?"

"Was he?"

"He went out to use the privy, sir, about midnight. He'd drunk a bucket full of ale. I fell asleep. It seemed to me that he was missing a while but I could not tell, for I too was rather far gone with drink. I slept most of the time. When I woke in the morning, he was back and asleep snoring."

"Thank you."

I was about to turn and leave when a thought occurred to me.

"Young Master Caspar. You all know him. Was he here on Friday?"

Mistress Ashley scoffed. "We haven't seen him this two weeks, sir."

"Oh!"

"He used to visit us regularly but now, I think he thinks us too lowly for him."

"Why do you say that?"

"I passed him on the street the other day and he looked right through me."

"Perhaps he's just grown up, Mistress Ashley," I said. "And I happen to know he has had some rather bad news of late."

"Bad news. Does that mean his father won't let him visit now then?"

"Is that something he used to do? Forbid him to visit?"

"He never had any money," said Mistress Ashley, "he ran up a large debt."

"Why did you allow him?"

"We liked him, didn't we girls?" They all nodded, especially the girl who was the doorkeeper.

"Ah mistress," said that girl, "Surely, you remember, he paid everything he owed, didn't he? To the last penny two weeks ago? You told me when you paid me my due that Caspar had paid up at last."

"He suddenly had some money?" I asked.

"Yes, he did," said Mistress Ashley. "But like I say, he hasn't been here since."

Johannes cleared his throat, "The man called Nattie? Nattie MacAlpine, was he here on Friday? With his other friends?"

The women looked at each other.

"The one with the black beard to his navel. No sir. I don't believe he was," said Sela. "In fact I thought I saw him from the window. I was hoping he would visit 'cos he is a good payer and he always goes that little bit extra to please...."

"He didn't turn up here?"

"No sir. Like I say, he was walking up the lane, but then someone called him and he went back."

"Did you see who that was?" I asked.

"No, sir. It was dark."

"Early or late?"

"Early" said Sela, "but still dark enough."

"Thank you ladies. You have been most helpful."

I made for the door with Johannes behind me.

"We will always be helpful to you sir, if we can. To you and to your lovely friend here," said Mistress Ashley.

"That reminds me," I said turning back as Johannes opened the outer door.

"The young girl whom you threatened. The one who was taken ill at St. Peter's. You weren't very friendly to her, were you? You did know her, didn't you, madam?"

Mistress Ashley smiled but the smile didn't touch her eyes. "Yes sir, I did, but that was not what you asked me that day. You asked me if she had worked here and I told you truthfully, that she did not."

"No, you didn't quite lie but it might have been more truthful to have told me that Anthony Chapman brought her to you."

The smile left her face.

"And that you refused her help when she so desperately needed it."

"I don't think..."

"You didn't directly deal out her death, madam. Others are guilty of that, but you did not help when she asked you. You threatened her, treated her very poorly. I think perhaps when you next make confession, it would be good for you to confess to your priest that you did not aid a fellow human being when it was obvious she was in dire need. Quite the opposite, madam; you frightened, threatened and harassed her. A little while later she was dead."

"I have not..."

"Do you believe, as many do, that those who die quickly and unshriven may walk, seeking retribution from those who spurned or wronged them in life?"

Mistress Ashley paled and wrapped her light blue supertunic tightly around her bosom.

"I would seek comfort in the church if I were you, mistress. And quickly."

We left.

As we walked up the alleyway, Johannes turned to me with a puzzled expression.

"Merewenna did not die unshriven, Aumary."

I smiled. "No, Father Columba was there at her end, was he not? But Mistress Ashley doesn't know that does she?"

Johannes chuckled.

Chapter Eleven

"Where does Caspar have his warehouse? You must know," I asked Nicholas Barbflet the next day when I saw him at work at his corn mill.

"He has, as far as I know, one small one here in the town," said Nick, "Up the hill from the rope works; one in Glebe Lane and another out Manton way. A large barn like building. Oh, and an office on Angel Yard. Why?"

"Where am I likely to find his son?"

Nicholas scoffed. "By all accounts at none of the warehouses. He's a free spirit that one. In London one moment, Marlborough the next. As Caspar said, I don't think he has any interest in following in his father's footsteps. He's hardly ever seen at the business premises."

"Caspar more or less said he was of no use to him, didn't he, the afternoon of your dinner?"

"Aye he did," Nicholas laughed. "He has to marry off his daughter to 'import' a useful son into the family to take over when he's too old to work any longer."

"Ah... yes… well. We shall see about that."

"What...?"

Nicholas put down his pen and inspected my face thoroughly. "Aumary Belvoir, what do you know that I haven't heard?"

I scratched my nose. "Just that I don't think the marriage of the delectable Hilda to her handsome paramour, Anthony, is now likely to take place. Not without a lot of fuss."

"Like I say, what do you know?" he grinned.

"They've fallen out. It's off. At the moment."

"Ho, ho! How do you know that?"

I shrugged. "I was there at the Caspar house when she broke off the betrothal."

Nicholas looked at me with narrowed eyes. "Now, tell me, what were you doing at the Caspar house, my friend?"

"My duty Nicholas... my duty."

His eyes narrowed further. "Hmmm. What are you up to, Belvoir?"

"I am following a trail which may lead me to the murderer of our visitor to the castle."

"The man we found at the bridge?"

"The same. His name was Alan of Windsor and he was a King's lawyer."

"It was murder then, as we suspected? He did not drown?"

"Two wounds to the back."

"Hmmm. Can you tell me or must this remain a secret? I have heard, as has the whole town, that there are some Scotsmen staying at the castle. Is this anything to do with them?"

I laughed. "I have tried to keep their presence quiet but they are determined to thwart me at every turn. I have been charged with their safety. Already one has been done to death...."

"In addition to our King's man?"

I nodded. "And now I hear that the young Caspar, well I'm guessing it was Cecil Caspar, was at the castle just before the man was killed, searching for one of our Scotsmen."

"No!"

"Peterkin saw him skulking about that night. The guard spoke to a young man answering his description a little earlier. I want to know what he's about."

"Best search first at the house, then. What time is it...about the third hour? He might have stumbled from his pit by now."

"Manton you say?"

"Yes, it's close by the Grange."

"Is it now?" I said heavy with emphasis.

*****

I did indeed visit the Caspar house. Neither of the men were at home. I was told they had gone to the warehouse at Manton.

I saddled Bayard and jogged at an easy pace along the road once more.

The building was a large lapstrake built one looking rather like a square ship. It was close to the river, but like the Grange barn, far enough away from flooding. Indeed I could see that very building from this edifice. There was a gated track leading to Caspar's place, where some carts were being unloaded. I remembered Caspar saying that he was awaiting some deliveries from south of the river. He'd wanted them across the bridge before the rains washed it away and was chafing because they did not make it and could not reach the town. If he had a warehouse here, why was he so worried about goods coming to Marlborough? Surely they were safe enough here?

I stood down and opened the gate. A few people looked up and I noticed two burly men at the front doors. A man came towards me.

"Sir Aumary isn't it? Lord Aumary Belvoir?"

"Yes. Master Kelner I believe?" Kelner was the Caspar overseer.

"Yes sir. I see you occasionally at the castle when I have cause to visit."

He stretched out a hand. "Come. The master is here. Would you like to see him?"

"It's the young master I'd like to see, Kelner, if he's here."

Kelner's face split into a grin. "Yes… for once you're in luck. He *is* here."

"Good. Can you take me to him?"

He bade me walk into the large building where bales of cloth, unspun wool, all manner of items for the clothing trade were laid out in rows on decks of wood. In a separate area I saw people sorting and carding wool and winding threads. All was busy.

"Is this place just for the fabric side of Master Caspar's business, Kelner?"

"Most of the finished stuff is near to the dyers and weavers at Angel Yard in the town. Here sir, we have the raw materials, unspun wool and fleeces, and sheepskins. There is a carding shed here too, as well as one on Chantry Lane. And some hides."

“Anything else?”

“Master Caspar has been buying up armaments lately...hoping to sell to the King for the upcoming… trouble,” he answered. “Arming the ships, sir.”

I nodded.

“What role does young Master Cecil play in all this, Kelner?”

“In the past year....nothing, but of late, he is accompanying his father, to learn the trade I suppose. It seems he has had a change of heart, sir.”

“Oh?”

“He did not want to be part of the business, now it seems he’s changed his mind. Youth eh?”

I laughed with him. Maybe Cecil would turn out to be the beautiful butterfly emerged from an ugly chrysalis, after all.

A small office was situated at the back of the building. Here Cecil lounged on a stool and contemplated the wooden wall of the warehouse. He saw me enter and jumped up as if bitten.

“My Lord Belvoir?”

“Master Caspar.” Kelner closed the door.

“My father is at the other end of the building. Shall I have him fetch...”

“It’s you I’ve come to talk to, Cecil.”

“Me?” His tone was squeaky, like a boy whose voice is not yet broken, but this young man was nearly eighteen.

“Not more about that girl, whatever her name was.”

“When last I saw you, I thought you were saddened by her death, young man? Are you now not so upset about your part in her downfall?”

“I was sad. And I am contrite. Do you think I’d be here at this God forsaken place if I was not paying a price for my involvement in her death?”

“Your penance?”

“I spoke with my mother. She tried to make me see that the girl was not worth my concern. I disagreed with her.”

“She is a hard woman, your mother.”

“I wanted to do something to make amends. Mother suggested I come here, every day. Of course it's not truly a penance. It's just working for my father. I hate it but no doubt after a while I'll get used to it and it'll no longer be painful."

Your mother knows that you hate it?"

"Aye, I have no doubt she does."

"I came to speak to you about the night you came to the castle."

"The night I came to..."

"And asked for a Scotsman."

"Scotsman..." Cecil looked away. "What Scotsman would that be? I didn't know there were any Scots at the castle."

"Come now...you know there are. Every Tom, Dick and Harry in Marlborough knows that a party of Scots are staying at the castle. I haven't been able to hide it, though I have tried."

"Why would I be wanting to speak to a Scotsman?"

"I have come to ask you that."

"I didn't..."

"Master Caspar. I can tell by the look on your face when you are lying."

"I didn't..."

"You were seen and recognised. What did you want with our Scots guests?"

"I...I...I met one of them at Madam Meretrix'"

"Which one?"

"I can't remember his name."

"What did he look like, this Scotsman?"

"Bearded. Old. He was stocky. They all look alike don't they?"

"What did you want with him?"

"I thought he might like to accompany me to the..."

"Master Caspar. If you were not nearly eighteen, I would put you across my knee and teach you the futility of lying to me. My patience is only so thick." I put up my finger and thumb to a half inch distance.

"The truth!"

Caspar sat down on his stool with a bump.

"I saw him with Merewenna...that was her real name wasn't it?"

"Yes. When?"

"The evening before she died."

"Where?"

"On South Field. They went into Wat's bothy together, the old one."

"She wrote of it in the last pages of her book," I said.

"I was going to follow them in but then I thought, I can't. The man will no doubt give me a beating for interrupting his pleasure."

"No doubt."

"So I waited. He left. I followed Merewenna to Figgins Lane. She wouldn't speak to me."

I nodded. "So why did you want to find this man again? You weren't particularly friendly with him?"

Caspar licked his lips.

"I'd seen him before."

"When? What was he doing?"

"Hanging around father's warehouse"

"This warehouse?"

"Everyone thinks I haven't been within a mile of this place before...but it's a good place to bring a girl after dark and I have a key."

"What was he doing?"

"I don't know," said Caspar, but.... "On my way home, he jumped me."

"You walked home and he attacked you?" I said, surprise in my voice.

"Well, he didn't attack me really, he just knocked me to the ground. Before I could mount my horse."

Ah, Caspar had been mounted.

"Whatever did he do that for?"

"He wanted me to...tell him something....get information for him."

"And he'd pay you?"

"Yes. He'd pay me a lot. You know I have debts."

"I know you paid your debt at the brothel."

Caspar nodded. "I shan't go there again..."

"No? You weren't there last night?" I asked.

"No."

"So where had you been all the time, from my guard seeing you at the castle early to my informer seeing you on Figgins Lane later on?"

"Waiting..."

"On the lane to see if the Scotsman turned up?"

"Yes."

"Did he?"

"Yes."

"So why did you want to see him so badly?"

"Because I think he killed...."

The door opened quickly. "Cecil my lad..."

The elder Caspar in a furred gown stood in the doorway with his mouth open.

"My Lord Belvoir. I thought we'd seen the last of you," he said after a while.

Cecil fidgeted.

"Forgive me Master Caspar, I have unfinished business with your son."

"Not here you haven't, sir," said the merchant, lifting his chin pugnaciously. "I have an urgent need to speak to him about wool, sir."

"And I to speak to him about murder, Caspar. I think my need outweighs yours."

The elder Caspar spluttered like a landed fish.

Suddenly seeing escape, Cecil stood and rushed past us both.

"Forgive me, I *must* go to the privy...something I ate..." and he fled.

Caspar and I stared at each other angrily.

I growled at Cecil's father. "Fetch him back, Caspar."

"I will not, my lord."

"Then I'll wait."

"You'll wait an age then. He's taken his horse and gone."

I ground my teeth.

"I will speak to your son again, sir. At home. Tell him."

The man bowed but I saw he was shaking. I couldn't decide whether it was anger or fear made him do so.

*****

I passed the Grange barn on my way back. I too was seething. I had been so close to Cecil telling me whom he thought was a murderer. It was most certainly one of the Scots. But which one was it?

I decided to go in one more time and check the place. My last investigation had been cut short.

The door was partly open. I pushed it. It moaned like a ghost.

Once again the rats rushed for cover.

I breathed in the sweet smell of the hay and I searched for my pitchfork. Ah, of course it would have been taken by the coroner as deodand.

Once more I quartered the ground. I scuffed up the edge of the hay with my boots. Nattie had been murdered just there on the beaten earth; there were scuff marks and blood there; signs that the three tines of the hayfork had pierced his body and struck the ground beneath. The body had then been dragged up to the top of the pile and hidden; then the hay was scattered to cover the signs and the fork dug into the pile. It all looked as innocent as a baby.

Where would you take a girl to lie her down if not here in the hay? No sign remained of Merewenna and Alan of Windsor. The pile had been too disturbed.

I stood back and my eye raked the pile of dried grasses. You would certainly want to make yourself comfortable. I smiled as I thought back to my youth, to my father's barns scattered across the estate and the two girls I used to meet there, before I married my sweet Cecily, my first wife, at the age of nineteen.

Oh yes, comfort was important.

I turned to walk away. As I did the sun came out once more and slanted its rays through the barn door; it had been a grey day so far. I blinked as motes of dust danced in the sunlight.

Half way up, I noticed something red glinting.

Once more I scrambled up the face of the hay and plunged my arm into the dried piled grasses.

"Ouch!"

Pulling back my hand, I noticed something sharp had scored across my thumb. I stuck my finger in my mouth and sucked like a child.

I have had wounds of many kinds; sword, dagger, crossbow quarrel but none of them sting at first and as nastily as does a simple pin prick.

I reached in more carefully this time. Out came a sizeable brooch, one with a red enamel decoration surrounded by a rope edge of bronze with a lethal point on the pin in front.

The missing cloak brooch of Alan of Windsor.

Carefully I pulled apart the hay.

There was a depression which had been covered over. And blood. A lot of blood.

More blood than had been spilled from Nattie's body who'd died almost immediately.

Here was where Alan of Windsor was attacked and unconscious, lay bleeding for some while before he was dragged a hundred yards or so to the rising river and thrown in.

He had, it seemed, stayed here in the warm hay after he had coupled with Merewenna. Perhaps he slept, meaning to resume his journey later. Perhaps he did not intend to sleep but fatigue overcame him.

I do not think he ever woke.

*****

I left the barn and made straight for the Caspar house but young Cecil had not gone home.

I would have to surprise him the next day, I thought.

That next day was one of the two days of the year when the South Field became the place where archery was practised. It became the butts.

Targets were set up at the far end by the river. Demonstrations of quarterstaff and pike drill were made. The townsfolk pitted themselves against the professional soldiers. The day had the feel of a fair about it, with food sellers doing good trade and peddlers going round with their wares.

I sauntered about early, nodding to folk I knew. There was much laughter and friendly rivalry. The air was filled with the thrumming of the bow strings and the thud of the arrows on the targets.

I passed the place where men competed with quarterstaffs. I saw Hardcastle beating back one of the tall lads of the town, going down on one knee and felling the lad with a swipe to the lower leg. There was much laughter and friendly cat calling. Hardcastle lifted up the smiling lad and slapped him on the back. There was no animosity; I realised it was his son John.

I passed on and standing at the back of the crowd, watched the competitors at the butts loose their arrows at the targets. I saw John of Dunfermline, his feet wide planted, aim at the target and let go his arrow to land smack in the middle of the straw bale with a circle painted onto a piece of wood. His friends Tam o' the Dale and John of Doune congratulated him.

There was no sign of the Lord David nor Donald Baird, nor at that moment Coagie Firmin.

The English negotiators had wisely chosen to stay in the castle this day.

I looked around me. It all looked calm and safe, though I was aware that at any moment a stray arrow might be loosed at one of the Scots.

I shouldered my way through the crowd and leaned against Wat's old bothy, where I'd found the coin. I scanned the field and the people.

There was Coagie on the edge of the field, by the roadside. I watched him rake the field with a practised eye and step out onto the still damp grass. He was heading it seemed for a pie man.

My eye left him and I sought out the Lord of Doune and John of Dunfermline once more. They were now watching the archery with interest.

I turned my back to the river. Some of the soldiers from the castle were bringing out the stand which held the spears. After the archery, there would be a competition for throwing these too, at a target.

I knew who would win. He always did. John Burton, one of the castle guards. This didn't stop the townsmen and some of the man's fellow guards trying to beat him.

They placed it at the rear of the garden yard wall of the house belonging to Mistress Ashley, which backed onto South Field and started to fill it with the short spears used in this competition.

At three passes each, I noticed fifteen spears loaded into the stand, which was a wooden, upside down v shaped rack, with bracing, creating spaces for the spears to nestle. Five men would compete, it seemed.

The rack was about four feet tall, with the spears protruding and the wooden storage structure started at about three feet from the ground with splayed feet for stability.

A cheer went up. Someone else had achieved the centre of the target at archery. His friends were slapping him on the back. I noticed it was Harry Glazer, the cordwainer's lad.

I smiled.

The smile died on my lips as my eye lit upon a furtive Cecil Caspar, leading his horse through the people standing on the Pewsey Road,. He stopped just for one moment, to look ahead then walked on past the castle drawbridge and towards the town bridge.

I set off at a jog towards the young man and his horse. I didn't want him to escape me a second time.

Coming up behind him, I said quickly, "Cecil, where are you off to in such a hurry?"

He jumped and turned quickly. "Oh my Lord Belvoir. I..."

"We haven't finished our conversation, my lad," I said.

I came up level with him and took his horse's reins.

"I think you were about to tell me yesterday, who you'd seen on the road to

Manton that day. The Scotsman you'd thought had murdered the man who lay with Merewenna?"

"No sir, you're mistaken."

"Aw c'mon Cecil. You went to the castle the night before last to find the man who paid you the money to tell him....what was it you were going to tell him?"

Caspar vehemently shook his head. "No sir, I can't tell you."

"You were all set to do so yesterday."

"I've had time to think."

I let go of the reins and folded my arms. "You can have plenty of time to think, sitting in the gaol at the castle, Cecil."

He made to set his foot in the stirrup of his horse.

I rounded the horse's head and pulled the beast away.

"No Cecil… you're not going until you tell me."

"I can't. They'd have my hide."

"How do you know them?"

"I don't know them. Not all of them. I told you. I was coming back from the warehouse and he jumped me. He wanted me to spy for him. He said that the warehouse building was a good place from which to see the river path and he was looking for someone."

"Was he now? Who?"

"He didn't tell me the man's name but he would be richly dressed and would be riding a grey horse."

"You were to look out for him and...."

"Tell the man immediately where he was, where he went."

"For this he'd pay you a lot of money?"

"Yes...I didn't know that he was going to kill him did I?"

"Did you see the man he was looking for?"

"No. But later on I saw Royse...Merewenna on Figgins Lane and she told me she'd seen the rich man at the Grange barn. That she'd lain with him and left him there."

"Ah… I see."

"I went immediately to town and met with the Scotsman at Madam Meretrix' and got my money."

"Can you see him here?" I asked "Your Scotsman."

Cecil looked ahead. "I...I can't say..."

I stared at the young man. "You really suppose that I will believe that you had no idea what this man was going to do with this information?"

"I didn't know he'd kill him..." he said, panic in his voice. His eye travelled past me to the field where the archery was still taking place. "I didn't know who he was or the rich man."

Coagie, David and John of Doune were now in a huddle. I could see them scouting round looking for...perhaps another of their party.

"I must go," shouted Cecil.

I held onto his horses' reins.

"Where are you going?"

He pushed past me and ran up the road to the bridge.

I followed towing his abandoned horse.

"Cecil!" I shouted...

At that moment, Donald Baird reared up over the slope of the sunken meadow and jogged onto the slightly raised road by the bridge. He walked nonchalantly back towards the castle drawbridge.

Cecil saw him, stopped. He turned tail, pushed past me...grabbed his horse's reins and made for a gap in the crowd on the field's edge. He mounted at a run and rode for the furthest edge of the South Field at the border of the High Street where it passed St. Peter's.

Where on earth was he going?

He tried to double back but Hardcastle, hearing me yell at the lad, had planted himself on the road and was all set to grab the horse as he passed.

There was no escape that way.

Cecil Casper turned his horse's head back towards the field. People scattered as he passed along the edge where folk had thought themselves safe from the press of people watching the events. They grabbed their children to them and swore at the reckless young man, tearing along on his dun horse. Women who wanted to keep clear of the closely packed crowd of men with weapons but who wanted to watch the competition screamed as divots of wet grass from Cecil's horse's hooves landed on them.

The ground was still quite boggy in places; after all, it had been under water here not so long ago.

Then I realised that he was going to try to jump the six foot wall at the back of Mistress Ashley's house. He could be down the alley way and off before anyone saw where he was going.

Cecil's horse thundered along the field edge. I saw Coagie turn and look at the commotion. He set off at a lope up to the wall. John of Doune followed him at a close distance.

Cecil reached the wall he was going to leap, just as Coagie, John and two others drew level with him.

The young man drove his heels into his horse's flank. The dun leapt the wall and cleared it, landing in the garden yard of the brothel.

Young Caspar tottered momentarily on the back of his horse and then, before the horse had cleared the wall toppled sideways with a cry.

It was as if I saw it all slowed down; as if I could watch every movement paced over a slow inbreath instead of the heartbeat it took to happen.

There was an earsplitting scream.

Everyone turned to the wall at the edge of the field.

A hundred or more voices were stilled.

The scream ended in a bubbling piping.

Then there were more screams. Women fled their place by the wall. Dogs barked incessantly.

Children screeched and ran for their parents, blubbering, slipping and sliding, bumping into each other.

I pushed my way through the silent and momentarily stilled group in the middle of the field.

The wrestlers had ceased to wrestle. The quarterstaff men parted to let me through.

Gayle came running up to my side. It had been he who had been organising the soldiers who were to begin the target throwing of the spears.

"God's breath, Aumary, what in..?"

Some brave people had stayed by the wall. As I came up I noticed Coagie was one of them. He stood a little way to the side of the wooden contraption which held the spears.

A woman was screeching and someone slapped her face and she fell into muttering sobs. I noticed she was splattered with blood.

The men in front of me fell away as I walked up.

My eye fell on the spear rack and then I turned away, my gorge rising. I swallowed and looked again.

Cecil was lying rigid on the side of the inverted V which held the spears. His body had been pierced....I counted...by eleven of the fifteen spears held in the rack. One to the throat, one to each shoulder. One to each of the out-flung arms. Three across the torso, one to the groin and one to each thigh. His mouth was open and was filled with blood. He made no sound now. His eyes stared at me pleadingly and then the light went out of them and he slumped, as much as he could, being held as he was by eleven vicious spikes.

I turned away again.

"Fetch the doctor..." I shouted. "And the priest."

*****

The field soon cleared. Once I had organised a party of men to lift Cecil from the spears, I too turned for the castle.

Johannes came running up.

He saw my face and looked behind me to the body they were lifting onto a blanket. They'd had a devil of a job to get the young man free of his imprisoning spikes.

"God's teeth Aumary; what happened?" he whispered.

Gayle came up at his elbow.

"I think he was attempting to vault the wall and he slipped from the horse's back. He fell on the rack of...." Gayle shielded his eyes with his hand. He could not carry on.

I turned back to see Coagie and John of Doune close together, staring at the bloodied spears. Not a word was said.

"Aye, that's how it happened," I said. "It's my fault. I made him bolt."

"No, Aumary..." said Johannes gently, "It's not your fault."

"I pressed him to tell me what it was he knew and he fled. If I'd left him… he would not have..."

"Shall I send someone for his father?" asked Gayle.

"I think he may be at the Manton warehouse," I said with a sigh.

Gayle turned away and jogged back up to the castle.

Johannes slipped his arm around my shoulder.

"Aumary, you were not to know he would try to run," he said. "It was an accident. A terrible accident."

I shook my head.

"He would not have suffered long. The shock will, if nothing else, have stopped his heart, I'm sure."

"He was alive for a while at least, I think...I saw his eyes. It took me a few heartbeats to reach him; he was alive then." I looked down at my boots. "God, that look will be with me for the rest of my life."

And do you know, Paul, I was right. I still see his face sometimes, in dreams. Or are they nightmares?

"Come… come up to the house with me," said Johannes, trying to turn me around but I would not be turned.

I stared at the Scotsmen now all grouped together. They were watching the deposition of the body in the blanket.

"He saw Donald Baird coming up the road. It made him about face and run back."

"Come, Aumary..."

I saw Nicholas Barbflet arrive. He stared at me across the field with a vacant face. I know now that he accompanied the body to the church.

"And then he saw John...and made for his horse. Then Coagie....."

"It was an accident...you cannot think it..."

I looked up. "No Johannes," I said. "I don't think it was. An accident."

Chapter Twelve

Johannes walked with me back to the castle, while the body was removed to the church of St. Mary. Gayle had offered to go up to the warehouse to Master Caspar and Nicholas to the house on the High Street to inform Cecil's mother, and to send a runner to the coroner.

It was, thank goodness, out of my hands.

We sat in my small office and Johannes took out a flask which he kept in his purse.

"Burntwine. It will do us no harm to take a little. It's good for shock," he said.

I told him what the young man had managed to explain to me before he died.

"So," he took a sip of the burntwine. "Cecil was approached by one of the Scots. He would pay him, he said, to inform him when Alan of Windsor was on the road to the town?"

"That must have been the very day they arrived, Johannes," I said, puzzled. "Or soon after."

"Cecil then meets Merewenna by the river who tells him about the man and where the man is," I said.

"A piece of luck that Merewenna had seen him but not so lucky for Alan or, ultimately, the girl."

"No. However it didn't leave long for one of the foreigners to learn the news and get to the barn to kill him," I said.

"Cecil tells him that he is there and our murderer seeks and finds Alan of Windsor in the barn and kills him," said Johannes.

"I found the spot where he died at the Grange barn. He was then dragged out and sent on his way in the rising waters. We found him the next day."

"The Scotsman must have been one of the last people back across the bridge that day. The day before the water demolished it and you found our body," said Johannes.

"Cecil told me he saw Merewenna a little while later with the Scotsman. According to her book, they came back from the riverside together," I said.

"And then onto South Field."

"Where Cecil saw them go into the bothy. Before the water rose up to that level."

"This was when Merewenna learned that her man was dead. The Scotsman told her?"

"I suppose so," I said. "The Scotsman must have been on his way back from killing Alan of Windsor when he met Merewenna," I sighed. "That's how he knew."

"The last page of her book says that the Scotsman paid her with a foreign coin." I fished in my scrip. "This one I think."

Johannes reached for it..."Where did you…?"

"I went to Wat's bothy. It was on the floor."

Johannes turned the coin around in his fingers.

"You realise what this means, Aumary?"

I nodded and took a sip of burntwine.

"Cecil Caspar committed treason, for he betrayed an officer of the crown to the enemy."

"Not only that, my friend," said the doctor, "the girl realised it. She also realised that she had unwittingly given Caspar the information he needed and that he'd used it. He'd betrayed Alan of Windsor to his enemy, sadly with her help."

I sat up straight. "That is why she was mumbling the word traitor and that is why the last page of her book is a diatribe upon a wicked man who'd used her. That man was Cecil Caspar."

"I fear it. She could not live with that thought," said Johannes. "The rest we know." He handed back the coin.

*****

Later that afternoon, Johannes went back to his house at the head of the

High Street.

A note came back quite quickly. Would I meet him at the church of St. Mary? There was something I had to see.

"The body has lain in the crypt, Aumary, all this afternoon," said Johannes as we descended the steps. "The women have finished laying him out. One of them came to me, a little puzzled. She knows of our friendship and our professional liaison and asked that I let you know what she had found."

Johannes peeled back the cover which had been lain over Cecil Caspar's naked body.

I grimaced to see the wounds to his young flesh.

"Eleven spear heads pierced him as he was thrown onto the rack. This woman knew this for I'd told her so."

"Yes, I counted, when I first saw him lying there."

"You will have seen this then...one to the neck. Left hand side." Johannes took his metal probe and pointed." One here and another here to each shoulder."

"Yes and three to the torso, one each to the outspread arms."

"And these two to the thighs," he pointed again. "The last is to the groin."

Johannes grasped the body by the right side and pulled it up.

"What we could not see until he was undressed, cleaned and laid out.... was this."

He pointed once more. This time I had to lean over and peer at the side of the corpse.

"Here. This wound was not made by a spear head."

"It's a knife wound."

"It's a side swipe. Yes, with a knife." He let the body down gently and covered it once more.

He reached for the cotte worn by the lad and laid it out on the ground. It was stiff with dried blood.

"Here we can see the spear rents. The two to the arms and legs aren't on the cotte but in the under tunic. And the one to the groin doesn't show because the split cotte flew open but we do have...this."

I peered by the light of a candle.

"Yes. I see it. The slash of a knife to the side."

"You were right Aumary. The lad did not *fall* off. It wasn't an accident. He fell because he was knifed. Oh, it was not a life threatening blow but it was enough to unseat him and drive him over his horse's saddle and onto the spear rack."

I pictured in my mind's eye, the scene as Caspar made to jump the wall. I saw everything slowed down, as I'd seemed to see it as it happened that morning.

Caspar had tensed to jump the wall, he'd leaned forward to encourage his horse. His left side was facing me, though I was still some way off.

The horse lifted its front feet, Cecil swayed and called out, a cry of pain. He let go of the reins. The horse's back feet left the ground and leapt the wall. Cecil's feet cleared the stirrups, he could not hang on. He turned sideways and fell. As he fell he rotated onto his back and the spears pierced him with a sickening squelch.

I looked up at Johannes. "This is murder," I said. "Whoever struck him knew that there was a good chance he would end up on the spears."

"Did you see who was on his right hand side?"

"Aye. I did," I said. "But which man struck him I cannot say. It was all over with so quickly and after the event I was too distracted to see fully who was standing on the other side."

"No doubt they will have moved off pretty quickly," said Johannes.

"There were the three Scots and one other young townsman."

"Which?"

"Coagie Firmin, John of Doune and I think...Donald Baird."

"All three have been regulars at Madam Ashley's?"

"They have."

"Then, my friend, you must question all three."

*****

"And you still do not have any idea why Nattie would be at the Grange barn that day?"

All the Scots looked at each other.

"He's never been here before, in this part of England. I've no idea why he would go there."

"Or what he was doing when he got there," said first the Lord David and then Sir John of Dunfermline.

"I have reason to believe that he was going to Mistress Ashley's earlier but he was called back by someone who hailed him from the end of the lane."

They all shrugged.

"You, John and you, Coagie, you were at Mistress Ashley's that night but Nattie didn't arrive as planned, did he?"

"I thought he'd stayed at the castle to drink the night away. Like m'lord said, he had certainly had a skinful that afternoon. Perhaps he did'na think he was going to be of any use to the ladies," said Coagie giggling. "But now you tell me he followed us and stood back."

"What would you think if I told you that I thought that Nattie was killed because he'd seen something or knew something? That he had to be silenced."

The lord of Doune sat down on a bench.

"And what might that be?"

I shrugged. "Nattie was at the scene of the shooting of the Lord David. Perhaps he saw who loosed the arrow."

David looked up at me and narrowed his eyes.

"He was later poisoned. Everyone knew that Nattie tasted all food before the Lord David ate it. If it weren't for the quick work of my friend Johannes, he probably would have died then. It wasn't the Lord David at risk that day. It was always about Nattie."

The Prince of Scotland stood up slowly. "Then you are saying that it's one of us, me, John Coagie, Dunfermline, Tam or Baird who killed Nattie?"

"What did he know, my lord?"

"It's absurd," said David through clenched teeth. "Better look to one of your own, laddie."

I walked to a clear space in the room. "When I was a younger man, my brother had a tutor, a very learned man called Quimper. I used to discourse with him on all manner of subjects. He was well versed in the classical histories. He told me about a man called Cicero. This man lived a very long time ago, in Rome. He too, Tam, was a lawyer. In the course of his work he developed an idea, if you like. I suppose it was not something which was readily pondered upon in those far off times. It was something new. In Latin - cui bono..."

"Who stands to gain?" said Tam folding his arms. "Aye, I too have heard of him."

"I have tried to apply that logic to every murder I have investigated since the day I learned about it. Nattie's too. Who benefits from his demise?"

"None of *us*," said Baird with a growl. "Nattie was a good friend."

"Maybe his death was nothing but accidental," said Coagie, smiling. "He was out in the night and stumbled upon a courtin' couple. A pair..." he rubbed his nose, "if yer catch me, who should'na been there together. The man snatched up the fork and..."

"You think Nattie couldn't defend himself against a peasant with a hayfork, Coagie?"

The man shrugged.

"He knew his killer I'm sure. Felt safe, perhaps." I said. "Cui bono. Who benefits? None of my men in this castle benefit," I said again. "Not by his particular death."

They all glared at me.

"One man of the town benefitted however from the death of Alan of Windsor."

David's brow puckered.

"One man was paid by one of you, to inform on the whereabouts of the lawyer."

Donald Baird shifted his feet and put his hand on the pommel of his sword. "Why should we do that?"

"To waylay and kill him of course."

The men, as one body, roared aloud and started up, taking steps towards me. I stood my ground, my hand on my own sword.

"Why that makes me feam… Nay, laddie… watch what you say," snarled John of Doune breathing hard.

"I'm sorry to say it but there is no doubt he was killed by one of your party," I fished in my scrip. "I have evidence."

"Yer planted it!" shouted Donald.

"Why should I?" I held up the coin I had found in Wat's bothy. "I found this in the Grange barn." They weren't to know I hadn't found it there. "Any of you admit to losing it in the barn? I doubt we have many Scotsmen in the area so loose with their coin that they can afford to toss away such money."

"It was Nattie's!" cried out Donald Baird, "Musta bin."

"Aye...," said David at last "Aye, it's true. Why, why should you put it there?"

"There's no doubt you as a party benefitted from the death of Alan of Windsor. You said yourself sir, he was a feared lawyer of great intellect."

David sat down again. "Aye...I did. I'll admit it. I did know what manner of man your King had sent against us. But I did not order his death, if that's what you mean."

I nodded.

"One of you paid a man of the town to keep an eye on the road and tell him when Alan of Windsor was travelling. Once he knew, it was an easy matter to go and kill him. I found the place where he was killed. Grange barn, the same place but a little way off from the spot where Nattie met his end."

"It's a dangerous place this Grange barn," said Coagie with a snort. "You'll no catch me goin' there."

I smiled, though I didn't want to. The tension released.

"Who's the townsman?" said David tersely looking at me from the corner of his eye.

"The man who informed on Alan of Windsor is the young man who died an awful death today at the South Field. His name was Cecil Caspar."

The Scots were silent.

"You don't know who the Scotsman is, do you?" asked Tam o' the Dale at last. "You would be telling us now if you did."

"The lad took the name to the grave with him but then I doubt he ever knew it."

I turned and walked around the knot of men at their backs. "He knew the face though and he saw that face today at the fair and he fled from that man, in great fear."

"He does'na know," said Tam to his lord.

"No, I don't know. I admit it."

Tam turned to look me in the eye. "If you knew and you accused the man there's nothing you can do. The man is a man of Scotland and as such subject to his lord here, David, and ultimately to the King, William."

"No, you're correct, I couldn't arrest him."

"You'd have a job laddie," said John of Doune under his breath.

"Wheesht Johnnie," said David, "Put your beard back on your face!" He swivelled in his seat to stare at me. "No lad, you couldn't arrest him. But maybe I would."

I bowed. "That would be my hope, sir."

"It was a terrible accident," said Donald Baird, shaking his head. "The lad who took the money. I saw it happen."

"He was eighteen, gentlemen. Eighteen. And no, Donald. It was not an accident."

Tam took in a sharp breath. "Another life taken?"

"As he prepared to jump the wall on his mount, someone sliced him sharply with a knife, hoping, I think, that it would unseat him and that as close as he was to the spear rack, he would fall and..."

"Jesu," said Tam o' the Dale, crossing himself.

Coagie hissed through his teeth.

"It was not a planned murder but a perfect opportunity to get rid of someone who could identify the killer. I have a feeling that Cecil's days were dwindling anyway. And he knew it. I think he wanted to get away today and was prevented."

"I saw him on the road running from...you my lord," said Baird.

"Then I saw you join your countrymen close by the spear rack, Donald."

The smile left Baird's face. "Are you accusing me, m'lord Belvoir?"

"No more than I can accuse Coagie Firmin here, or Sir John of Doune. You were all within striking distance I think." I shook my head. "All three of you jogged at a pace to the wall when you saw the commotion made by the passage of the young man's horse."

"I thought to stop him," said Baird angrily. "I was trying to do you a favour, Belvoir. I knew you wanted him for I heard you cry out."

"I will not deny it," I said. "And I feel in part responsible for the poor lad's death."

The Earl David turned in his seat to stare at his men. After a while he said resignedly,

"Aye well. What's done is done. Now, we must concentrate on the job we were sent to do."

"I will request that from now on you stay in your quarters when you are not in the Queen's house with Masters Argentum and Lingan. If you wish to go out *please* will you inform me. I'll have soldiers accompany you. For your own protection."

"Pah!" said John of Doune, turning away. "We are not children that we need nursemaiding."

"I am concerned that there will be another attempt to destroy the talks. I'll have no more deaths."

All the Scots looked at each other. David cleared his throat. "We will do as you ask, Sir Aumary. Aye we will..." he snarled as John and Donald protested. "We're not afrit, you understand, but it makes sense not to put our heads in the devil's mouth."

"Thank you, sir, for your...understanding." I bowed and left.

*****

I stomped back to my room and threw myself into my chair. Gayle's head popped around the door and he scratched on it to attract my attention.

"I've seen Johannes. He tells me it's murder."

"Yes, Pete." I scrubbed at my face and yawned. "Caspar was unlawfully killed."

Gayle came into the room and closed the door. "You look as if you could eat and drink a mountain. You've had nothing since you broke your fast I suppose."

"No, you're right, Pete. Nothing."

"I have food in my room. Come on… come and help me eat it."

I stood wearily and followed Peterkin Gayle into his little room, the room next to my own.

My friend poured us some wine, set out cheese and meat, some radishes and a dish of sallet leaves.

"My my, Pete. Where did you get these so early in the season?"

My cousin Philomena, she has a plot out back and grows them as early as she can."

"They're good," I said, biting into the peppery red root.

I put the radish down on the table. "Pete, how did....Master Caspar...and Mistress Caspar..."

"As you would expect. The woman dissolved into hysterical tears and was no use at all, Nick tells me. Master Caspar sat in silence when I told him. It doesn't always go in at first, does it?"

"No, there is a time of disbelief. When you think it's all completely wrong and it's not your loved one."

"Aye...you'd know," said Peterkin gently. "Then he denounced him as an idiot...and what was he doing anyway trying to leap the wall… and similar things."

"That too is normal, I think. You seek to find someone or something to blame."

"And then… I'm sorry to say he blamed… well... he blamed...."

"Me."

"Yes, he did," he said sadly.

"Said that you had, from the first, hounded the family for some imagined slight. None of them were safe from your wrath, Caspar said."

I breathed in harshly.

"Aye he would. After the Merewenna business."

"Ah yes...I remember you telling me."

"He is bound to feel that I sought revenge after that. Even though I said that I would do nothing to them. Any of them. Of course he knows nothing of the business of his son and the Scots."

"No. Shall you tell him?"

"Depends on what he does."

"Ah yes...what he does..." said Gayle fingering the mole on his chin nervously.

"Pete...what did he say?"

"That you have brought about the ruin of his family. That he no longer *has* a family. His son is dead, his wife estranged from him, his daughter ruined.... That he'd kill you, that's all."

I scoffed. "Yes… well, he can try."

"He is a very rich man, Aumary. He won't do it himself of course. He'll pay."

"He'll calm down Pete, I'm sure, in time."

"No doubt you're right."

I reached for a slice of beef. "My, this is good fare. I can see why you go out two nights a week to your cousin's."

Peterkin laughed. "I'm so glad Philly came to live here. She was going to stay in London but she'd no one to stay for. No children you see. And well, there's just me and Philly and Dagget..."

"Dagget?"

"My older brother. Part of the King's privy wardrobe at the Tower in London."

I nodded. I remembered Pete telling me he was born in London.

We chatted, tossing personal information back and forth till late afternoon or so. Gradually I began to feel better, less wearied and more convinced that I had done nothing wrong on the South Field that day.

We were chuckling at something one of the gate guards had said earlier that morning, when we heard an almighty thud.

"That came from next door," said Pete, cocking his head.

I must have looked perplexed for Pete asked, "Did you lock your door, Aumary?"

I thought back. "No, I didn't. I usually do but I was so weary with it all, I just followed you in here, I didn't..."

We stood and raced for his door. He drew his sword. Mine was still in my room.

I stood by the door panel and Peterkin placed himself at the other door jamb. I pushed open the door quickly. Peterkin leapt into the room. I followed.

The room was empty but where I might have been sitting in the back of the chair, a cross bow quarrel had been released into the wood.

It gouged deep into the back.

A discarded crossbow was dropped on the floor by the door.

Peterkin Gayle turned to me.

"I think from now on, my friend," he said, "you lock the doors at all times."

I walked up to the bolt and with difficulty, pulled it free.

"Castle issue, perhaps?"

"Looks like it. Who knows? Tomorrow we can examine it further. In better light," I said.

Peterkin looked up at me. "Aumary, I mean what I say - watch your back."

"You think Caspar has moved this quickly, Pete?"

He shrugged. "His warehouse doesn't just hold fabric, I hear."

"Hmmm. But then. It might not be him."

"Oh..?"

"He's not the only person I've annoyed today."

Pete's brow furrowed.

"The Scots. I damn near accused them all of murder earlier."

Gayle chuckled, a dry bubbling sound. "Oh God, Aumary, when you do it....you do it properly!"

*****

"And so sir, if you are willing, I should like to show you hospitality at Durley Manor on Saturday. You might like to stay for divine service on Sunday and return to Marlborough, to your task on Monday?" I asked Master Argentum when I met him crossing the bailey.

"Indeed it would be wonderful m'lord. I have long had a hankering to see this beautiful forest of yours. I'm told it's one of the finest in the country."

I laughed. "Well I would say *the* finest, but you might think me a little biased Master Argentum."

"Please do call me Stephen, my lord Belvoir."

I bowed. "And likewise sir, you must call me Aumary."

The King's man smiled. He held out his hand. I grasped his arm and the matter was settled.

We walked back to the Queen's House together, Master Argentum to his task as negotiator and I to find my two men at arms, Stephen and Peter, and send them to Durley to warn my wife we were coming. Then I would gather a party of men to accompany us to the village. I'd have no unexpected attacks on my two Englishmen as they wandered through my forest.

With that accomplished, Stephen Dunn and Peter Devizes jogged through the gateway of the castle on their rounceys. I turned to find the Lord of Huntingdon on my heels.

"So you invite two men who do not hunt to your forest, Belvoir, and not us; men who enjoy the chase and who've been here twiddling our toes in boredom these several weeks?"

"Sir, I would with all my heart invite you but I must have a keen eye to security now that..."

"Pish… man!" said the Earl David, "Like John said, we aren't swaddled babes that we must be nursemaided all the time."

"My Lord David, one of your men is dead. I have a duty to….."

"Nonsense, Belvoir. Unlike you, I don't think we're now in danger, any of us. It's nonsense."

"My King has charged me with your safety..."

"My safety is my own affair, Belvoir," he said, scowling at me.

I stared at him for a moment. He held my stare. "As you wish, my lord," I sighed. "Please do accompany us to Durley. We should be pleased to entertain you." I bowed.

Turning away I swore under my breath. Now the trip to the forest might not be the pleasant diversion I'd planned.

Now, I'd have to be on my guard the whole time.

*****

We hunted in the forest. The Scots were impeccably behaved and followed every suggestion I made for their safety. We took down two fine beasts and Matthew my cook did them proud, cooking, the meat in imaginative ways, so that it melted in the mouth.

The two English negotiators did not hunt but stayed with John Brenthall, my forester, and Hal of Potterne, my man at arms, and followed the horses, marvelling at the beauty of our spring forest.

At the end of the day's hunting, I don't mind saying, I heaved a huge sigh of relief when we clopped through the gate and nothing untoward had happened.

My steward Henry met us at the bottom of the stairs and Lydia stood at the top. I winked at her and saw her exhale as if she'd been holding her breath all day.

Henry took our Scottish guests off to the hall for a drink. I stayed with Masters Argentum and Lingan, apologising that their two days of relaxation had to be spoiled by the tagging along of their opponents.

"There was nothing you could do, Aumary" said Stephen Argentum, "and still remain on good terms with them. They are without doubt the most intransigent men it has ever been my misfortune to meet."

I smiled. "They will not be advised, will not brook questioning nor...."

"No, indeed. I do not envy you your job."

"Nor I yours, Stephen," I chuckled.

I unbuckled my sword belt and wound it round my hand. "I promise tonight at supper I will sit with you both and we shall have some interesting discourse."

"I look forward to it," bowed Stephen Argentum.

We sat at the high table; I placed the Lord David to my right and Stephen to my left. Etiquette dictated that the man at my right hand should be the most elevated of the company and a King's brother outstripped a King's lawyer.

My wife Lydia sat to the left of Master Argentum. The Scots were all placed on my right. Lydia and Stephen began some chatter about Oxford. My wife was born there and the lawyer had studied there. They chattered and laughed their way through the first remove.

I heard Lydia talking about people they both knew about in Oxford. Then the conversation passed on to the town of Windsor, where Lydia's mother had been born.

"You did not know our sadly departed cleric, Alan, madam?" asked Stephen

"No, not at all," answered Lydia. "My grandparents lived in Windsor until they died but I visited rarely, so I know few people there." She chuckled her tinkling laugh, "I doubt I would know anyone at all in the town now."

"I spend some time there with the King and even I know few people. Places change so rapidly."

"Marlborough is a point in case," I said, leaning forward. "When I was a lad it was barely a castle and a few houses clustered around it and a few dwellings up the hill on the Green. Now, it grows like a fungus."

"Oh, Aumary...is that a way to speak about our lovely little town?" said Lydia laughing.

"Well, when I was a boy, there were few shops, no market - not like we have now, just one church, the castle was very basic. We had no chandlers, no fullers' yards, a very small weaving industry, no glass makers and no silver goods to be had on Silver Street."

"Ah yes...the Jews are there now, are they not?" said Lingan.

"Yes. They came from London; I believe at the invitation of King Richard. If we wanted anything special that was where we had to go - London. Now we can get most things made here or fairly locally and have all sorts of skilled artisans working in the town. That has happened in my lifetime."

"From rope to robes, candles to cloth, fleece to flowers...," said Lingan, sitting back in his chair and rolling his wine cup in his fingers. He obviously enjoyed the sounds of words. "Brooches to bread... glass to gloves...."

"Our Richard is not called Lingan for nothing," chuckled Stephen.

Lydia's brow puckered. "His name means tongue, Lady Belvoir," said Stephen, "in Latin."

Richard Lingan's shoulders moved up and down with suppressed laughter. "And the two of us together... why, we are silver tongued..."

"Ah yes... my name does mean silver - I wonder if one of my ancestors was a silversmith perhaps," said Stephen.

"If you enjoy the sounds of words and if you like music, then I have a treat in store for you," I said. "One of my villagers is very skilled in singing. I also have a couple of men who play instruments of one sort and another. We might make music and perhaps have some dancing when we're finished eating, if this meets with your approval, sirs."

I caught Henry's eye and asked him to relay a message to our village singer, Martyn Summersete and to Johnathan Reeve and Bill, one of my grooms. They both played well.

"My wife too has a fine voice" I said, leaning to catch her eye. She blushed and denied it saying that she could only sing for the family.

Donald Baird turned in his seat. "Our Coagie here is a fine dancer," he said.

"Well then, we *shall* have dancing tonight," I said.

Coagie snuffled into his wine cup. "I only dance alone mind...I don't allow anyone else in the way lest I lose a toe or two."

We all laughed at that. Coagie looked up. "You think I jest, eh?"

The Earl of Huntingdon's voice rose above the general hubbub. "Aye Coagie. You shall dance alone tonight. Best sharpen your dirks."

Tam o' the Dale entered the conversation.

"I think my lord David," he said, looking at the Earl, "our hosts are a little confused." He turned to me and leaning back in his seat and talking around the back of the others said,

"Coagie dances the ancient war dance of the Highlands. It's done with two sharp swords and any mishap can indeed result in the loss of a toe...or two."

"Ah," I said. "In that case, I am anxious that Coagie does indeed dance alone."

*****

We had our promised singing and music. Martyn Summersete, our peddler, sang. Johnathan and Bill played. Donald Baird fetched a bagpipe from his quarters and at first the thing groaned like a dying duck and then he set to, playing a lament which had us all sniffling.

Then the tables were cleared and a space made for dancing. Coagie would begin and then we would all tap our feet to the tunes played by our village musicians, joined by Baird in those tunes he knew.

Coagie took off his cotte and his boots. He asked that the floor be swept and a bare space created for him and so Janet, Martyn's wife and a few of the women tidied him a clear area.

Stripped of his shirt, down to his braies and barefooted, Coagie Firmin strutted to the space on the hall floor. He lifted his arms. Tam o' the Dale brought out two swords, smaller than my own sword and wickedly sharp, and laid them in a cross shape on the floor. Donald Baird blew a long note and Coagie began to step over the swords.

Faster and faster went the music, faster and faster went Coagie's bare toes around the sword blades.

Coagie jumped and twirled, he turned a somersault on the spot; his hands placed perfectly between the swords; and landed surely on his toes between the blades.

He pirouetted, his hands held to his waist, then above his head. He tapped out a rhythm with his toes between the swords and never once, no matter how fast he went, did his toes come into contact with the wickedly sharp blades.

People clapped in rhythm with the music, they whooped and sang, laughed and cheered.

Coagie's face became pink and sweaty and suddenly with a swish of his hands, he stopped. The last note died.

Everyone cheered and congratulated the Scotsman. He beamed and wiped his face with his shirt which Tam returned to him.

Coagie Firmin donned his shirt and took his cotte from Donald, shrugging them over his head. He approached the dais, bowed and reached in his purse which was now hanging from the belt he'd just buckled at his waist.

He fished out a small brooch and pinned it to the front of his cotte, to hold the two edges together and keep it from falling from his shoulders. This was accomplished without looking for he was bowing laughingly the whole time to me, to his lord and to the assembly.

He stood up chuckling happily, smoothing down his beard and ran his hands through his disordered hair.

My eye travelled to his breast.

There, pinning his tunic, was a brooch, the like of which I had seen before. It was bronze with red enamel decoration surrounded by a rope design. Smaller than the brooch worn by Alan of Windsor on his green cloak but precisely the same design. This was the small brooch missing from the dead man's cotte and which had left a mark and a hole in the material.

Coagie turned to disappear into the press of people and fetch himself a drink. I shouted him back.

"That was a fine performance, Coagie, thank you. We have never seen the like."

He bowed once more. "Thank you, my Lord Belvoir. It's not so often I get to dance with the swords now."

Donald had swept them up and was polishing them in order to put them back into their scabbards again.

"I have however, seen the like of your fine brooch there. Mind telling me where you got it?"

Coagie swallowed and looked puzzled.

I frowned. Everyone grew deathly quiet.

"My brooch?"

"The one that is pinned to your cotte, Coagie," I said stepping forward.

Chapter Thirteen

The silence persisted, then Coagie shook himself.

"Oh it's merely a little thing, but it has some sentimental..." He grabbed a handful of his cotte and turned the brooch right way up to his eyes, "value..." He stopped.

"Oh...this is no mine."

He unpinned it with a sigh and fished once more in his scrip.

Out came a small silver brooch of the same size but with no enamel decoration. Onto the circle was scratched the likeness of a bird.

"This is mine," he said, grinning.

"Where did you get that?" I repeated, pointing to the unknown brooch.

Coagie held the red bronze brooch on his palm. "I dinna know it. It's no mine."

The Earl of Huntingdon came forward, pushing away the folk gathered round, Scots and Durley folk.

"What are you insinuating, Belvoir?"

"I'm laying down no charge but merely saying that it bears a remarkable likeness to the brooch worn by Alan of Windsor, the man slain and thrown in the river. The man sent by the King to negotiate with you, my Lord David."

"Where is this thing, this other brooch?"

I threw the key to my office to Hal and asked him to fetch the brooch which lay wrapped in a scrap of material on top of my chest.

He was back quickly. Coagie was protesting again and again he'd never seen the brooch, his chest heaving with his exertions and with the stress of what seemed like an accusation of theft and possibly murder.

Hal put the brooch in my hand. I held it up for all to see.

"The man had a matching knife pommel."

Master Argentum now came up to the front. "May I?"

I handed him the brooch. I signalled for Hal to fetch the knife from the chest, handing over my key which was always kept on a chain around my neck.

"I can confirm this is indeed Alan's," said Stephen Argentum. "He liked to wear fine jewels and jewelled items. I believe he once had a ring to match."

The brooch was passed round to a few folk and came back to me.

"I have never seen it before I tell you," said Coagie. The room was silent.

Hal returned with the knife.

"Yes, this is Alan's," said Stephen Argentum. "He had a few matching pieces like this, as I said."

The Lord David drew himself up. "Where did you get it, Coagie?"

"My lord, I promise, I've never seen it before. It's no mine and I didn'a steal it."

My eyes went from one man to the other.

"Coagie, Coagie. Did you kill the man for me...did you think that it would help me...?"

Coagie fell to his knees before his lord. "Ach no. Why would I do that? On my mother's heart, I've never seen this pin before, my lord. You all know I only have ma small silver bird."

The Earl of Huntingdon fingered the pommel of his sword and I did wonder if he was about to whip out the weapon and strike off Coagie's head. I stepped forward.

"My Lord David. Might we confine Coagie a while in my lock up whilst we make some enquiries?"

The Lord David stared at me as if I was mad.

"This is a Scots matter, Belvoir."

"I beg to differ, my lord. The man killed was an Englishman. We are on English soil. If Coagie is indeed guilty of the death of Alan of Windsor, then he shall be handed over to you to deal with as you see fit, but for the moment...."

John of Doune came forward. "If you've thieved it Coagie Firmin, then best to say and be done with it."

"I tell you, I have never seen it before."

"How did it get in your scrip then?"

"I don't know," said Coagie, trembling. "The first I saw it, it was on ma clothes in place of ma small silver thing."

David of Scotland turned to me. "Aye lock him up... and we'll get to the bottom of this. If he is the murderer of the man Alan then I'll deal with him."

I asked Hal and a couple of the lads along with John of Dunfermline to go with Coagie and make him comfortable in the lock-up, a small building at the back of the privy by the manor wall.

"My lord, might I call you into my office," I said when they'd gone. "There are a few things I'd like to impart to you...alone."

David took a moment to decide, then nodding to John of Doune, he followed me to my office. The promised dancing never materialised and the hall fell into a disappointed hush. People went home to their beds, cheated of the dancing but full of the excitement of the unmasking of a possible murderer.

I quietly closed the door to my office. Tam and Hal of Potterne stood sentinel outside.

The lord David sat in my chair. I offered him wine which he declined. I perched on the corner of my table.

"My lord, are you certain that Coagie is a loyal servant of the crown?"

"Why do you ask that, laddie?"

"The men who came with you on this mission. You handpicked them?"

"Aye; my brother William the King, and I."

"So they are men trusted by you both, with a long history of loyalty to the Scottish crown?"

"Aye. They are. They and their fathers before them. Coagie in particular, as his name signifies - their family name means loyalty," said David, "Steadfastness."

"Is it likely that Coagie would kill Alan of Windsor?"

David stood and walked around a little. "I'd like to say that none of my men would do such a thing. I trust them all. Many of them I've known all my life or from early manhood." He stared at the wall as if seeing those far off days.

His eye came back to fix on me. "If one of them mistakenly thought they'd be helping me by getting rid of the man Alan of Windsor, I'd be surprised. But I can't say it would be impossible."

"Might any of them, forgive, me my lord, be a traitor?"

"T' my brother?" came back the retort immediately.

"Might any be in an English purse?"

David sat down heavily. "Then why kill the man Alan?"

"I wondered at one point if we had two murderers," I said.

David's eyebrow flew up.

"One without doubt lured Nattie to his death at the Grange barn. I suspect that Nattie saw the attempt on your life at the copse in the wood that day and so he had to be silenced. The same man, maybe, paid the Caspar lad to tell him when Alan was on the road to Marlborough and went to Grange barn to slay him. "

David scoffed but his eye was worried.

"We have another possibility. Perhaps it was Nattie who tried to kill you and one of the others got even with him."

"The poison then, Aumary?" I noticed for the first time the man used my given name.

"The first attempt at killing him, yes. It would look as if someone had tried to get at you."

David shook his head slowly. "Nattie MacAlpine and I were cradle brothers, Aumary. I cannot think he would try to kill me."

"Pardon me, you didn't seem too upset when..."

"Aye, well...it's not the done thing for a Prince of Scotland to weep into his beard over a retainer, is it?" The Lord David looked down at his hands. "I shall miss him though. Like a blinded man misses the daylight."

I cleared my throat. "Sir, I don't think that Coagie is the culprit."

"Then why do you lock him up, man?"

"I watched his expression when the brooch was discovered. There was, as far as I could tell, true shock on his face. The item might have been planted in his purse whilst he danced. No one watched what happened to his things, his clothes, his purse. They were handed to Donald and left on the table. To answer your question. I have locked him up for his own good. Someone may next try to kill him."

"What for?"

"Someone has tried to frame him. We need to ask why."

"Frame Coagie?"

"If Coagie was taken for the crimes, we would all relax and the true perpetrator would then go about his business unrestrained."

"What's his task?"

"To make sure the talks do not happen. Or if they do, that Scotland, or rather your brother, is the loser."

David took a moment to register that.

Then he stood and looked at me with one eye almost closed.

"Belvoir. That is what *you* want isn't it?"

"No, my lord. I am as much an Englishman as you are a Scotsman but I have no interest in the outcome of these talks. I do not *personally* care if Scotland takes the north of this country. Nor do I *personally* care if my King retains it. My King has asked me to look after you and the English delegation whilst you thrash out a solution to this knotty problem. It is not my role to take sides. I must treat both sides in the same manner."

"I have said it before...you Englishmen and your honour!" he chuckled dryly.

"I am the constable of this part of the county, Lord David. It is my appointed role to bring to justice those who take a life, who commit murder. I am as equally worried by the death of a visiting Scotsman as I am a young Englishman. I must investigate both deaths. I cannot be partisan, sir. Murder is murder. I do not like murder, my lord."

David unclenched his fingers.

"What must I do, Aumary?"

"Leave Coagie locked up and no one must visit save with one of my men." I came to sit on my stool, opposite the Lord David.

"The day Nattie disappeared, I told you I think he'd been called away by someone when he was approaching the brothel. We need to know who was missing. Who called him away."

"I can see if I can find out..."

"We need also to know who went to the small bothy with the girl who died that night by the church of St. Peter. That man knew that Alan of Windsor was dead for he told her so. The only way he would know was if he killed him or saw him killed, and knew who the culprit was. We also need to find out who struck the lad Caspar..."

I told the Earl again what had happened to Cecil Caspar to make him fall.

"That was a bad thing, Aumary," said the Lord David, with feeling.

"Who struck the lad Caspar before he fell onto the spears? Three men were by the horse then, for I saw them myself. Coagie, Donald and John of Doune. Donald Baird was on the other side of him and I think that you came up shortly after. No Englishman was near enough, though there was another man on the other side of the horse whom I couldn't see clearly."

"I think that was me, Aumary. Tam was on my right hand side and not near to the horse."

I nodded.

"Must it be one of them?"

"I cannot see how it is not."

"Yet you think Coagie innocent?"

"I cannot say for sure but I think so, yes."

"Then the only thing that makes sense is for Coagie to have seen who struck the young lad Caspar."

"That is why he's been singled out," I said. "We must be careful."

"Shall I speak to Coagie? See if he will tell me who it was he saw striking out, if he did see it?" asked David.

"It would help us but...we must be very quiet about it."

David stood...and hesitated. "This means, lad...I cannot trust any one of my men."

"Sadly sir, no you can't."

"But I can trust an Englishman eh?"

I stood. "With your life, sir," I said.

*****

The Lord David promised me that when all his men were asleep that night in what I fondly called my guest rooms on the south wall of the manor courtyard, he would slip out and talk to Coagie. Stephen and Peter, my men at arms would be guarding the lock up and would let him in and out.

I don't mind saying that I was worried, for the Earl was attempting to learn which man of his party was a traitor to his cause and I wasn't sure if, at the last, he would tell me what he'd discovered.

The next day was a Sunday. We all filed into the church of St. Mary for mass.

The Earl stood by me. I could see that his face was set like stone. He'd learned something that night, which perhaps he didn't care to know. As the service began he nodded to me and then bowed his head in prayer.

He whispered through the side of his mouth. "You were right, Aumary. Coagie did know. He did see. With a little coaxing he told me."

"Good," I said. "Perhaps we shall take a turn around the village when we are done here?"

Again David nodded and his face set once more as he applied himself to the mumbled liturgy.

Once the mass was complete and with Tam following us out of the church, the Earl David and I set off to walk to the river. There we thought we'd be private and not overheard.

"No Tam, you stay here," I said as the lawyer started off after us.

"No, my Lord Belvoir, one of us must stay with our Lord. How do we know you are not going to harm him?"

"We have no weapons Tam, coming straight from church. Go away now and I'll meet you in the hall."

People streamed from the building and made their way home. Tam stood a little way up the bank for a while. Then we were alone.

The alder tree leaning out over the river gave us shade from the sun. With our backs to the water we began to speak about what Coagie Firmin had heard and seen.

"At first," said Prince David, "the man wouldn't say anything."

"You told him that his freedom and possibly his life depended on what he told you?"

"Aye, I did."

"Did he say why he hadn't spoken up at the time?"

"Aye he told me that too. It was because..." the Earl of Huntingdon licked his lips, "because he was afraid I wouldn't believe him."

I turned to the river and scanned the water for trout. The earl turned with me.

"That I'd believe he was throwing the blame onto another in order to make mischief."

"Did he know who called Nattie back?"

"Aye… he did, but he didn't make the connection until I put it before him."

"Was it the same man who was missing at the brothel and who went into the bothy with the girl Merewenna?"

"He was missing, though Coagie knows nothing about this girl. He tells me this man was possibly the man who struck out at the Caspar lad, though Coagie can't be absolutely sure about that. He had his back to the goings on, he said. He was looking at the horse and was going to try to catch hold of it before it jumped. He too had heard you call the lad as if you wanted him to stop and so was trying to help."

"I think..."

Suddenly out of nowhere came an arrow. We heard the whoosh of it and it struck the alder right by us with a thwack.

The two of us dived to the grass and wriggled closer to the bole of the tree and the vegetation growing at the river's edge.

"Jesus' body!" cried David. "That was a mite too close for me."

"I thought we'd be out of range here." I raised my head an inch. "Can you see anything?"

The earl leaned out a little "No. But the man is behind your barn."

"And hidden from the manor by the wall. No one can see him at his work," I added.

I risked another look to see if anyone was by the river, further away at the back of the southern manor wall where it abutted the dove cote. Another arrow came streaming out and missed me by an inch. It was Sunday; all were at their own business.

"I'd say we must part and run two ways but then our man would have to go after just the one of us and I know who he'd go after," I said.

"Me."

"Yes. Somehow he knows you have spoken to Coagie and are about to tell me. He must kill you before you betray him. Then naturally he'll kill me."

"Then just in case either Coagie or I do not manage to cheat death…I must tell *you* who our man is," said David. "Then if you can, you must bring him to justice. English or Scots."

"I think I know who it is….and I know how it must have hurt you to learn his name."

I spoke the name of the man whom I thought had tried to kill the Earl David and had killed Nattie and Alan of Windsor.

"Aye…" David sighed, looking out with narrowed eyes over the grass of the meadow between our hiding place and the threshing barn. "We think it is. God help me. He's the last man…"

I put my hand on his arm, "I know."

At that moment Hal of Potterne came around the corner by the dovecote. He scanned the meadow looking for us.

"Hal!" I yelled. "Man at the back of the barn with a bow… Be careful."

After surveying the ground he spotted us lying down in the vegetation and waved in acknowledgement, quickly sprinting for the cover of the wall.

"What's goin' on lad?" he shouted.

Our bowman was slightly distracted and an arrow flew in Hal's direction bouncing harmlessly from the western stone wall.

"Trying to kill the Earl David, Hal."

I saw him stretch to see if he could catch sight of our attacker but he was now too far round the wall.

"Can you run back and get help?"

Again Hal lifted a hand then he was gone back the way he'd come.

The earl chuckled deep in his throat. "He must be spitting stones that he's missed his chance, eh, Aumary?"

Suddenly from the roof of the threshing barn a couple of wood pigeons who had been happily sitting there trying to mate, bowing, bobbing up their tails and stretching their breasts, rose up with a clatter of wings and flew off over the nearer forest.

I looked up. Our man had moved slightly nearer.

The earl lifted himself on his elbow to look. "Bastard!" he yelled.

An arrow came whizzing out from the threshing barn wall. It caught the earl on the side of the head as it flew past and skittered to a halt in the grass. The earl threw up his arms and rolled out into the open meadow, blood pouring from his head. I risked a quick look back to where he lay. The arrow was not embedded in his head but it had given him a nasty wound as it passed. He lay unconscious in full view of the enemy.

I grabbed the earl's legs and hauled him back into the vegetation at the base of the alder tree just as Hal and several others rounded the southern wall.

I saw John Brenthall with some more villagers making their way carefully and cautiously around the northern wall of the manor.

Our bowman was trapped between them.

*****

"Here...quick" I yelled, "The earl is hurt."

Hal reached me first.

"Does 'e live still?" he asked.

"He's alive but bleeding, copiously as you do from a head wound."

I'd pulled off my cotte and was tearing up my linen shirt to staunch the flow of blood.

"Get the earl to the manor and send for Johannes. I'm going after our bowman."

I saw Hal signal to the other men. I strapped the earl's head as best I could. Hubert Alder the blacksmith, who was big and brawny, threw the earl across his shoulder and bounded for the wall. I watched as they disappeared around the corner. No further arrows followed them.

John caught up with me and together with Wilfrid and his friends, Cedric and Edward, the grooms, we ran, bent double and in spurts to the door of the threshing barn.

I jumped into the space between the sets of doors. It was a bright day and the sunlight had made my vision dim. I could see very little in the darkness of the huge stone barn. No arrow followed my progress along the open space.

John came in the other door. "Gone, sir."

"How? Did no one see him?"

All three men shook their heads.

"Came round behind us perhaps. Went on into the orchard," offered John.

"Or followed behind Hubert around the wall," said Edward.

"Aye, you'd never look back if you were getting an injured man to safety quickly," said Wilfrid.

"Damn. That was my fault. I took my eye from things just as..."

I sighed and ran my hands through my hair. "No point in hanging on here. Let's go back and see how the earl is. Our bowman is away now."

Hal had rushed off to saddle our fastest horse; Fitzroy, and had asked Bill to ride like the wind for Johannes in Marlborough. I passed the stables on my way to the rooms we had given the Scots as their guest quarters, where the Earl of Huntingdon had been laid out. Hal came out of the stable building and caught my arm.

"Sir, you need to know that..."

"Later Hal..."

Hal didn't relinquish his grip..."The lady Belvoir asks you go to her quickly, lad," he said. His face was grave.

"Where is she?"

"In the lockup."

I ran the few paces from the stable to the small building which acted as our gaol.

There was Lydia kneeling on the floor.

"Aumary..." I noticed her hands and dress were bloodied.

"Lydia!" I stepped forward, a sinking feeling in my guts.

"No...No, not my blood," she cried, seeing the expression on my face.

I leaned over.

Coagie was lying on his back, gasping, his eyes huge and terrified.

"His throat has been cut but it's not a complete job," said my wife. "I've seen Johannes stop the bleeding by applying a deal of pressure to the wound." She pressed down. "We must send for Johannes now...quickly."

"Already done, my love," I said. "Here; show John what to do....and then Cedric. Take it in turns to keep the poor man alive until Johannes gets here. I must go to the earl...a moment only."

Lydia inclined her head and applied herself to the task of showing Cedric how to stem the flow. I saw him nod as I turned for the door.

*****

Henry was supervising the placing of David, Earl of Huntingdon on his bed in the guest room.

Hubert laid him down gently. The man was alive but still unconscious.

I lifted my makeshift bandage and looked at the wound to the side of his head. The arrow had gouged a furrow to the right side of his skull but luckily had not pierced it.

I sighed. I doubted he would die from this wound but, who knew, as Johannes often said, what damage had been done to the brain beneath.

"We can do naught but wait. Everyone stay here and guard the Earl. Let no Scotsman in. No matter how hard they plead."

I made my way back to the lock up.

Lydia was standing watching, looking pale. Her light blue dress was covered in blood; her hands were rusty red. Coagie continued to breathe but poorly.

"How did you come to be here with...?"

"I walked back from church with Hawise. I sent her on, thank Heavens I did. I just glanced at the wall and saw that neither Stephen nor Peter were outside the door of the lock up as you'd requested. Then I thought you must have allowed them rest, for they'd been there all night."

"Aye, they were relieved this morning. I asked Tostig and Hal…" I said, and as light dawned, "ah… I see."

"Hal came out to find you after we found this man. In the change of guards Tostig was alone at the door for a moment. He was waiting for Hal to join him when he was hit from behind and fell to the floor."

"Is he all right?"

She nodded. "He is. He's gone home to Alysoun. He's fared better than this poor man. We both looked down at Coagie.

"Hal came up a moment later to find the door open, Tostig out cold and this man here gasping for breath and I saw it from the courtyard. I came in quickly and... the rest you know."

"Praise the Heavens you were alert and there when needed, my love," I said, drawing her to me. "Can we keep Coagie alive do you think? Until Johannes gets here."

"We must keep pressure on the throat. It must be constant. The blood will clot and the bleeding will not be so severe but, his life is still in the hands of the Almighty, Aumary."

"God's Cods," said Hal, coming in at last. "We must keep 'is blood in 'is body lad but not throttle the poor man, Cedric. 'Ere. Let me 'ave a go."

He rolled up his sleeves and took over for a while from Cedric.

Thus we kept poor terrified Coagie Firmin alive for a goodly while. After a short time, he passed out.

*****

It was some time later when we wearily ascended the steps to the hall.

I heard Stephen Argentum take in a sharp breath at the state of our clothes and hands. He stood and stepped forward from a bench at the hall table.

"Not our blood, Stephen," I said quickly. "Coagie...one of the Scotsmen, has been attacked and we have pulled him from the jaws of death. Johannes the doctor is with him now."

"I heard that the Lord..."

"You heard correctly, but he too is out of danger." I whispered so that none but they would hear. "He is still unconscious but the doctor feels he will awake soon." The two English mediators crossed themselves.

I saw two of the Scots standing at the head of the table, a few yards off, looking our way. They scowled.

"What's going on, Belvoir?" shouted John of Doune. "Nobody is telling us anything."

"Aye, I tried to get into see our Lord but I was turned away," said Tam o' the Dale in disgust.

I looked their way but didn't answer. "Where's Donald Baird and John of Dunfermline?" I asked.

They looked at each other. "How do we know?" said Tam. "We haven't seen them since mass."

"You two will stay in the hall. I will have some of my men take you to your quarters where you'll be locked in until I deem it's safe."

"You can't do that!" shouted John, taking a step forward. "We..."

"This is my manor and I will do as I see fit. We have a murderer loose about the place and I will confine everyone until I feel it's safe to let anyone free," I answered in a firm voice.

Tam o' the Dale reached out and took John by the arm. He shook his head.

Lydia took my arm shakily and we ascended the solar steps. Looking back, I saw John Brenthall come in with a couple of men and they began to escort the two surly Scots out of the hall and to their rooms.

Then Lydia and I changed our clothes and washed off the blood.

"What will you do, Aumary?" asked my wife with concern in her voice.

I sat down tiredly on a stool and replaced my boots.

"I cannot let the killer know I'm aware who he is yet. If I do that, he may bolt. He might even do that anyway. If I can get all the Scots confined, I have them secure and the killer can do no more harm."

"Well, it isn't Nattie and it isn't Coagie...so..."

I told Lydia who our traitor was.

She sat down on the edge of the bed. "Oh no, Aumary, it can't be. You know that will hurt the Lord David greatly."

"It has hurt him."

"I know that the death of Nattie was a great blow to him," Lydia gave a sad smile. "He told me at supper the other night. He said he'd like to have the privilege of sewing the murderer's shroud, for Nattie's killing."

I nodded. "That I can believe. He was close to Nattie and grieves for him greatly. David is the killer's liege lord. He may do as he wishes with him."

"Why is the killer doing it, Aumary?"

"I can only think it's English silver which has been his undoing."

Lydia sat up straight. "Oh Aumary...do you suppose? ...No it's unthinkable."

"That John our King has a hand in this?"

"Yes," said Lydia breathlessly.

I shrugged "It's not beyond the realms of possibility. If I thought that the disputed lands were anywhere near the man's own, I might think the killer benefits from the annexing of the northern lands of England to Scotland. But his lands are to the middle of Scotland..."

"And he has killed both English and Scots," said Lydia in irritation. "Oh, it's all too complicated."

"Perhaps it's a personal feud of some kind," I said. "I do know there are rival Scots for the kingship which William holds. William's realm is by no means secure, even after so long. The heir is a young boy and that's never a good thing for a country. Perhaps our man backs a different king."

"But then surely he'd stay in Scotland and join the rebels?"

I shrugged again. "I will only know the truth when and if I can get the man to confess. "

"Oh my love," said Lydia. "I don't think he's the sort to do that."

"No. He'll brazen it out. He's doing that already. I don't think he knows that Coagie is alive and he hopes against hope that David hasn't managed to get the truth from Coagie and that he hasn't told me."

"He hopes his lord will die of the wound he gave him?"

"Maybe we shall let him think that the truth then," I smiled.

Chapter Fourteen

Donald Baird and John of Dunfermline came strolling into the manor a while later. They had been out birding, they said, in the forest. Both of them carried a bow, and to give credence to their story, several pheasants were swinging from a branch which they carried between them. I didn't remind them that this was the King's forest, my forest and that technically, they should have my permission to hunt any creature.

I told them their lord was badly injured and not likely to live. I told them that Coagie's throat had been cut. I gave them over to John Brenthall and Hubert Alder and confined them to their quarters. They looked shocked and Donald Baird swore at the news. They protested but there was little they could effectively do.

The pheasants were delivered to the kitchens to be stored.

I breathed a sigh of relief as I wandered over to the room Johannes normally used when he was here at Durley.

I had our murderer under lock and key and he thought himself safe. What I didn't know - did he have an accomplice?

I scratched at the door and Johannes let me in. Hungerford stood by the opening, his quarterstaff firmly clamped in his hands. I nodded to him. "No one to pass...no one, Rob," I said and he dipped his head.

Coagie was lying in a clean shirt on his back on the second bed in Johannes' room.

A cover was drawn up to his breast and his throat was bandaged with sparkling white linen.

"I have given him a draft of soporific, Aumary, to help with the pain. He sleeps peacefully now for a while."

I sat down on a stool. "Can he speak?"

"I am not encouraging it yet but I think he will make a full recovery. You and Lydia..."

"And Hal and Cedric and a few others," I said.

Johannes chuckled. "Yes, all of you did a good job. He's lost a lot of blood but he is alive."

"Most of the blood was on Lydia, it seemed."

"Her quick thinking saved his life."

"I think the killer was disturbed; he made a poor job of slashing Coagie's throat," I said.

"He attacked him from the front, Aumary, and that's always more difficult. It's easier if you can grab the victim's hair, pull back the head and slash deep."

"But he didn't slash deep enough?"

"No. Oh, enough to do a great deal of damage but not enough for certain death."

"I am putting it about that Coagie is dead and that the Lord is thought not to recover."

"Oh?"

"When it's dark I shall move the Earl David here. Do you mind a truckle bed?"

"Not at all."

"You can look after them better if they're together and also it will not seem as strange as if we had two rooms occupied by invalids. After all Coagie is dead and in the mortuary isn't he?" I raised my eyebrows.

"Ah. I see."

"How is the earl?"

"Still unconscious. The wound is like that of a blow...."

"Like that which Martyn Peddler sustained that winter?"

"Very similar."

"That rendered him senseless for weeks."

"It's just the same and naturally the scalp is also flayed. That will take a while to mend. He will come to his senses eventually."

Johannes turned back to his potions. "Did you find the arrow?"

"Aye, we did. It's not one we recognise."

Johannes turned back to me. "You'll look for its mates?"

"I am off to do that very thing right now," I said, smiling. "I just want to be absolutely sure that I have the right man and that he hasn't got an accomplice."

"Ah… right," said Johannes, "That would be awkward."

*****

I took Hal, Stephen and Peter with me.

John of Dunfermline had shared a room with Coagie. Now he and Baird were billeted together.

"Gentlemen. Can you tell me where you went when you left the manor earlier to go birding ?"

They looked at each other, a little puzzled.

Baird folded his arms across his chest. "We'll tell you, if you tell us what's going on, my Lord Belvoir."

"Gladly. Coagie, as I told you has had his throat cut and the Earl David lies in a stupor tended by Doctor Johannes who thinks he will die shortly. He's been hit in the head by an arrow. An arrow fired by one of you Scots, I'm sad to say. I am confining you all until I know the outcome. Then you may all go home."

Baird narrowed his eyes. "I want to see the Earl."

"That is not possible. He is gravely ill."

"I want to see him."

"You shall do so when he recovers or dies. One or the other."

Baird stared at me malevolently. "Johnnie and I went out beyond the village to the fields up the hill. We took our bows and beat the hedges for birds. It was just by your large fences we found them"

"Ah yes. Our deer fences. Thank you."

I picked up John of Dunfermline's bow. "This yours?"

"Aye. It is."

"And the arrows?"

Dunfermline reached beyond the bed and brought out a quiver of arrows. I took one out and examined it.

"Thank you." I handed it back. "And you Donald?"

"The bow is there." He gestured to the table. "I have no arrows left. I used them all."

"He's no such a good shot with the bow," said John, grinning. "Loses more arrows than he hits birds!"

"Does he?" I smiled. "Well, well. And you were together all morning?"

"Aye, we were."

I made for the door.

"When can we get out?" asked Donald.

"When I say so," was my parting shot.

*****

I next visited John of Doune and Tam o' the Dale.

John's face was thunderous. He jumped up and I noticed he'd changed his clothes.

"Belvoir! You cannot keep us here without telling us what's going on!"

"I will tell you, gentlemen. Your lord is sore hurt and like to die. He has taken an arrow to the head. The doctor is with him and is doing what he can for him."

"Who did it?" asked Tam, white faced.

"That we do not know but I'm looking at everyone's weapons to find a match for the arrow which pierced him."

"There's mine," said Tam, pointing to a bow and quiver of arrows hung on a peg on the wall.

I took one out and looked at the fletch. It did not match.

"John...?"

"I do not have a bow."

"None at all?" I knew he'd had one that day up on the downs.

"I left it at the castle."

"You came to hunt in the forest and you left your bow?" I quizzed.

"It was an oversight."

"So you have no arrows?"

"None."

"Hmm."

"Tammie here will vouch for that, won't you Tam?"

The man's eyes swivelled to his friend. "Aye, I suppose I can. He didn'a bring it."

I turned to leave.

"Who did it?" asked Tam. "May a wheel run over his skull."

"I shall find out," I said. "Thank you gentlemen. I hope to have some news for you soon."

Hal closed and locked the door giving the key to Henry my steward, who kept all keys to the manor.

"So 'oo's lyin' then?" asked Hal as we crossed the courtyard.

I chuckled. "The killer thinks himself safe, his mission accomplished. There will be no talks because his lord will be dead and Coagie is cold and ready for the ground. No one can point the finger at him."

Hal chuckled into his long grey beard.

"My Lord Belvoir!" A voice hailed me as I crossed to the hall steps.

I turned to see Cedric, cleaned up and sporting a new blue tunic.

"Cedric?"

"My lord, can you come to the back wall...there's something you should see?"

"Lead on - through the sally port, I think," I said.

We rounded the kitchen and passed through the small gate; Hal, Cedric and I crossed the grass, passed the threshing barn and reached the place where the manor wall started to bend round the north western corner.

There, just parked by the wall was a small hand cart full of straw.

"We passed it by sir, never thinking..."

Cedric parted the straw. "I came out to look to the horses we have in the paddock at the back of the threshing barn. This was here. It was going to the stables but it got stopped. I looked in it and found this, sir."

In his hand was a bow. I reached into the straw. There was the quiver. The arrow which struck the Earl David was the exact match for those remaining in the leather holder.

"What's more sir...looks as if there's been a man burying himself in the pile."

I looked down. There was a depression in the straw where someone had indeed lain and covered themselves.

"Well done Cedric. Looks like we've found the place where our killer hid after he struck the earl. We thought he'd run but no, as cool as a cat, he hid."

"Awful thing is, we missed him completely" said Cedric, clucking his tongue and shaking his head. "We walked right past him."

*****

We returned to the hall.

A message was waiting for me. Would I go to Johannes' room. The Earl had regained consciousness.

The man was still lying down. He looked very frail and he was pale around the eyes and lips.

I nodded to Johannes. "How is he?" I whispered.

"I have the devil of a headache, Belvoir, but there's nothing wrong with my ears," said the man in French.

I chuckled. "My lord. I'm pleased to hear it."

I approached the bed and bowed.

"I have all your men in custody, sir. With your permission and help, we can confront our killer."

"Coagie...," he licked his lips, "Coagie was attacked too." His eye flew to the next bed where Coagie still slept.

"Yes sir," said Johannes. "I've stitched the wound. He's very lucky that no further damage was done. His voice may be changed by this and he'll bear a scar..."

"It won't be his first," said the earl.

"Nor the last I warrant," I said.

"He'll not worry about a scar or two. It'll give him more credibility, an attraction for the ladies."

I smiled. "The doctor tells me he mustn't be moved for a little while. Will you be up to moving to the hall later tonight? I don't want to drag this out. I want to confront the killer tonight."

Johannes began to protest but the Earl of Huntingdon met his eyes with a determined stare, full of steel.

"Aye, give me a wee while."

I sat down on the stool. "I have put it about the manor that you are like to die of your wound, sir, for the arrow pierced your head. I have also made it known that Coagie is dead. The killer feels himself safe."

"Damn his eyes," said David through clenched teeth.

"Why do you think the man is trying to end the talks, sir? He's been a loyal subject of the Scottish crown for years, I think. Why now has he turned traitor?"

I could see that the earl wanted to shake his head but thought better of it.

"I don't know. Except that... wheesh I don't know."

"Except that?"

The earl lifted himself up on one elbow in his bed.

"I'll tell you. Aye, I will. He's my bastard brother...our bastard brother and there may be some..."

"Resentment?"

The earl's chuckle ended in a cough. "You might call it that."

"Has he shown himself untrustworthy before?"

The earl looked to the floor. "No. Not in so many words but... he's a temper and… William, well William has.... William the King is too trusting of him. Aye, I have been too." His face took on a wistful look. The eyes focussed on nothing.

"I know this is very painful for you, sir."

"Aye, aye it is."

The earl suddenly sat up straighter.

"I'm sorry, Sir Aumary, that we have been such a trouble to you. Nattie would still be alive if I'd listened to you and Coagie wouldn't have been in such danger had I not been so set on my own way."

I bowed but did not answer. That was the nearest I was going to get to an apology, I thought.

"So there is no real reason you can think of, no reason why your brother should play you false in this way?"

"Why do you need to know? He has and there's an end to it."

"I always like to know why a man has done something, sir."

I saw the earl's hand clench.

"He's my brother....my half brother. You will not know what that's about, Sir Aumary. He's my blood. My father's son...."

"Oh but I do, sir," I said enigmatically.

The lord David looked up at me and his eyes locked with mine.

"I do know what it's like to have a half brother. Mine is dead sadly. Dead and buried in Rouen," I said.

The earl thought about that for a moment. "Aye well. Mine's alive and a murderer."

"We must confront him, sir. Then he will be your man to deal with as you wish."

"Aye, I suppose we must." He tried to swing his legs out of the bed. He was very unsteady and Johannes was there in an instant to prevent him from falling.

"A little while longer, Aumary?" said the doctor.

"Aye, I'm no longer a young man," chuckled the earl, "to deal with bangs on the head like I did when I was young."

"Rest sir...a little while longer," I said, and Johannes smiled a grateful smile at me. "We shall wait till nightfall to get you to the hall under cover of darkness and then we'll begin."

*****

We crossed the courtyard in a black night without a moon and with a very wobbly Earl David, supported by Johannes and myself. We got him up the steps and into my office where we laid him down on the daybed I kept there. The man was fifty five and, as he'd said, didn't take knocks well now.

We covered him with a blanket and Johannes stayed with him.

Then John, Hal and I went to the guest range to let out the Scots, first John of Dunfermline and Baird, then John of Doune and Tam.

We led them to the hall. Hal locked the outer stair door. I opened the door to my office and left the hall door open so that the Earl David could hear everything that was said.

The rest of the Scots could not see their lord just a few feet away.

I walked to the dais and sat in the central chair.

"Gentlemen. This evening we shall go through the events leading up to the shooting of the Lord David and the blow delivered to Coagie Firmin which ruptured his throat. Please be seated."

I leaned forward. "We shall begin with you, Donald. Where were you this morning after mass?"

Baird folded his arms across his chest "I've already said. I was out in yon field with Johnnie. We took our bows and killed a few birds for the pot."

"Nay" said John of Dunfermline, "That's no quite right."

"Oh...it isn't?" I said.

"You couldn'a hit a bear if it reared up its arse and farted at you," he said to Donald. "He couldn'a hit our lord, Sir Aumary. Sober his aim is as bad as a drunken man's. I killed most of 'em. Birds that is."

I smiled at the vision. "You were together all the time?"

"Aye all the time, save a few feet," said Baird. "And a long way from your manor."

"You'll find his arrows a way off in the forest" said Dunfermline again. "If you care to look." He smiled sideways at his friend.

"Aye. We tried to recover them but there's a damn big fence between us and the trees. I wasn'a goin' to scale it I can tell you," added Baird.

"That's our deer fence. It keeps the beasts of the forest away from the village and in the forest deer park where they belong."

Baird nodded.

"John, you were with Donald the whole time?"

"Aye. In my eyes the whole time."

I nodded.

"Tam, where were you?"

"I was here in the hall."

"Alone?"

"No, John here was with me."

"How long were you here?"

"After mass until you came in, Sir Aumary and told us our lord was dying and Coagie was dead too." He crossed himself.

"John. Is this true?"

"Aye, it is."

"Except when he went out to the privy," added Tam.

"You left the building?"

"For a heartbeat only. I was soon back."

"Tell me Tam, this trip to the privy, was it long enough to perhaps recover a bow and a quiver of arrows from a cart of straw at the back of the manor wall and shoot a few at us at the little stream? Or maybe to run to the lock up and kill Coagie?"

Tam's eyes narrowed. "I can't say."

I turned to John who had not been seated and who now stood straighter and taller.

"You changed your clothes, sir?"

"Aye. It's not a crime to take off a cotte and hose is it?"

"Perhaps it is, if that cotte and hose are dark and are obviously covered in tiny pieces of straw, the bits one picks up when one has been hiding in a cart of straw to evade detection."

John of Doune folded his arms and stared at me. "You cannot prove it."

I nodded to Stephen who stood by the open door of the hall. He came forward with the clothes Doune had worn earlier.

"These clothes, perhaps, which we have taken from your room?"

"They aren't mine."

"They are also splattered with the blood of Coagie Firmin, John."

He shook his head. "Someone has planted them there." He pointed at me. "You have planted them there."

"The thing is, when you attempt to cut the throat of a man, it's best, the doctor tells me, to be behind him. There's less splatter that way. You couldn't get behind Coagie could you, for he was wary of you. You slashed at him from the front. You had little time to do the job properly before you were out and away through the sally port, up by the wall and retrieving your bow from the cart left there. Then you crossed the meadow and slipped into the barn emerging at the other side to loose at us, your lord and myself, by the river."

"Nonsense. Why? Why should I do that?"

"Because you feared that Coagie had told your lord he'd seen you wound the young lad Caspar that day at the fair."

"It's rubbish I tell you."

"You heard that the Lord David and I planned to walk by the river and saw your chance. Both of us in one go. Just to make sure there would be no one left to know anything."

"And what *did* you know?"

"That you were the killer of the English envoy, Alan of Windsor, and that you killed Nattie MacAlpine of course. Nattie who had seen you loose an arrow at your lord that day in the forest. You lured him to the barn at Manton with the promise perhaps of some sport with women, women for whom you wouldn't have to pay. Unlike those at the brothel."

"No one knows that, Belvoir," snapped John of Doune.

"Cecil Caspar knew. He saw you going into the bothy with the girl he knew as

Royse. He identified you to me before he died. You told her that Alan was dead."

"I was never with any girl called Royse."

"Wait!" shouted Tam o' the Dale. "This is just your word, my Lord Belvoir. Bring witnesses and we shall listen to them."

"We have no witnesses Tam, save perhaps one. We'll call him in a moment. No, John was very careful to get rid of everyone."

"John, answer no more questions. He has no proof."

I stood up. "Peter, do you have the quiver and bow?"

My man at arms came up to the dais and passed me the weapons with a nod.

"This is the bow which we found hidden in the straw in the cart." I blew on the leather quiver. "See, there are still small pieces sticking to it."

"Can anyone tell me to whom it belongs? The fletch of the arrow is very distinctive. Heron I believe."

I saw John of Dunfermline shift and scratch his nose. He'd recognised the weapon.

No one spoke.

"This," I reached behind me to a small table, "is the arrow which was used on the Earl David. I put them together. "You see, gentlemen, they are very similar fletchings."

I turned to Doune.

"Is this your lost bow, John?"

"It's mine, but I've not used it. It went missing this morning."

"Then why did you not tell me that when I asked you earlier?"

I looked at Tam, "and why did you not tell me the truth? That John had a bow here with him at Durley but that it went missing?"

The lawyer looked down at his boots. "Us Scots have to stick together," was all he said in his defence.

I jumped down from the dais. John leapt round his hand on his hip and faced me.

"This is an English lie to discredit us Scots!"

"Tell me John, how much were you paid to kill Alan of Windsor and destroy any hope of a Scots victory over the northern territories?"

John roared and leapt for my throat. I fended him off. Hal was there in an instant, a sword poised to skewer the Lord of Doune.

"Easy there my man. I'm an old fella, I'm a mite jittery with me sword in me 'and nowadays," he said.

Tam had run forward and had grabbed John's arm. "No John. It's not the way."

I pulled down my cotte and adjusted my belt. "Why would you wish to scupper the talks so that your own lord, that lord who trusted you would have less of a chance of..."

"Belvoir, you go too far."

"Is it right that you are the King's and Earl David's half brother?"

John of Doune shrugged off the hand of Tam o' the Dale holding him back. "Aye. They're my brothers, what of it?"

"Makes it worse doesn't it? Treachery to one's family and to one's King and country."

John of Doune was breathing hard.

"That's a *lie.*"

"I know what it's like having a half brother. I had one once. There's quite a resentment sometimes...."

"I've no problem with that. The King has been good to me and so has David. I want no more than I've been given."

"No, you're lucky in your siblings I think. As you say, they're good to you. They treat you well and make sure you are part of what is going on in Scotland. But you have another master don't you?"

"It's not an Englishman if that is what you're thinking."

"No John. It's another Scotsman isn't it?"

John of Doune scoffed. "Yer daft laddie."

"I am a little unsure exactly who it might be but I do know that this is all about the rivalry for the crown. I think it's something to do with the fact that there's a whole swathe of Scotland which isn't behind King William and his hankering after English lands. I think they prefer to secure their own lands first. They think it's a consummate waste of Scottish funds to pour money into the borders. They can't be doing with William and his foolish plans. Scottish politics is beyond me..."

"Then stay out of it, laddie," spat Doune between clenched teeth, "You can't meddle in what you don't understand."

Tam o' the Dale stepped up and put his feet together to stand before me. "Shall I explain it, Sir Aumary?"

I sat down again on a bench. "I'd be pleased to know, Tam," I said smiling broadly.

"The Scottish kings have long held the view that the frontier between our two lands should not lie along the River Tweed. They believe, not wrongly I think, that the towns of Carlisle and Newcastle are essential to our national security. The lands were ours under your King Stephen. Malcolm the Fourth foolishly surrendered them to your King's father, Henry. William was ambitious to regain the lost counties and assert his independence."

"That much I know Tam."

"Henry took our king in battle and imprisoned him in Normandy, obliged him to do homage for his own country and forced him to surrender his strongest castles. Imagine that."

"Yes. I can," I said. "And I do know that William came here to Marlborough."

"King Richard was eager for money to go on crusade and William the Lion was given the opportunity to buy back his own country."

"For ten thousand marks I believe?"

"An enormous sum for a country such as ours."

"In addition, your King made the mistake of backing Arthur of Brittany and conspired with our King's enemies."

"Aye, he did. I must say he did."

"John has a long memory, Tam, and is not the most forgiving of kings, unless, of course, there's money to be made.."

"William did homage to John at Lincoln in 1200 but there has been bad blood ever since between us."

"Yes I know it. William flirted with the king of France too, I hear."

"He made…approaches… to Louis of France, yes, but it came to nothing."

"I know this too."

"The Lion has fought a war within his own country for years. The Norse Scots have no particular loyalty to our Scottish kings, Sir Aumary. The Lords of the Isles and those in the Highlands nip at our heels the whole time. They fear domination by the lowlander Scots. They are a stubborn people, proud of their independence and their antipathy has much to do with their attachment to their beloved Celtic language and a heritage which they fear will be lost should they bow their heads to the English speaking Scottish crown."

"There are those who believe that William is wasting money on such frivolous ideas of expansion. They believe that Scotland should look to her northern and western edges, that The Lion should look to his own and secure Scottish lands and not stretch out his hand to English ones?" I said.

"You have the right of it, my Lord Aumary," said Tam, standing back. "The Crown has no love for the Highlander ; even less the Isleman, sir."

I turned to John of Doune. "Is this how you feel, John?"

"John," said Tam, "say nothing."

John drew back. "I will say this. I didn't kill Coagie. I didn't kill my brother."

"No John. You didn't," I said.

I called out, "Johannes."

The doctor came in leading the aged David Earl of Huntingdon, the blanket now around his shoulders. His barrel chest seemed to have sunk and he was very pale.

Johannes led him to a chair and David sat down with a smile to him. Johannes and Stephen disappeared out of the hall as I had requested.

"Your arrow failed to kill your brother. It wounded him and he has been unconscious this past day. I kept it quiet for I thought if you were kept in ignorance you would not bolt, and I could keep you at Durley and face you with your crimes."

I saw John of Doune glance at his brother and put his hand on his sword pommel. Peter and Hal came closer to the earl.

Earl David lifted his chin. "I'm sorry you felt you had to kill me, Johnnie," he said. "Aye, I'm right sorry."

"It was not me, Davie. I didn't try to kill you."

"No, don't add lies to your other sins, Johnnie" said the earl. "Coagie told me it was you who stuck that poor young lad with your dirk to make him fall. I know it was you."

The remaining Scots drew closer to their earl. John of Doune stood alone.

I looked at Donald Baird squarely. "Donald...tell me. Did you see John of Doune prick the lad Caspar with his knife that day on the meadow?"

Donald looked at Doune. "I cannot say truly. But maybe he did. Aye."

"You lie! Coagie lied. He lied, I tell you. It was Firmin all along. He was the killer of Nattie and the Englishman. He loosed an arrow at you..."

"He cannot have done John, he was in our lockup, bleeding onto the ground," I said.

"It was Coagie...I tell you," shouted Doune, "on the downs that day."

There was a strangled cry. More breath than cry and Coagie erupted from the arms of Johannes who stood in the doorway and threw himself into the room, shaking his fist and pointing at Doune.

There was a shocked silence.

Donald Baird took a step back. "He's a ghost."

Tam looked round. "He's not a ghost, you lummox. He's alive."

"Thank my wife for that," I said.

I held out my hand and Coagie, glaring at Doune, staggered the few steps towards me. I helped him to a bench.

"Coagie, I want you to answer me a question. Will you point to the man who tried to kill you by cutting your throat earlier today?"

He looked up at me and his eyes first sought out his lord, David of Huntingdon.

Then he lifted a hand, pointed a finger and swivelled it round to John of Doune.

He mouthed, "It was John."

*****

Everyone was shouting at once and I had to bellow for silence.

"Thank you Coagie."

I turned to Doune.

"You now have a chance, my lord, to speak in your own defence. We are listening."

He did not look at his lord but at me as he addressed him.

"My lord, this is preposterous."

"I can only repeat the charge I have made against you, sir," I said.

"It is either malice or stupidity makes you..."

"Then refute it and be done. Provide evidence it was not as we say."

John of Doune planted his feet wide. He drew his left hand from his sword pommel. His head came up. "Then I shall."

Before any of us could work out what he was doing, he reached for the riding glove tucked into his belt, lifted it and threw it at me.

It hit me squarely in the chest and fell to the hall floor.

"As God is my witness, I'll have justice from you, Belvoir, for the lies you have told."

I watched his face, angry and guilty at the same time. His face had grown red and heated with exasperation.

"I offer proof of my innocence with the strength of my arm and body. I offer that claim to innocence upon the body of Aumary Belvoir, in combat to the death."

I looked at the man in front of me. He was confident. He thought me an easy opponent. He was sure he could send me out of this world.

I looked long at the glove on the floor. I reached down and picked it up.

"I accept your challenge," I said.

"To the death," said Doune.

"If you wish," I answered.

"On foot, here at Durley, in the courtyard?"

"As you say, and with swords."

Then I heard a high pitched, "Noooo!" issue from behind me.

Lydia had been standing on the solar stairs silently listening. I turned my head.

"No, Aumary."

"Laddie, you don't have to do this," said the Earl David quietly.

I shrugged. "Us Englishmen and our ridiculous honour, my lord," I smiled.

Chapter Fifteen

After the furore had died down the Earl David stood shakily.

"My Lord," I cried out. "Your man John of Doune will not have purgation by oath, it seems, but would rather take out his ire upon my body! I have accepted his challenge."

This ordeal was one which was left in the hands of the clergy and I sought out the face of my priest.

"Father Crispin, are you willing to aid us in this? Three days of prayer and fasting…"

John of Doune stood up tall and shouted across my words.

"I need no prayer or fasting, Belvoir. We do it now."

I turned to face the King of Scotland's brother, the man who should have the last say in this matter.

"My Lord of Huntingdon?"

David planted his feet wide. "If you are willing, my Lord Belvoir, I would have you fight at first light tomorrow. No, John!" said Earl David as John of Doune began to protest. "I have spoken. Tomorrow."

I took a deep breath and answered. "I am willing." There was a flurry of noise from the onlookers. This was a departure from the usual ritual.

"Then I shall have no prolonged battle between you," said David. "You shall wear maille but no helms and no maille coifs. No horses since we fight here in the courtyard which is the statutory sixty feet, enough for a fighting square. I'll have the matter settled quickly. Tomorrow, first thing." He signalled to Baird that he wanted to go and the man caught him up by the arm and took him down the stairs.

We heard him shout up to us, "Confine the man until tomorrow. I'll not have him escape this. It's of his own making."

I thought I knew what it was costing him.

John of Doune was led away.

Johannes, shaking his head, followed Coagie and the Earl down the steps.

Lydia ran down the solar stairs and stood a way off.

I sighed and turned to face her.

"Is there no other way, Aumary?"

I tried not to smile but my mouth betrayed me. "Do you think I'd do this thing if there were any other way left to me?"

"You could have let his brother deal with him."

"Not when a challenge is issued. You either accept and fight or you back off and let the other party win. I cannot let him win, Lydia."

Tears had begun to stream down her cheeks.

"And if he kills you?"

"Then his brother, I think, will have him."

"But if he kills you then he is deemed innocent."

"I think the Lord David will see to it. I'll not go unavenged."

Lydia scoffed. "*That* will do Simon, Hawise and myself a lot of good."

The hall had emptied now. The only person left was Hal and he stood watching, looking first at me and then at my wife.

"Lady Lydia," he said "Doune is older and not so good on 'is feet. 'E hasn't the reach Aumary 'as. 'E's not quick and lithe...."

"He's not much older than you are, Hal," said my wife.

"And for the past few weeks I suspect 'e's not kept 'imself in trim, sitting at the castle, eatin' and wenchin'. Whereas if I know Aumary...."

"Yes Hal. Stephen, Peter and I have been at our usual practice every day in the castle bailey."

"There you are, see," he said coming up to stand beside me.

"Besides, Aumary's got the right of it. God won't fail 'im."

Lydia threw her arms around her body in a comforting self-hug. "I'm glad you have so much faith, Hal, in God and in Aumary," she said and then she turned and ran up the stairs sobbing.

Hal shrugged. "One of the reasons why I 'en't never bin married, see," he said.

*****

At last I stood alone in the middle of my hall. I looked around. The new fireplace I'd created where none existed before: the good wooden oak floor, laid where there had been nothing but rough planks in my youth: the glass in the lancet windows. All mine but transient. As fleeting, as the old song said; the song Martyn Peddler sang; as a sparrow flying in one window out of another, momentarily lit by the fire of a hall. So is the life of man, I thought. Here one moment, gone the next. Would I be gone from all this, this time tomorrow?

Ah no Paul, obviously not. I'm still here forty years later!

Father Crispin came breathlessly up the steps and skidded to a halt in the doorway.

"They've just told me," he said.

I sat down heavily on a bench.

"I had no choice, Crispin. I let him go free or I fight him. He's a murderer twice over. He was part responsible for the death of a young girl and he tried to kill his liege lord and his friend. What choice do I have?"

Crispin came to sit by me. We were boyhood friends and he slid close to me. Our legs touched. His arm came over my shoulder. "I understand. Plenty out there..." he threw a hand behind him in the direction of the village and courtyard, "don't understand it. They are sore worried for you and themselves. If there was any other way..."

"There's none. It's done now anyway. It cannot be undone."

"Aye." He sighed. "Well then, we had better make your soul as white as a summer swan. Come, let's go to the chapel."

"A moment...I must speak with Lydia. She is very hurt by this. Go and pray for me. I'll join you soon."

I dragged myself up the steps. Lydia was sitting on the side of the bed, Simon was playing on the floor at her feet with a toy horse which Hal had carved for him.

Hawise was standing on a stool, looking out of the window, her doll Thomasina, another present from Hal, clasped close to her. She turned and stared at me.

"I've told mama not to worry," she said with certainty. "You will win. I know you will, because you always do. You are a good fighter. And God will not let that bad man hurt you."

She ran to me and buried her face in my side.

I sat on the bed close to Lydia and picked up Simon. He giggled and chewed the horse. Lydia tutted and took it from him, giving him instead one of the small wafers he adored.

I hugged him.

"Aumary, Hal tells me you will win. What if you don't? What happens to us?"

"I have monies laid by for that eventuality, my love. For you, Simon and Hawise. If the King sees fit to remove the title of Warden of the Forest and bestow it elsewhere then Durley still belongs to you. Simon is my heir. Someone will take him into wardship. The village is mine. It's unlikely John will take it away. It can be run just the same by all the trusted folk who run it now."

"How can we live here without you?"

Hawise began to cry. I grabbed her and hugged her to my other side.

"You shall not."

"Will you spend all night in a vigil with Crispin in the chapel or will you sensibly sleep all night here beside me and get rest. You'll need every ounce of...?"

"I shall be here."

She turned to me and took my head in her two hands. "Then go and be shriven and come back clean and eat with us here and..."

I smiled. "I'll be back soon," I said and kissed her hard on the lips.

*****

I knelt before the Earl of Huntingdon and bowed my head. John of Doune was kneeling on my right hand side as we asked for the lord's blessing. David was not *my* lord but I felt better asking him to sanction what I was about to do.

I had given five pence to the church as one is supposed to do, one for each of the wounds of Christ. Crispin had taken them with a nod and had made the sign of the cross over me.

The day had dawned cool but the sun was now rising over the eastern wall of the courtyard, stripped bare of all the usual paraphernalia and swept clean. Hal had helped me into my maille. Peter Brenthall, though not training to be a knight, helping him, had acted as my squire and had scoured it and ensure it was in good condition. Under it I wore my padded gambeson for ease of movement and protection. The Earl David dictated that we both have a sword each and a knife and that we wear no helm nor carry any shield.

Early that morning I had been to the stables to look at my dogs. I'd fondled the ears of my wolfhounds Mildred, Jocasta and Ben and had patted and stroked my smaller dog Holdfast. I squeezed into the stall and spoke to my old horse Bayard and caressed the muzzle of my fiery racehorse Fitzroy.

As I exited, into the yard came Andrew on his old horse Classis. He threw himself from his back and ran up to me.

"The news got to me this morning," he said breathlessly. I sent up to Pete and Gilbert. They are fast coming up behind me."

I shook my head. "They can't help."

Andrew snorted. "You know that's not why they want to be here."

I grasped his hand, "I'm glad you are here."

Johannes came out of his room supporting Coagie. He sat him down on the bench by the wall.

"The doctor is here already," said Andrew. "Good. Let's hope we shan't need him."

*****

Now, I rose from my blessing from the Earl and took up my sword and paced away to the southern end of the yard. Doune did the same, springing up lithely from his knees and flexing his shoulders and stood at the northern end. No sun would blind us as we fought, initially at least.

I turned to the hall steps and bowed to my lady. I saw her hands tighten on the railings I'd had made by Alfred Woodsmith. Was it really only two years ago?

She caught her lip with her teeth. I could see she had been crying.

Lydia leaned down. "Do not fail, Aumary," she said quietly, "I am not yet ready to be a widow."

Hawise had been shepherded away by her nurse Felice. No doubt she too would be biting her nails.

Hal stood behind me. Baird took up his place behind the Lord of Doune.

The Prince of Scotland stood, rising from his chair at the northern end of the yard with a slight wobble. It seemed as if he'd aged a few years overnight. The white of his bandaged head was strong in the early sunlight.

"The Lord Aumary Belvoir of Durley is challenged by John, Lord of Doune. The Lord Aumary contends that John Lord of Doune is a murderer and a traitor to his king. The Lord of Doune refutes that accusation. May God decide the truth. May the seconds come forward."

Hal and Baird stepped behind their men.

Lord David's hand fell.

We both walked warily to the centre of the space. A long drawn out sigh floated around the yard. Through the open gate manor folk were crowding as far as the eye could see. In the front was Walter Reeve with his staff of office planted as if to keep folk back from the fray. I noticed all my grooms ranged along the open doors of the stables. Father Crispin was on the bottom step of the hall stairs, John behind him. Andrew Merriman, Gilbert Cordwainer, Nick Barbflet and Peterkin Gayle who had come in a few heartbeats before, were now pressed against the guest house wall at the southern end of the yard. Matthew, my cook, was hiding around the corner of his kitchen wall as if he needed to be there but could not bear to watch. My steward Henry was standing at the top of the doorway of the manor steps with my housekeeper, Agnes Brenthall.

Many folk had climbed the gatehouse stairs and were ranged along the wall walk. I saw Wyot with his huge mastiff Thibault, on a chain. There too were some of my verderers and foresters.

Peter, his hound Maxime sitting beside him, was up there too and had a good view of the proceedings. He caught my eye and waved. Then I saw no more but the eyes of my opponent.

There was no doubting Doune's skill for he went straight for a disabling blow and he was, contrary to our expectation, light on his feet. I too was light and danced away from harm turning his stroke.

Another blow caught me on the upper arm but the rings of my maille deflected the blow and it merely stung. I hit back, catching him on the upper leg but his maille protected him also. He backed to the western wall and with a huge cry came at me for a two handed downward blow. I turned to my side and cannoned into him, pushing him against the stone. The blow was never delivered and his sword rang harmlessly on the stone of the kitchen wall.

I backed off into the middle of the yard again and Doune followed me. Once more two handed, he tried to cleave me in twain but I ducked and swiped him a light blow to his middle. Again his maille saved him.

We traded blows back and forth until an unguarded moment allowed me to catch him with my edge on the forearm where his mailed glove had fallen back. He drew away with a hiss and blood flowed freely from the wound and down his gloved hand.

I took the advantage and lunged; he parried and off balance, fell on one knee. I swapped my blade to my left hand and went for the neck.

Doune twisted backwards, and eyes widening at the change of hands, wriggled back thrusting his sword up, catching me a light blow on the lower stomach, where my maille parted.

I drew back. I had learned to fight with two hands; Hal teaching me when I was a lad, and it often disconcerted opponents. Doune panicked, stood and ran back, giving himself room and breathing space. I saw his eyes flicking from my right hand to my left.

I came after him, sideways on, my sword arm fully stretched and providing as small a target for his blows as I could.

He lunged, I leapt forward and grasped the blade of his sword with my gloved hand, wrenching it sideways and pushing it into him. The side of the blade, close by the hilt, caught his nose and cut him. His head snapped back and he heaved the sword away.

Blood trickled from his nose and he shook his head to clear his eyes.

He came at me again with a blow to the legs. I jumped, and once more transferring my sword, swiped him in the middle. I missed but he growled and grimaced.

He backed off and then wiped his arm across his sweating forehead. I waited for him to focus again.

I tried a blow to his shoulder but he parried it and slid his sword across mine and down to the hilt. We struggled closely and his knee came up and caught me a blow to the lower ribs.

The pain was sharp but I pivoted my sword down and dropped it straight, snatching it up again immediately as it bounced from his mailled foot. It did not pierce but it must have hurt. Hurt as a stubbed toe does.

We parted and walked around each other.

Hal was suddenly behind me and he called over my shoulder. "'E doesn't like the left 'and lad. Try the left 'and."

My breath had returned and I went after him with my right hand trying a blow to the head. At the last moment I shifted to my left hand and I caught the man right at the side of the head. His ear lobe went flying out onto the cobbles of the courtyard. He had not dressed carefully for his maille coif had fallen back on his shoulder.

John of Doune yelled and threw up a hand to his head.

I heard Hal shout, "That's the way Aumary!"

People were now yelling and cheering. I smiled at Peter, who caught my eye, jumping up and down on the wall walk.

My opponent had backed off. Blood coated the side of his head and beard, and dripped onto the cobbles from his ear.

John of Doune came at me again recklessly throwing lunge after lunge at my middle. I backed and backed until I felt the step of the manor stair at my heel.

John, Crispin and Lydia had retreated further up. I could see the black of Crispin's cassock, the blue of John's cotte and the green of Lydia's skirt but I couldn't see their faces.

I gave back a blow with my left hand and with my right grasped the Lord of Doune's sword hilt as it fell to meet mine. I turned it down and pushed him.

He stepped back and immediately came on for a disabling blow to my sword hilt. The blade snapped and flew across the courtyard. I heard the ring of it on the cobbles.

Doune grinned ferally. I saw the white teeth in the grey speckled, bloodied, black beard.

Throwing away the useless hilt I reached back for my knife at my right hip.

Etiquette demanded that Doune also cease to use his sword but he didn't.

I heard Prince David shout, "Throw away your sword Johnnie or you'll be disarmed."

Doune came on following me to the bottom of the steps again. He swung a huge swipe at me. I heard Lydia cry out behind me.

I sat down abruptly on the second step and lifted my leg to catch the man in the midriff. I pushed him. His sword missed my leg by an inch.

Whilst he was off balance, two of the earl's men, Baird and Dunfermline, ran up and grabbed him. Baird wrestled the sword from his hand.

"Aye, aye. All right. I hear ye," shouted Doune, relinquishing his weapon. Breathing hard, he took out a wickedly long dirk.

Bending, he waved it in front of me and gave me a feral smile.

Swipe after swipe with the weapon saw him catch me on the upper leg where my mailled cotte swung open and where my mailled chausses did not protect me.

I went down on one knee to rest the injured thigh for a moment and stabbed up to his body, trying to get between his cotte and breeks.

I made contact but did not quite push far enough to disable him.

He leaned over me and took a swipe at my back.

The crowd hissed.

I stood. Both of us were breathing hard as we were tiring a little now.

John of Doune backed off. I came away from the steps and turned so that my back was to the stable block.

I saw Lydia run down four steps to stand half way down the flight.

From the corner of my eye, I saw Johannes working his way round the edge of the stables to the corner of the hall. John was now at the edge of the steps by the opening to the undercroft. Matthew had come out of hiding. Crispin was on the bottom step of the hall stairs. Hal was behind me still.

'I am surrounded by friends, by people I love' I thought, 'and people who love me.' That gave me a warm rush to my veins; I leapt forward and engaged the lord of Doune in a sliding stab that pushed him against the wall of the hall.

He grimaced as we pushed harder and harder into each other. Our knives were locked in front of our eyes.

I slipped my leg behind the man's calf and kicked back. He slid downwards landing on the floor on his seat with a bump. His knife went skittering away.

"Cry Craven, Doune," I yelled at him. "You are vanquished."

I saw the Prince of Scotland rise out of the corner of my eye. I turned to ask him if he wanted me to finish his brother. It was almost my undoing.

I heard Lydia's voice cry out, "Aumary!"

Just a flicker of an eyelid later and I would have been skewered in the back by Doune's long dirk.

Somehow he'd righted himself and lunged across the cobbles to pick up his weapon again.

He threw it, like a throwing knife. I bounced onto the westernmost wall of the stables to avoid it and immediately went for him again.

He stood lifting his hands.

"What say - we start - again with - swords...these knives - aren't for proper - knights?" he breathed.

I nodded and looked towards the earl. He inclined his head.

Two new swords were procured and Doune tested his by waving it over his head in a display of dexterity.

Hal came up and offered me his own sword, hilt first across his arm.

I smiled. I'd used this weapon many times when Hal and I had sparred. My opponent's sword was totally new to him.

Once again we stepped out into the middle. Once again Doune tried a huge blow to the body. Once more I parried it.

My thigh was stinging and stiffening but I danced forward to receive a blow which I swung round in an arc. I felt that my opponent's strength was ebbing for the force of the blow had lessened.

We drove back to the gate and forward to the steps again.

Doune's boot heel met the edge of the first step and he fell with his back on the step. His maille prevented him from breaking his spine but it jarred him and he cried out.

I noticed that Lydia was just two steps further up, her violet eyes large with fear as John of Doune stabbed up and caught me a blow to the shoulder. It pierced my maille though truthfully I didn't feel it at first. It was merely a bruise under my gambeson. I lifted my arm to catch him a blow to the body, supine as he was.

He rolled and my sword hit stone.

He jumped up, turned and before I could follow him, he'd grabbed Lydia from the step above him and pushed her before him.

The crowd screamed.

John of Doune pulled his sword blade up to Lydia's throat.

"Back off Belvoir," he said, through gritted teeth, breathing harshly.

I stood down and pointed my sword blade to the cobbles. My sides were heaving. I lowered my head but my eyes never left his face.

Doune, realising that he was vulnerable to a blow from behind, from one of my men, backed onto the manor wall and slid down step by step, dragging poor Lydia with him.

She couldn't see where she was going for he'd got her head so high to avoid the blade, she was stretched almost on tip toe.

"Leave her, Doune," I managed to say. "This isn't the action of a knight. It's dishonourable to act so."

"Ha! Ha! You Englishmen and your honour, as my brother says."

He was now on the final step. I moved forward and Doune pulled Lydia closer to him nicking her neck, through her white barbette. A red stain appeared quickly but Lydia didn't make a sound.

The Earl of Huntingdon was making his way close.

"Johnnie," he said, "It was you who insisted you fight and you who wanted it to the death. Put the girl down. It's not right."

Doune took no notice. "Get me a horse!" he yelled.

No one moved. "A horse I say! Now!"

"Johnnie. We'll not let you go," said Earl David gently.

Doune rounded the wall in the direction of the stables. I saw Hawise appear on the top step of the stairs and noticed her push her fist into her mouth.

"Hawise...go in," I shouted.

She did not obey but came down to the fifth step.

Suddenly she screamed with all her might.

"If you hurt my mama, I'll kill you, you bad man."

Doune was momentarily distracted. He looked up.

Lydia lifted her head a little more, risking a further nick of the sword blade and bit down for all she was worth onto the exposed wrist of John of Doune. He had foolishly turned back his mitten. He yelled. Lydia then, like one of Matthew Cook's famous jellies, became as pliant as a withy and dropped from his grasp, sliding gently to the floor.

I quickly pulled her up and behind me.

Once more I reached out with my sword.

"Shall we finish this like gentlemen, Doune?" I said.

"You'll no be needing to," I heard the Earl of Huntingdon say, as I saw his hands move quickly, swiping his sword, two handed, hard, in a cutting motion.

Blood sprayed everywhere, I caught a swathe of it as it passed, splashing on my beard and upper torso. I shut my eyes on impulse to avoid it and turned away.

John of Doune's head fell from his body and bounced on the cobbles, rolling to lie at the feet of Donald Baird.

The body stood for a moment then wavered and crumpled in a heap, blood fountaining from the neck.

*****

There was a terrible hush and then the whole place erupted. People jumped up and down on the spot. Those outside the courtyard ran forward in a wave to stand in the fighting space and stare at the head. No one passed it.

Hal came trotting over and took his sword from me. He slapped me on the back.

I reached behind me and caught Lydia's hand; she swung round and hugged me close, blood, wounds, maille and all.

Hawise careered down the steps and flung herself at us both, weeping and laughing by turns.

I looked up at the earl. He was standing stock still staring at the body of his erstwhile brother. The expression on his face was one of shock and sadness. And something else.

I disengaged from my women folk and walked towards him. He did not see me.

"Sir."

He looked up and he cleared his throat. I noticed there were tears on his cheeks above his grey beard.

"Thank you."

"No lad, it's not me needing your thanks. It's your wee lass."

I smiled.

"Thank you sir," I said again.

"He didn't fight fair, Aumary."

"No sir."

"He made the rules and then he bent them. He was always so when we were... childer...." His eye went wistfully off for a moment.

"God moved you to action, I think." I said.

"Aye, right has been seen to have been done. It's all done now."

He gestured to one of his men: he only had four left and one of those was an invalid. He waved his hand at the head and the body.

"Reunite them if you will," he said.

I watched as Father Crispin went to the body and began his prayers for the dead. Even for an enemy, I thought, it has to be done.

I'd seen Coagie rise when John of Doune's head had gone flying across the cobbles. He was still standing staring at it. What must he be thinking?

The earl turned his back and walked away to the room where he was staying and closed the door. No one followed him.

Johannes came up. "Let's see to your wounds, Aumary. You'll stiffen and cramp soon enough. Best we do it now."

I smiled. "Aye, I know. You have some salve or other for them, I suppose."

Johannes guffawed loud and long. "Aye, I probably do."

Hawise looked up at him from under her mother's arm. "But you can't put heads back on can you, uncle Johannes?"

"No, my dove... that I cannot do."

I stretched my back and as I did I caught the look Peter and John Brenthall gave me as they came up.

"Well done sir," said Peter, "You were wonderful."

"Thank you, Peter, but I didn't kill him."

"No," said John, looking back at the earl as he closed the door of his room. "You didn't have to."

Andrew, Nick and Peterkin Gayle came up next, buffeting me and joking. In their banter I could tell how relieved they were. Gilbert Cordwainer came up looking rather green. He shyly shook my grubby and bloodied hand.

"I'm right glad you're alright," he said quietly.

I embraced him swiftly, turning my head so that he wouldn't be too bloodied.

Andrew threw his arm over my shoulder. "God'sTeeth, Aumary. You must show me a few of those tricks of yours. I've never seen the like."

"Hal's the one you want," I said, nodding in the direction of my man at arms who was organising the swilling down of the yard.

"He and my father taught me everything I know."

"That old crock? Nah… never!" said Andrew louder than needful and he laughed.

" 'Ere! Mind 'oo you call an ol' crock you 'airless babe," grinned Hal.

Andrew slapped Hal on the back. "You may teach me any time you're at the castle Hal, old man."

I tried to extricate myself but it wasn't easy. Everyone wanted to congratulate me; say how happy they were that I'd survived; tell me how much they loved me as their lord and they didn't know what they'd do without me. I was truly blessed that day.

*****

Eventually I crawled up the steps to the manor and up into the solar. I'd peeled off my maille at the foot of the steps and given it back to Hal and Peter. Now pulling off my braies, chausses and tunic, I gratefully sank into a bath of warm water and bathed my hurts. The only one really causing me distress was the cut to my thigh; Johannes looked and said it would probably need a couple of stitches. The wound to my shoulder was on top of the scar tissue from a previous fight and was sore but all right.

That done, clothed and sitting in my monk's chair…

Yes, the one I'm sitting in now, Paul. I do not nor ever have owned a better chair. So comfortable. The best kind of chair for an old man for you can lean against the sides and there's no fear of you falling out if you fall asleep.

...I kissed my wife, hugged my daughter and cooed at my son.

I dozed a little.

Half way through the day the earl came to me.

I bade him sit and talk to me in the solar.

He came in tottering a little on the arm of his man Donald Baird.

"I'm away back to the castle, Aumary," he said.

"Sir, please do not leave us now. You aren't yet fit and certainly Coagie..."

"Coagie can follow when he's able."

I nodded.

"I don't want to be here, you understand."

"Yes," I said. "I do understand. What will you do with the body of John, with your brother's body?"

"I'll get a coffin made and he'll go back to Scotland, along with Nattie. I can't leave him here on foreign soil, no matter what he's done."

I nodded again. "He is your brother, sir."

"Yes."

"I had to leave mine in Rouen. It wasn't easy."

The earl's eyes widened. "I didn't know."

"How could you?"

He reached out and grasped my forearm. "We aren't enemies, Aumary."

"We never have been, sir," I smiled. "I'll see you before you go back to Scotland? Will you continue to negotiate or..."

"No. I don't think so. I'm tired of it all. We cannot win just now. Maybe next year my brother will try again eh?"

"We'd be pleased to see you back here in Durley, my lord," I said.

David gave a slight shake of his head. "I won't be going back to Scotland. I've had enough. I have plans to retire to my lands in Huntingdon."

I don't mind saying, Paul my scribe, I was rather surprised by this.

"Not return?"

David of Huntingdon swivelled his eyes to Heaven as if he could not look at me.

"I cannot go back to stay...I have my reasons."

He saw my quizzical expression and took a deep breath.

"When my brother the King was childless…"

"Before young Alexander was born?"

"Aye. Alexander. He's nine now."

"A son of William's old age." I said. The King had no legitimate sons earlier in his reign.

"Yes. I was his heir. My brother's heir. For years. Do you see how that was? And now how that feels?" He turned a red rimmed eye on me. "I was his heir and then when Alexander was born...I was passed over."

"No sir, surely…."

"I was ousted. We have a nine year old heir. I was no longer important. If anything happened to William it would not be me who would be King of Scotland. After all I had done for her...for years...not me."

Suddenly it was as if a fog had cleared and I thought I began to see this whole mystery plainly as if for the first time, Paul. I don't mind saying, a lump rose in my throat.

"I accused John of Doune of being partisan," I said slowly, "I thought perhaps he had a master outside Scotland. God forbid, I even wondered if John of England had had a hand in it all," I sighed. "No, it was not our monarch, was it?"

I stood and faced David of Scotland.

"John of Doune was not loyal to William your brother, was he? He was loyal... to you. To you and you alone."

The Scotsman chuckled, a dry coughing thing, "Aye, to me. It seems he'd do anything he could to scupper the plans of his elder brother. Anything he could to benefit me, as he saw it. He thought I should be King after William, for you know that William is not a well man. He told me he thought I deserved it; not some mewling infant. He knew that William and I were not on the best of terms, not now. Not nowadays. I'd offered to come down here in an effort to patch things up between William and me. William asked me so I came in advance of further talks. Our brother John thought I'd want it all to fail, I think. I know now that *he* did."

"And did *you*?"

The man shook his injured head and shrugged. "I am...indifferent. Now"

"And so he set about his plan to kill Alan of Windsor, to make sure the talks would not take place."

"What he did, he did for me. He knew I felt slighted."

"So why did he try to kill you?"

Again the dry almost coughing laugh came from his lips. "At first it was not *me* who was in danger. Nattie died because he saw John loose an arrow in the woods which was meant for *Tam*. It was never meant for me. It was an accident that I was hurt. I think John believed If we had no lawyers, we could not proceed. No Alan of Windsor and no Tam o' the Dale"

"Tam?"

"Aye. Then Coagie saw him stick the young lad Caspar. He had to be rid of him because he'd seen him with Nattie the night he died and knew that John was our likely killer."

"That I'd guessed but…"

"And after all that John could no longer trust me." David tiredly wiped his forehead with shaky fingers. "Like you, I do not like murder and once he knew that I had the truth, he knew that I would not allow him to escape blame."

"Why did you kill him?"

"Aw…. I'm not really sure myself," he said. "I've had enough. Enough of Scottish politics. I think I realised that John would never let me rest. If I couldn't be King then...maybe *he* would." His eye suddenly became steely. "Maybe another insurrection with John at the head? And then what? A swift knife to the ribs one dark night… his loyalty to William was only ever skin deep. I know that now. How safe would our boy King be eh? Our nephew?"

Another King, another nephew, another feud suddenly leapt into my memory and I was taken back to Rouen, to the France of 1203 when King John's nephew Arthur was killed.

"And he didn't fight fairly. I didn't want him to kill you," said David, smiling.

I don't mind saying, Paul, my heart was hammering as I said,

"I hear that you have refused to swear fealty to William's heir, sir, the young Alexander?"

David's eye grew agitated.

"I could not do it."

I stepped a little nearer "And now?"

"Maybe I shall. But I'll live out my days on English soil. Oh, I'll go back to Scotland in my coffin. It's my desire for my bones to lie in Lindores Abbey, in Fife. I endowed the monastery there, you see. It's a fine place for a monument."

"So I've heard."

"But Scotland will get no more from *me* living."

Ah, Paul my scribe - it never happened. When the man died, in 1219, they buried him in Sawtry Abbey, Huntingdonshire, in England, far away from Scotland. Yes...yes, you're right; I suppose that is quite sad. I heard also that he had relinquished his claim to the throne, legally. Given it up of his own free will but I cannot substantiate that. It's just hearsay.

Part of me did wonder if David had known what was going on all along. Even that John of Doune was operating at his instruction. Perhaps he did after all, want the crown. Again I can't prove it.

*****

I rested for two days. Coagie gained in strength and struck up a friendship with Martyn Peddler who added a few new songs to his repertoire.

Coagie kissed my wife's hand and whispered his thanks for saving his life. She blushed and smiled sweetly at him. I think she liked the amiable Alexander Firmin.

Together on the third day we returned to the castle and on the following day the Scots left us to travel for the coast and a ship which would take them to Glasgow, all around the western coast of our island. The Lord of Huntingdon left for that county the day after with the loyal Donald Baird.

The English negotiators who had stayed in the hall and in their quarters throughout the troubled day of the fight and death of John of Doune, left for London to make their report to the Justiciar, FitzPeter. I have a feeling it was all too much for them, but I do think I remember catching a face staring out of the window during the fight. So perhaps they were interested after all.

I wrote to John the King and told him everything. I had no idea what he would think but there was nothing I could do but tell him the truth. I'd always done that and he told me he loved me for it.

In the following year John himself went up to Northumbria to settle, as he'd promised, the problem of the disputed lands.

It was an odd war...which wasn't a war at all, I'm told, but that, Paul, is another story. No, no, that's for another time.

What? Oh yes... Hilda Caspar did marry Anthony Chapman. They hated each other for the rest of their lives. Their children, two boys I think, moved away and after Anthony died when he was about forty, I think, Hilda lived in penury for the children would for some reason have nothing to do with her and took the business and money elsewhere.

What happened to the senior Caspars, do you ask? Master Caspar was laid low with some wasting disease about four years after my tale. He took a long time to die, I think. Mistress Caspar married again but her husband beat her and one day he beat her so badly she died. That's for another tale perhaps.

Yes, Paul, in a way it was justice.

I reached home, so pleased to be out of the castle and away from politics; out in my beloved forest which was approaching the season of high summer; doing those things I loved doing best.

I jumped down from Bayard's back, forgetting about the wound to my upper thigh.

"Ouch!" It still hurt. I think it was about time the stitches came out.

Lydia was at the top of the steps.

"Ah...so you have condescended to visit us again, have you?" she joked. I noticed she wore a loose head cloth and nothing across her throat for I think it was still painful. Neither of us went unscathed in that terrible fight.

She disappeared into the hall. I followed.

Hawise poked her head up from her lessons with Father Crispin at the large hall table.

"Oh dada, you're back. I think mama is a bit cross with you, so be careful."

"Why's that, sweetling?"

"I don't know. But she said she'd smack your bottom, 'cos you needed it," she giggled.

Crispin shrugged, looking vacant. He had no idea what was going on.

*****

I followed my wife up to the solar.

"So why do you want to smack my bottom?" I asked, throwing my sword belt and gloves on the bed and peeling off my cotte.

"Hmmm?" said my wife.

"C'mon Lydia...it's not fair to keep a man in suspense, so..."

She turned to me, her hands on her hips.

"I have seen Felicity today."

"Felicity Barbflet has been?"

"Yes, she came to dinner so that Hawise and Aedel could play together for a while."

"Hmmm?"

I dropped down on the bed and crossed my ankles. I folded my hands behind my head.

"Boots, Aumary..."

"Ah yes."

I pulled them off and dropped them on the floor.

"And so...?"

"She tells me that....that....Alyson..."

"Their maid?"

"Had told her that you have been seen....."

"Yes?"

"Seen at..."

"Yes, for goodness sake?"

"Going into the..." Lydia hesitated as if she didn't quite know the right word to use.

"Brothel, Aumary."

I lay back and laughed and laughed and laughed until my sides ached.

A bolster landed on me and I was whacked with serious strength.

"The house run by Mistress Ashley, I believe," she said.

"Ah, yes, well..." I laughed some more.

The pillow hit me squarely on the jaw. I seized it.

"No! No! It was nothing. It's like this Lydia... You see I...."

~ ~ ~ ~ ~

GLOSSARY

Adamant - A compass, magnet.

Afrit - Afraid (Scots).

Alembic - Consisting of two vessels connected by a tube, an alembic is used for distilling chemicals.

Alkanet - Plant of the borage family, *Pentaglottis sempervirens* typically having a hairy stem and blue flowers.

Angevin - Of Anjou in France. The ancestral home of the Plantagenet dynasty.

Apothecary - Primitive chemist.

Atte - From.

Backstool - A stool with a back. A chair without arms.

Bailey - The outer courtyard of a castle, surrounded by walls.

Balls - Bowls.

Barbette - A linen cloth worn by women under the chin and secured in the hair with a band.

Billhook - A tool having a sickle-shaped blade with a sharp inner edge, used for pruning or lopping branches or other vegetation.

Bliaut - Voluminous overgarment worn by both sexes (but mostly women) and pleated to the waist or under the bust.

Bothy - Small, simple building often of daub and wattle, roofed with thatch and having a beaten earth floor.

Butts - The place where targets for archery are set up.

Carnaptious - Easily riled. Ready to take offence (Scottish).

Caul - A decorative net in which ladies fixed up their hair.

Clap - A sexually transmitted disease.

Clipping of ears - A punishment meted out to thieves and criminals. Taking off a small amount at a time.

Coif - Close fitting linen cap.

Consanguinity - Closeness of blood - too closely related.

Cordwainer - A shoemaker.

Coroner - Sometimes known as the Crowner. The man appointed by the Crown to deal with unexpected deaths. The coroner was the man who drew up the jury of twelve men to decide the cause of death and if need be, impose fines.

Cotte - A long sleeve shift or tunic. A coat.

Crabs - The old word for cancer.

Curfew - Comes from the French phrase *"couvre-feu"*, which means to cover the fire. It was a time when all fires should be extinguished and people should be off the streets.

Daub and wattle - Building material consisting of hazel withies and mud and dung.

Deodand - Some personal property, such as a horse or a spade, was considered a deodand whenever a coroner's jury decided that it had caused the death of a human being. In theory, deodands were forfeit to the crown, which was supposed to sell the chattel and then apply the profits to some pious use.

Diaper - A decorative motif of a diamond shape.

Dirk - A long knife (Scottish).

Downs - Chalk hills with steep coombes and valleys, thin soils and few trees.

Dun - A pale coated horse.

Dwale - A painkiller based on *belladonna* or deadly nightshade.

Excommunicate - One who is /has been excluded from and is outside, the Christian church.

Feam - Froth at the mouth with anger (Scottish).

Fustian - A thick, hard-wearing twilled cloth with a short nap, usually dyed in dark colours.

Good conduct - Reference.

Grange - An outlying barn belonging to a monastery, castle or estate.

Herald - A government courier.

Hurling - A game resembling hockey.

Justiciar - A king's right hand man - his deputy and one he trusts to run the country in his absence.

Ken - Know (Scottish).

Lapstrake - Or clinker built. Built like a ship's hull, one plank overlapping another.

Madder - *Rubia tinctoria*, a plant which is used for a dye of very light fast crimson red.

Mordant - A fixative for fabric dyes.

Murrey - A scarlet cloth, fashionable in the 13th and 14th centuries.

Palfrey - Small boned horse, ridden by the clergy and women in particular.

Pallet - Straw filled mattress.

Paunch - Disembowel a deer.

Pommel - Handle of a sword or knife or part of a saddle.

Portcullis - A metal gate of spikes lowered into a castle gateway.

Quarterstaff - Staff being made from hardwood of a tree split or sawed into quarters.

Remove - A course in a banquet or feast.

Rouncey - A smaller horse used as a workhorse often ridden by servants. Rounceys were not fast but they were possessed of great stamina.

Saffron - A dull yellow colour. Dyes made with the stamens of the crocus plant.

Sally Port - The small door in the wall of a town, castle or manor which allows one person to enter or exit at a time.

Saracen - An enemy of the Crusades. A person from the Middle East.

Scrip - A pouch worn at the waist on a belt or slung over the shoulder if larger. A purse.

Shriven - A person confessed of their sins has been shriven.

Surcote - An over tunic, sometimes with sleeves.

Swaddle - To bind closely with a cloth like a baby.

Tawny - Brown orange colour cloth.

Tonsure - The shaven circle on the head of a priest.

Town reeve - Head of the town council, an office which later became mayor.

Truckle bed - A low bed on wheels that can be stored under a larger bed. Often used by servants.

Twill - A fabric so woven as to have a surface of diagonal parallel ridges.

Uskebeaghe - Whisky (Gaelic).

Vitriol - Old name for sulphuric acid.

Wattle - Woven hazel withies.

Watchet - A blue cloth woven in the west country.

Wicket - Small personnel door in a larger gate.

AUTHOR'S NOTE

The Scottish border was in dispute for much of the latter twelfth century and into the thirteenth, and William the Lion spent much of his long reign trying to regain the lands along the English side. There was a great deal of opposition at home to his spending so much money and effort on this project. David of Huntingdon was indeed his brother though I don't think he ever went to Marlborough to discuss the thorny problem; my meeting is fictitious. It's not known if he was with his brother when they embarked upon talks again in the next year, further north. During the long reign of William the Lion (1165-1214), there were many rebellions and various claimants to the throne, none of whom succeeded.

David was the heir until William produced a son late in his reign. It seems they may have fallen out over it and David retired to his English lands, having nothing further to do with Scottish politics. However when the legitimate line of William the Lion died out later in the century, David's descendants came into their own. The two most notable claimants to the throne, Robert Bruce, 5th Lord of Annandale (grandfather of King Robert I of Scotland), and John Balliol were his descendants through David's daughters Isobel and Margaret, respectively.

His final resting place was in Arbroath Abbey, Scotland.

The poem A Parcel of Rogues was written by Scotland's National poet Robert Burns in 1791. He vilified those members of parliament who signed the Act of Union with England in 1707, intimating that some of them had been bribed. There is enough evidence to suggest that this was true.

The dispute over the northern boundary rumbled on for centuries and was only settled by that union. There were two further rebellions in 1715 and 1745; uprisings to restore the Catholic monarchy, but they were put down ruthlessly.

I have used this poem as a starting place for my story, even though it antedates the fiction by some five centuries. The roots of the conflict go a long way back.

The language spoken at the Scottish court was French, as it was at the court in England. David would also have known early middle English. It seems inconceivable that he wouldn't have had a smattering of Gaelic.

With the spread of Christianity across the north of Britain by the Columban Church the Gaelic language slowly moved eastwards and southwards across the lowlands of Scotland. When Northumbrian lands were incorporated into Scotland in the eleventh century, Gaelic became the prestige language there and had some influence, but the south east remained largely English speaking. In the far north, Viking incursions brought Old Norse speakers into Caithness, Orkney and Shetland. By the thirteenth century the languages had changed; largely English spoken by the southern dwellers and Gaelic by the northern people and the islands.

The parcel of rogues is either the perfidious English or the treacherous Scots - whichever it is, you may decide. The Caspar family too are another parcel of rogues....every one. This story makes a passing nod to J.B. Priestley's An Inspector Calls. I have often wondered how it would be, taken back a few centuries.

Acids were not widely understood in the thirteenth century but they certainly knew about them and could make them. Sulphuric acid was known as vitriol. Its primary use at this time was in the dyeing and moneying trades.

Trial by combat was a method of law to settle accusations in the absence of witnesses or confession. The winner of the fight was deemed to have God on his side and if he was the accused party, was proclaimed innocent. Wager of battle, as it was often called, was introduced into Common Law after the conquest of 1066 and remained in use throughout the early Mediaeval period, being superseded by Trial by Jury in 1215. If the plaintiff cried out "craven" and gave up the fight, he was deprived of his privileges and was liable for damages to his opponent. Sometimes the loser was hanged; often they were declared outlaw.

The storage of spears in the way described in this book is documented in various manuscripts both in words and drawings.

Now to Aumary. He is a minor lord, not terribly wealthy and more a businessman than pure aristocracy. As warden of the forest he has quite a practical job and needs to know about the forest and its trades. He is a knight - yes, but first and foremost, a forester. I have made him a sympathetic character as so many folk of his class in novels, are portrayed as proud, haughty and nasty. I fail to see how many of them could be so. They were dependent upon their peasants for their livelihood. If the peasant didn't prosper, neither did they at this level of society. Grander folk perhaps could be less amenable. Aumary takes every man as he finds him and isn't averse to rolling up his sleeves and getting on with it.

Susanna M. Newstead © April 2020

ABOUT THE AUTHOR

Susanna, like Aumary Belvoir has known the Forest of Savernake all her life. After a period at the University of Wales studying Speech Therapy, she returned to Wiltshire and then moved to Hampshire to work, not so very far from her forest. Susanna developed an interest in English history, particularly that of the 12th and 13th centuries, early in life and began to write about it in her twenties. She now lives in Northamptonshire with her husband and two small wire haired fox terriers called Delphi and Tabor.

TITLES IN THIS SERIES

Belvoir's Promise

She Moved Through the Fair

Down by the Salley Gardens

I Will Give my Love an Apple

Black is the Colour of my True Love's Hair

Long Lankyn

One Misty Moisty Morning

The Unquiet Grave

The Lark in the Morning

A Parcel of Rogues

Please visit the website for further information

https://susannamnewstead.co.uk/

Printed in Poland
by Amazon Fulfillment
Poland Sp. z o.o., Wrocław

56945456R00161